PRAISE FOR JACK WAKES UP

"Harwood sucker-punches crime fiction. It's not a fair fight, he's waiting for you to look the other way, then you get a blackjack in the back of the head. Then he kicks you in the nuts, and you actually thank him for it."
-- **Scott Sigler, bestselling author of ANCESTOR and IN-FECTED**

"If Chandler had been tapped to write the first DIE HARD, and somewhere along the way Tarantino had been called in for re-writes à la TRUE ROMANCE, the result would have been a JACK PALMS tale. Hook-a-minute hardboiled dialogue and re-lentless action"
-- **Shannon Clute,** *Behind the Black Mask*

"A thrilling noir story that pulls the listener into the dark world of Jack Palms."
-- **Kevin Einarson,** *Spinetingler Magazine*

"Seth Harwood has the inventiveness and energy of ten men and it's always a treat to see what he comes up with."
-- **Charles Ardai,** *Hard Case Crime*

"I'm a Palms Daddy!"
-- **Allan Guthrie, author of HARD MAN**

"JACK WAKES UP isn't a novel -- it's a force of nature. Har-wood's writing brilliantly blends the brass-knuckled voice of Ray-mond Chandler with the slick plot twists of Jeffrey Deaver. This story goes for the throat, pulling the reader into a California un-derworld so seamy and believable, it's a wonder that Jack Palms, Harwood's unlikely hero, is a fictional character at all. Rock-solid crime noir that takes no prisoners."
-- **J.C. Hutchins, author of 7th SON: DESCENT**

"This is the stuff that will keep the PI around in crime fiction!"
-- **Jochem Steen,** *Sons of Spade*

JACK WAKES UP

SETH HARWOOD

BREAKNECK BOOKS
PUBLISHING COMPANY

www.breakneckbooks.com

Published by Breakneck Books (USA)
www.breakneckbooks.com

Portions of this book appeared previously in *Spinetingler Magazine* and *Storyglossia*.

Printed in the United States of America.

ISBN: 0-9796929-5-4
ISBN-13: 978-0-9796929-5-6

Cover Design by: Jerry Scullion

Visit Seth Harwood on the World Wide Web at:
www.sethharwood.com

ATTENTION: SCHOOLS AND BUSINESSES
Breakneck Books' titles are available at bulk order discount rates for educational, business or sales promotional use. They are also available for fundraiser programs. Please e-mail: info@breakneckbooks.com or write us at: Breakneck Books - PO Box 122 - Barrington, NH 03867 for details

for Joelle

JACK WAKES UP

"Let he who's without sin cast the first stone…"
-- John 8:7, as paraphrased by MF DOOM

1

Jack Palms walks into a diner just south of Japantown, the one where he's supposed to meet Ralph. As he passes the *Wait To Be Seated* sign, he wonders if these things didn't come standard issue with *Please* at the start not too long ago, back when the world was more friendly and kind.

But Jack knows what Ralph and the rest of the people who come to a place like this would tell him: fuck that.

The diner's built out of an old cable car, with a lunch counter along one side and booths on the other. Ralph sits alone at the last table eating, hunched over his plate, long brown hair hanging curly around his face, his blue and white Hawaiian clashing with the ugly checked wallpaper. He hasn't gotten any younger or prettier over the years: his pock-marked cheeks move like a rabbit's, his eyebrows form a thick mustache over his eyes. He wears wide sunglasses, the kind blind people wear, pushed up onto the top of his head.

Ralph smiles when he sees Jack. "Jacky *boy*," he says, showing Jack the other side of his booth with a big hand, not getting up. "You look good. Like you added a little weight." He winks. "In a good way."

"Thanks." Jack pats his ribcage. He calculates it's been three years since he last saw Ralph. Three years and then the phone call this morning, asking Jack to come in on a deal.

"You see that game against the Mets?" Ralph starts, saying no one should be allowed to pitch around Bonds, the steroids home-run machine, that the Giants lost because the Mets did just that. Ralph shakes his head. "I guarantee you: they pitch to Bonds, he puts that shit in the Bay."

"Just coffee," Jack tells the waitress, who's just come out from behind the counter. She stops with the brown-rimmed pot over the table, when Jack says, "Decaf," and it's clear she's not happy about having to go back for the other pot.

"And toast," Ralph adds. "He'll have a wheat toast, darling." The waitress, pushing forty and only a few years from when the days on her feet and gravity will own her, smiles and tips her head. "Thank you." He winks. When she's gone: "You got to have toast or something. So they know we're not camping." He tilts his head, forking more waffle into his mouth.

"Just don't eat it." He shrugs. "I'm buying."

"Right," Jack says. Next to Ralph's untouched water, two butts half-fill his ashtray: one coming in and one with his coffee, waiting for Jack and his food, Jack guesses. He's a quarter into his waffle and has a side of eggs and bacon that he hasn't touched. Ralph did a good job syrupping the waffle: buttered it first, went liberal, and stayed away from the fruit flavors—no blueberry or apple bullshit.

"Listen Jack." Ralph barely looks up, cuts the next quarter-waffle into strips. "I'm real sorry about how that shit went down with Victoria. How you handling yourself?" He looks up, pauses from eating.

Jack runs his finger over the rim of his coffee mug. "Getting by, Ralph. Thanks for your concern."

"Because I feel for you about Victoria telling people you hit her." He shakes his head. "That wasn't good." He looks at Jack, like he's trying to get it all figured out right then and there. "You didn't, right?"

"No, Ralph."

"And that wasn't cool that they pulled the money for your sequel, dumped the project." He forks a big piece of waffle into his mouth. "I'm sorry about that too."

"So what's the basics here, Ralph? The big picture?"

Ralph nods. "It's a buy," he says, mouth full, using his fork to point. "Easy and simple: a buy and a sell. One big trade, no small shit or breaking up of product. We each stand to make a couple thou for a few days work."

"You said on the phone we'd be set for good."

Ralph shrugs. "Shit, Jack. I needed to get you down here to hear this, right?"

Jack looks around the diner, thinks about how it'd feel to just get up and walk out. But then he considers the two thousand reasons to stay and the guy from the bank calling this morning about his missed mortgage payments.

"Keep talking."

A sip of coffee and Ralph cuts off some eggs with his fork and adds them to what he's already chewing. "You want this bacon?" he asks. "I'm trying to watch my cholesterol."

The waitress comes back with the decaf pot and fills Jack's cup until he stops her about an inch from the top. He's glad Ralph doesn't ask about the decaf, doesn't want to explain that he had his coffee at home and knows a second cup will leave him too jittery to deal with Ralph's shit. She drops off a small plate of dry wheat toast, lightly toasted, at the top of Jack's placemat. Little pats of butter line the side of the plate, the kind you have to peel the paper off of. Ralph drops two bacon slices on top of the bread. "Make yourself a sandwich," he says.

Jack adds a sugar to his coffee and stirs it with one of the diner's dirty spoons, adding a half-and-half. "So what's the who? The when?"

Ralph goes on eating. "The when is still up in the air, but I say it happens within the week. Thursday or Friday. The who you don't need now. I'd tell you, but it wouldn't mean anything. You're too long out of this game."

Jack nods, sits back in his chair and looks at the little white mug of decaf, thinking about whether he should walk out. "Tell me why you need me."

"Listen. You made that sequel, you'd be in a whole different world right now, financially and otherwise." Ralph holds up his hand, stopping Jack before he can tell him to shut up. "I know," he says. "Enough. But I'll just say I heard you're touching down on your luck, that maybe you could use a little money. That's why I called."

Jack takes a bitter sip of coffee, puts the mug back down. "I'm listening."

"I need a side, a guy who can come along, maybe drive a nice car and get us into some respectable places if these guys want a nice time in the city. You still got the Fastback, right?" Jack nods. "And that mug of yours can still get us past a few red ropes. More than mine anyway, probably more than any of the suckers' I know."

Jack lifts up a triangle of toast and looks at it, puts it back. With butter, maybe it'd be all right, but plain it looks like warm cardboard. "You see my name in the papers lately?" he asks. "No one gives a shit who I am anymore."

"Exactly, my man. They see you, people don't care, but maybe a small part of them remembers your face, knows you from the movie. I know it, you know it. That's why you wear the hat." He points to Jack's baseball cap, the Red Sox World Series Edition that he's taken to wearing when he comes into the city. "They recognize you and sometimes it's good: 'Oh, Jack Palms, you the man from *Shake 'Em Down*.' Then sometimes it's not good; someone says: 'You the guy got addicted to smack and hit his wife. The one never made a second movie.' Either way, bad or good, they like knowing you, recognizing someone they think is a celebrity. And we get the treatment we want."

Jack doesn't want to believe it comes down to this, to hear this is what people think of him, that he's down to the point where these are his options. He's been up in Sausalito for a long time now, two years of hiding away from the city, cleaning himself up, but he can't hide out forever, especially with his money from the movie running out.

Jack takes a deep breath. The flat surface of his coffee has no reflection. Bacon lies across his toast, grease soaking into the bread. He wonders how Ralph can still be eating like this and partying like he used to, how nothing's changed, nothing's come along and kicked his ass like the newspapers did when they came to take Jack's picture in handcuffs.

"I apologize, Jacky." Ralph puts his hands flat on the table, no longer eating. "But you know how it is. I know the papers got it wrong, but let's be honest about the street: you not the man anymore, Jack, but you still got *something.*"

Jack sips his coffee: cold already and bitter. He takes a deep breath, lets it out slow. "OK," he says. "I'm in."

Ralph nods, fluffs his eggs and forks in a mouthful. "Good," he says. "It's Eastern Europeans coming in from out of town, Czechs traveling big time, looking for a large chunk of blow. We meet them, take them out, show them The Guy and see that the deal goes off. It's easy."

"Right. And they'll pay big for that."

"Relax." Ralph stops eating for a beat, points his fork at Jack. "Why so skeptical? It's just a trade. Big trade. Don't doubt, bro." He forks up a big chunk of eggs, rubs it in the syrup. "I just need a backup. And for high rollers, I have to look good. That's why I call you. When I say we do this, I mean we do the fucker. No stops." He brings the fork to his mouth.

Jack nods. It's been a long time since he's worked *anything.* Maybe he's just getting nerves; maybe he just needs to be involved with something outside of his own house. He thinks about where he'd be right now if Ralph hadn't called: probably at the gym lifting or out on a morning run—activities that were good until they got old, things he needed at first to keep himself sane while he cleaned up. Now he's clean, needs something new.

"When do we start?"

Ralph laughs while chewing and catches some egg going down the wrong way. He coughs into the top of his fist. When he finishes catching his breath, he says, "That part you can just leave up to me, baby."

2

Two days later, after Jack's run his three miles and just started a coffee, Ralph calls again and says to meet him downtown on Stockton at eight, at the Hotel Regis. Jack doesn't know it but knows the neighborhood around it: the city's boutique shopping. The finest places: only designer names and upscale hotels.

Jack takes out a cigarette, his one of the day: the one he smokes with his cup of coffee in the morning, the one that reminds him of where he's been. He kicked the junk three years ago, one thousand, sixty-six days exactly, and hasn't had a drink in two years. No cigarettes, just this one every morning.

He looks out over the Bay while he smokes, through the huge kitchen windows that were the biggest selling point of the house, the thing Victoria fell in love with first. Now he's used to the view, to seeing the tiny sailboats move about on the water while he eats. As he takes a long drag, he feels the familiar nausea, and closes his eyes, eases into the comfort of his chair. The rest of the cigarette goes slowly, bringing the day to a crawl that Jack can appreciate now, knowing the afternoon will feature things he doesn't know and might not be prepared for.

When he's done, he snuffs out the cigarette, gets up and washes his hands, scrubs them vigorously with soap to remove any of the smell from his fingertips, knowing it won't ever work. He takes down the cereal and a ceramic bowl off the shelves that Victoria had installed when she remodeled the kitchen.

He skims the front page of the newspaper while he eats, looks out over the Bay, thinking about what Ralph's going to get him into with this and whether it's worth it overall. Compared to sitting around all day, there's hardly a choice. Compared to losing the house and looking for an apartment he can't afford either, he's ready to hit the shower and get dressed to go.

The phone rings and Jack waits it out, finally hears his answering machine beep. The plain voice of an agent from his bank comes on, the second call in as many days, asking Jack to call back, make an appointment to come in and discuss his loan. Jack knows what the bank knows—that he's late on the second payment in a row now and doesn't have the money. He's just transferred the balance from one credit card to another, buying himself some time, but the bank won't wait much longer.

Out in the Bay, a steamer makes its way toward the Bay Bridge, heading for the port of Oakland. Soon it will dock and the cranes will start to unload its containers; people will work to put its cargo onto trains, trucks; others will drive it across the country to places from California to Maine; still others will unload and unpack whatever the containers hold, putting items onto shelves to sell.

Jack dresses in jeans and a dark button-down, not tucked in. For too long he's been up here wearing sweats and track suits, going to the gym, and it feels good to be clean, dressed. Back in L.A. he dressed up for parties, went out to clubs all the time, had work to take care of. With Victoria, he'd dress nicer even: tuck in, wear a suit jacket every once in a while. But that was back then. Even before the divorce, after her first time in rehab, they stopped going out, mostly just stayed at home to nurse their addictions.

He stops at the mirror in the living room before going out to the garage. This is where he usually puts on his Sox hat, but now he leaves it on the rack. He looks at himself in the mirror, runs his hand over the short brown hair that he cuts himself every couple of weeks with electric clippers, smoothes the skin over his face that he shaves clean now every couple of days. In L.A., he used to have his hair styled and he'd wear a goatee or something else whenever he wanted, shaved himself with an electric and had a good time playing with the styles, but not now. Now he shaves with a razor, hot water, lather, and a badger brush. His face feels tight, the skin sensitive, but he takes his chin in his hand and looks at the side of his face, the bump on his nose from when he broke it playing football in high school. He's still in there, he tells himself, the guy he's known his whole life, alive and breathing, has the same looks that got him the movie, and has even added a little muscle since he made *Shake 'Em Down*, the movie where he drove the fast car, won all the fights, got all the girls.

The dark circles under his eyes are gone finally, the payoff of two years of getting a good night's sleep, running every morning and spending time in the sun. He stands up and looks over his body, patting his ribs like he did when he saw Ralph. He doesn't look bad, he tells himself, and does his best to try and believe it.

From Sausalito to the bridge, Jack opens up the engine on his light red, almost orange, '66 Mustang Fastback "K-code" GT. Here on the 101, early on a weekday evening, he can hear the engine roar, feel the torque and the power of the rpm's as he eats up the hills. He's replaced almost everything inside the car himself, repainted the body too. It was orange-red when he got it and he'd wanted blue, but something in him couldn't make the change. Something in him knew that this car was meant to be this color forever, new paint or old and faded. So when he put on the shiny new coat, waxed it, he had to stay with the original color.

He got the car after the movie, when he had money; this was the big thing he'd wanted, the thing he had to have: a '66 Mustang Fastback that could only survive in the clean California climate—no winter slush or salt to eat through the frame. Now, even without anything in the bank and the mortgage falling apart, he'd give up the house before this car.

Nothing matches the power feel of the Mustang "Hi Po" engine, the looks he gets on the street, or the feeling of knowing exactly what he's driving, a car so rare that even when they were being produced in 1965, 66 and 67, you only had a one in a hundred shot of getting a "K-code." And he's worked on it enough to know exactly how it runs and what pieces went into it. And the style. This car has more style than anything else on the road for Jack's money—any amount—the slick line and the rise in the back untouchable. And he's not trying to compensate for anything, as Victoria once suggested. The Mustang eats hills like they were bumps, a San Francisco must, makes a sound like a jet engine, and does what he wants. The car is Jack's love, the only friend from L.A. times that's still around.

In the city, heading downtown, Jack gets looks, especially in and around Union Square, where the traffic slows and the shoppers all look to see who you are. Jack keeps his sunglasses on, tries not to make eye contact with anyone. Whether they'd really recognize him or he just needs to get over his fears, he's not sure. But a part of him doesn't want to find out.

Jack pulls up outside the hotel and parks next to a new white Mercedes G-Class, a big boxy number like a cross between a German tank and an SUV. He'd guess this for the Eastern Europeans' car, but they're probably driving a rental, one of the sports cars, the convertible Porsche, or an S-class sedan. He sees a new Mustang parked here too, a convertible, but it's one of the recent releases he's heard so much about. Supposedly they're more powerful than his with the same size engine. Forty years later and they must have reengineered it to do *something* better, because it'll never look as good as the Fastback. They've only made a lighter body, it's likely, and that's no great feat with forty years of technology on your side.

Getting out of his car, Jack catches a quick second-glance from the parking attendant—the look Ralph described; people know Jack, recognize him still. As San Francisco goes, mostly sports stars and locals, not that many actors, Jack's face is one of the few that people remember.

He gives the attendant a five and hits the revolving door without looking back, still holding the keys to his car. If it has to be moved, they can page him.

Inside the lobby Jack looks around, trying to decide what he should do. The place has second story-level ceilings, fancy chandeliers and leather couches all over. A big guy wearing a designer suit stands up from one of the couches on the left side of the lobby.

Jack looks around for the bar, and the guy makes his way over, asks if Jack is "Mr. Palimas?"

"No." Jack shakes his head, taking a good look at the guy: big nose, face like an anvil. He tries to dodge the guy, more from habit than not, but the guy moves faster than Jack expects, cuts him off.

"You are Jack. I am told to wait." He holds up a small version of Jack's old headshot, probably clipped from a bad newspaper article. "Ralphie told me to meet you."

"Oh, *Ral*phie," Jack says. "In that case." He shrugs, holds his hand out for the guy to lead the way.

"I am Michal. Please to come." The big guy starts toward the elevators.

"Where did you get that?" Jack points to the picture.

"Ralphie has changed our meeting from bar to our suite. It is big." He turns and shows Jack an awkward toothy smile, as if he got an extra helping of teeth in the attributes line at birth and his mouth did its best to fit them all in. They run together at angles, jammed and overlapping. "Our suite is big so we can have party."

A bellman holds the elevator doors open and they enter. As the doors slide closed, Jack sees his reflection and that of the smiling suit. He's taller than Jack and wider; this guy can carry himself. Plus he's been lifting more than just the rocks they've got where he's from, and his suit is well cut, expensive.

Jack rubs his face. He leans toward the door and looks at his cheeks: pale and clean from this morning's shave. A couple dots of dried blood have come out along his jaw since he left the house. His eyes still look tired; he doesn't like what he sees. Though he's put on five or ten pounds of muscle in the past two years, his eyes still look deep-set in his face—like he's using—as if he needs a couple nights' sleep, even though it feels like that's all he's gotten for the past two years. His skin is pale, freckled, has been since the sixth grade when his mother moved him and his sister up from North Carolina to Boston to get away from his father and the sun. He takes a good look at his brown eyes and runs a hand over his hair. Would I believe me? He wonders.

He turns his neck to the side, leaning his ear to his shoulder, try-ing to loosen up, get a pop. In his movie, they gave him a big tattoo from his chest up onto his neck, out the top of his shirt. People liked that, were disappointed when they found out it wasn't real. Even when Jack first met Victoria, she ran her fingers around his neck and pulled his collar down.

As the numbers light up above the doors, Jack rolls up his sleeves. They're going all the way to the top.

3

The doors open onto a single large room, a two-story suite. White leather furniture fills the middle of the room beneath floor-to-ceiling windows. Jack is used to good views like the one he has up in Sausalito, seeing the Bay, but from here can see into the hills, clear to Alcatraz, Treasure Island, El Cerrito, Berkeley, and down over Alameda and beyond. The other downtown skyscrapers surround them, like seeing the skyline from inside it. Jack recognizes the Trans-America tower but doesn't know the others by name.

As he and Michal step out of the elevator, three men in suits stand to meet them, one of them wearing an awful green eyesore with wide lapels. Ralph is here, wearing another loud Hawaiian shirt.

Two guys come forward with hands extended, the one with the bad suit, and another, wearing a simple blue suit. Behind him, Jack notices a fifth man standing against the wall, almost blending in, wearing a suit that looks a lot like Michal's. Michal steps back and takes a position beside the elevator doors, fading back as if he and the other guy have been posted there. They stand with their arms crossed, like sentries on either side of the entrance.

"Shake this man down," the Czech with the green suit says, doing a funny dance in his legs, mostly, without any movement of his torso or arms.

The others laugh.

"Yes, man. You are the one from this movie." Green Suit bends his knees and shakes his legs, brings them apart and together. "Shake this down."

To stop this, Jack takes his arm in a two-handed shake and starts pumping, telling the guy he's glad to meet him.

"I am Al," Green Suit says. "It is a very pleasure to meet you." His suit is soft, some kind of ultra-synthetic fabric, shiny and dull at the same time, with a gold shirt underneath and a dark, wine-colored tie.

"Nice suit," Jack says, because it's clear he's looking.

"You like it." Al turns to the others. "This is good guy. Style, see. Loud, like the American Rock and Roll." He laughs, a full on, head-tilted-back-and-mouth-wide-open laugh that you have to go along with. He moves his hands along his sides, showing off the green fabric.

The other two come around and start shaking Jack's hands, the one guy in a blue suit and the other wearing a deep gray solid. Both of these guys come on reserved like their clothes. "I am David," the guy shaking his hand says. He has a glass of scotch in one hand, raises it in salute as he says his name. His hair is cut short, in a buzz that's grown out, or was cut recently by someone who wanted to make him look like a Chia Pet.

"I am Vlade," the third guy says, taking Jack in a hug. "I have still the good name from our country that I do not change like them." He looks at Al and makes a funny face, putting his lower lip up toward his moustache, as if he's smelled something bad. "*Al*," he says, with an intentionally flat accent, imitating how Americans must sound to him.

"Yes, sir, this is the man here: Jack Palms," Ralph says, stepping forward. He has a thick cigar in one hand and a scotch in the other. He sways as he moves. Jack realizes this is why Ralph asked him along: because he's planning on spending most of his time in the bag.

"Jack Palms," Al says, "Let us share with you some blow." More laughs and then Jack watches Al, Ralph and the others retreat to the couches. He can see a glass-top coffee table in the middle all ready to go, with the lines cut and set. Ralph sits down on one of the couches and starts rolling up a twenty.

Jack hesitates. Coke got him going in L.A., made him the rage at the right parties, introduced him to some of the right people, maybe even started his short movie career. But it also led him to H and his life falling apart.

Now he's spent two years in a place where life seems dull: either because he's taken too much out of it and he's evening out, or because he's got fewer dopamine receptors left to stimulate his pleasure cells—either the karmic or the biological explanation, Jack's not sure which he prefers. He smells the remnants of the morning's cigarette on his fingers. Even after the scrubbing, it's still there, like a trail of where he's been, a reminder of mistakes he's made.

Ralph leans close to the table and snorts a line. Ralph who's never had anything bad happen as far as Jack's known, Ralph who just keeps going and going and partying. Fucking Ralph.

Jack clenches his teeth. If he can stand here, watch these guys, play roving concierge, maybe he'll be cured, or at least on his way to getting paid.

David cleans up a line with a fresh-rolled bill.

"Mr. Jack?" Al says, pointing to the table.

"No thanks." Jack stays near the door, hooks a thumb at the sentries. "Just think of me like I'm these guys: here to work. To help you have the fun."

The Czechs turn to him. David says, "You do not want to join?"

"You do not enjoy the blow?"

Jack shakes his head. "I'm OK."

Ralph holds up both hands and says, "Serious downer." He leans toward the table, covers a nostril, and snorts a line. "Oh, yeah. Motherfucker!" He does another quick one, then lies back on the couch, powder on his upper lip. "Yeah!" he yells.

David's still looking at Jack, so he shows him three fingers. "Three years now," Jack says. David nods.

Vlade stands up and comes over to Jack. He claps his hands, rubs Jack's shoulder when he gets there. "This is all right. Seriously. It means there is more for us." He starts laughing. "There is the bar," he says, pointing to a small white refrigerator under a mirrored wall of glass shelves and cocktail glasses. He gives Jack a slight push. "Help yourself."

Jack starts to decline, then thinks better of it and goes over. He finds seltzer and ice, a lime, and makes himself a drink. As he turns, he sees David and Al's heads to the table, Vlade still watching him.

"Cheers, bro." Jack holds up his glass, just seltzer and ice, and squeezes in the lime.

4

An hour into drinking and snorting blow in the hotel room and the Czechs are ready to explore the S.F. nightlife. They have a small and dwindling stash of blow that they'll be done with by morning, that Ralph has assured them can be replenished—and then some— through his connection, a Colombian who is only in town for a short time. If Jack stays, this might actually work out; if he leaves Ralph to run this show drunk and coked up, his guess is it won't get too far. The Czechs keep pushing Ralph about how much they can get from the Colombian; say they want to stay in the U.S. and deal here, need a nest egg to start off with.

"You don't know the community we can connect to," Al keeps saying.

Every time he feels weak, Jack smells his fingers, the tinge of the cigarette smell, and thinks about his imperfection, the feel of the bottom rung that's not so far behind him. It's been so long since he worked a job that it actually feels good to be standing still, not partying, to Just Say No, like Nancy Reagan.

And then they start bouncing around the suite, hire a limo to take them around, and Jack has to share in a few laughs along with their bad jokes. But he can endure their coked-up ideas, like Al standing up through the limo's sunroof, and going to strip clubs will be a lot easier on the eyes than looking at Ralph and his boys.

At Ralph's suggestion, they head downtown to a place south of Market. "Shit is tight here guys. I fucking know you'll love this place."

The bouncers recognize Jack as soon as he steps out of the limo. To his way of looking at it, the stretch draws their attention, so they're looking closer at who gets out, getting ready to jar the part of their memory that might know *Shake 'Em Down*.

"Jack Palms," one of the bouncers says, nodding, shaking Jack's hand. The guy's got a good grip, a tight black shirt on that matches the color of his short afro, and a dark leather jacket. He wears nice shoes, shined, a tip that this place might actually be worth spending some time in. He leads the group to an alternate door and tells Jack, "V.I.P. section, Mr. Palms. I hope you guys have a good night." He claps Jack on the back as he shows them inside. "And I *loved* your movie, man."

Jack follows the Czechs straight to the bar, thinking that this is not bad, like he might be scoring himself some karmic points by staying away from the blow.

Here in the V.I.P. section, a large room, with as many dancers as men, Jack sits at the bar and watches a beautiful young blonde stand on a stage above Al and David, swaying in front of them, wearing only a small yellow thong.

Vlade sits down next to Jack, waves to a bartender with long brown hair and a pair of fake breasts that won't quit. She works without a shirt on, her falsies standing at attention as she works the bar, moves toward Jack and Vlade to make their drinks.

"Hi," Jack says.

She laughs. "That's a new line. What can I get you?"

"Seltzer. With lime."

She laughs again—"I got that."—and turns to face Vlade. Curly hair, long legs, big, delicate eyes. She can't hide her surprise at Al's green suit and gold shirt and she lets out another laugh, more of a short howl, then covers her mouth with her hand. Jack likes her already. She wears a tight black band around her neck. She looks back at Jack, looking maybe for an explanation about Al, one he doesn't have. Her lips have a glimmer, her eyes squeezed into smiles at their corners.

Vlade orders a scotch and two more for Al and David.

"And I'm buying." A short guy pulls back the stool next to Jack's, holds out his hand. "Tony Vitelli," he says, like his last name comes in two parts, the first rhyming with bite, the second with jelly. "It's not often I have a local celebrity in my establishment."

He speaks softly, with a slight lisp—Jack thinks of Joe Pesci—and wears a deep blue suit, a shirt with a high French collar underneath. His hair is slicked back and held behind his head in a tight ponytail. The guy's got a diamond on his finger as big as a dime.

"I like your place," Jack says. He shoots the bartender a look to let her know she's included, but she's busy squeezing a lime into Jack's drink.

Tony Vitelli waves his hand at the idea, says, "Shake this baby down, motherfucker!"

Jack nods, acknowledging the line from his movie.

"I've seen that shit like six times. It's no *Scarface*, but after *Pulp Fiction*, *True Romance* and a few others, it's on my shelf."

Jack wonders where that puts it, decides to try the waters, just to talk to this guy. He hasn't made conversation with someone in a bar or club for a long time. "So it's top ten?"

"Of mine?" Tony Vitelli slips up onto the chair. "I'm not sure I'd go that far. Top twenty maybe." He hits Jack on the back. "I'll give you that, how about?"

The bartender comes close again, sets Jack's drink down on a white beverage napkin. The more he looks at her, the more he likes what he sees. And this isn't only because it's the first pair of breasts he's been this close to in a long time.

Or it could also be that.

She smiles an extra-wide one at Jack as she puts a glass of ice on the bar in front of Vlade, starts pouring Oban over it slowly.

She bites her lip, steals another look at Al and brings her eyes right back to Jack's.

Vlade thanks her. As she moves down the bar to tend to the Czechs and Ralph—David is leaning over the bar with a hundred-dollar bill extended from his hand—she gives Jack a look, all eyes and big red lips, that would stop a train.

"Yeah," Tony says, "Top twenty." He takes Jack's hand again to shake it, already getting up off his chair. "We like your friends here, their kind of business," he says, looking around Jack and sizing up the cut of David's suit, the bill in his hand. Then he sees Al and he laughs, shakes his head. "That's nice," he says. "I got to get me one of those."

"The suit?" Jack asks.

"No." Tony smiles. "The monkey wearing that thing, he's a fucking holler."

Vlade holds up his drink in a toast.

Then Tony Vitelli leans in close to Jack, pats him on the shoulder and says, "For tonight we won't say anything about Mr. Anderino, your boy. But take it into consideration——" He holds up one finger on his left hand, the first finger, and Jack can see the diamond sitting at the other end of his fist. "Let it be known that he has been unwelcome here in the past."

Jack looks at Ralph. He just got his drink, what looks like a gin and tonic in an extra-large tumbler, something more like a bowl than a glass. He stirs it with his finger, licks it off and takes a long pull. He's got different sunglasses on top of his head, aviators today instead of the Ray Charles specials, but most of his curly hair has come loose around his face.

"Ralph?" Jack says.

"So you've heard me?"

"What?"

"Nice meeting you, Mr. Palms." He cocks his head, grabs Jack's hand again, squinting his eyes just slightly, maybe trying to tell Jack something. Before he moves away, he stops for a look at the bartender, tightens his ponytail and smiles at her. "Sweet thing," he says, to Jack.

"Thanks," Jack says, stupidly: he wanted to mean it about the drink, but it comes out like he's talking about the bartender. Tony laughs, an awkward sound, almost a bark, then turns and waves to one of his guys, points toward Jack's party, and he's gone. As he moves away, Jack looks up onto the stage behind the bar, where a tall blonde in knee-high white leather boots and a skin-tight leather leotard has just come out from a wing to Janet Jackson's "Nasty."

Later in the night, between the bartender—Maxine—slipping Jack her phone number and the Czechs working their way through a series of lap-dances, Jack starts to really enjoy himself, actually have a good time without coke or booze. He's thinking he should get out more often, when Ralph stumbles over and puts his arm around his shoulders. "We're doing well so far, brother," Ralph mumbles. Even leaning away, Jack can smell Ralph's breath. He can imagine how this must have been for the young stripper whose breasts Ralph's just been kissing—but that's if she's sober, which she probably isn't.

"Real well, pal," Ralph continues. "These boys having fun and that's the point. We just keep them happy, get a few girls to go and see what happens."

Jack moves away from Ralph's arm, ducks to go for his drink, and Ralph has to use both hands to steady himself against the bar, shuffle his feet to keep balanced.

"Sounds good." Jack tucks the bartender's number inside his jacket. "We keep them happy here. Then we introduce your Colombian friend and get this thing done."

Ralph turns to Jack and winks at him, opening his mouth to do it. "Good for you, right?" He looks at where Jack's just put Maxine's number. "You just make sure you keep these boys entertained."

Down the bar, Jack sees David and Al standing at the stage, holding bills up to a brunette putting one of her high heels on Al's green shoulder. As she bends forward to take Al's bill between her breasts, David is already laying a twenty across the bridge of his nose.

Jack laughs. "That shouldn't be too hard."

5

The next morning Jack wakes up later than his schedule—he didn't get in until after four—and when he gets into the kitchen, there are already three messages waiting on his machine. He hits the button and starts taking out a bowl and the cereal—fuck today's run.

First there's a beep and then, *"Hi, Jack. This is Maxine from The Coast. From last night. Hope you liked your seltzers with lime. So sorry you and your friends had to leave before we got off. I'll call you again later."*

Nice one, Jack thinks. The girl's aggressive. Not afraid to find his number or to call first. He considers calling her back, but she probably got in later than he did and is still sleeping it off. Jack thinks back to her breasts, the little silver cups over her nipples, the tight choker around her neck. He hears the second beep. *"Yo Jackie, this's Ralph. Nice show last night. I'm icing my head to wake up this morning and I just got a call from the Colombian. He wants to meet this afternoon and get acquainted. Know what that means? Anyways, come pick me up when you're moving and I'll tell you what's next."*

Jack guesses the Colombian will have some questions about this Czech money and if it's as green as he likes. That or he doesn't know Ralph as well as Ralph wants everyone to think. Probably the Colombian wants to feel Ralph out before he gets into any deals with his friends.

Maybe it's the cards he's been dealt, more payback for all the drugs he did with Victoria, all he took out of life after *Shake 'Em Down*, that makes Jack a hired hand in all this, the guy who has to go pick up Ralph at his house, but he can take it. He has to admit he had fun last night; even acting like a bodyguard-concierge, it felt good to get out again, better than anything he's done in a while.

He knows the longer he goes with Ralph, the harder it'll be to get out. But maybe he doesn't care. Maybe he's ready for something—even something like this.

The answering machine beeps again. *"Jack Palms, this is Sergeant Hopkins from the S.F.P.D. I'm sure you remember me from when we made that little visit to your house three years ago. The one your wife requested?"*

"Fuck," Jack says out loud to the morning. He remembers them taking him away in handcuffs as the papers snapped pictures of him like he'd just robbed the White House. How could he forget? Or forget Sgt. Mills Hopkins, the cop who brought him in?

"Well it's just come onto my desk that there may be a few new reasons for us to have a talk sometime soon. Do you think you could call me back at 559-6477 and save me the trip out to your place?" Jack can practically hear something like joy in the officer's voice. *"That'd be the greatest. Thanks."*

Jack can hear the sarcasm dripping from his final statement. Hopkins, the fucking Sausalito cop who took Jack away that time Victoria called, tipped off the papers about the wife-beater story and had a fun time doing it. Jack remembers the guy laughing in his squad car, his big thick neck-rolls contracting and expanding as his head moved up and down laughing, nodding at all he'd done and the reporters snapping pictures of Jack in the back seat as the squad car pulled away from his house.

Now that motherfucker's going to call? That makes sense, Jack considers, thinking it would be too much to ask for the good to start coming again that easy.

Jack pours the milk, looks out over the Bay to see this morning's sun coming out in force near Treasure Island. As usual, a stream of fog covers the Golden Gate and West San Francisco. Downtown, where the money is made and spent, is still in the sun.

He spoons the first mouthful of cornflakes into his mouth.

6

An hour later, showered and cleaned up but wearing an Adidas warm-up suit—because it's clean and why the fuck not?—Jack cruises across the Richmond-San Rafael Bridge toward El Cerrito to find Ralph where he lives. Jack likes the feel of being out of the house, doing something without going to the gym first, and the chill breeze coming in his window. No way he'll catch any visits from Sgt. Hopkins today.

The fact that Ralph's already been up and calling Jack doesn't surprise him. The old Ralph partied till morning four or five nights a week and still made all his meetings, talked the movie dicks blue until his clients got whatever roles they wanted. Now he'll probably do the same to the Colombian, which is why Jack's going along to make sure he doesn't fuck things up.

In front of Ralph's house, a tan one-family in the middle of a street of tan one-families, Jack sees a white pickup and a green Chevy sedan. Either way, Jack knows why they're using his car. On the lawn Ralph's planted a big "Beware of Dog" sign, but as Jack gets out of the car and walks up to the door, he doesn't hear any barking. Ralph, himself, is probably the dog to beware of.

Jack tries the bell and doesn't hear anything happening for a while, so he knocks twice, waits, then knocks twice again before trying the door.

It opens before he can turn the knob. At a normal person's house this could be weird, but at Ralph's, it's not that out of the ordinary. The last time Jack came over, he found the front door

unlocked and Ralph tripping his head off on mushrooms in an upstairs bathroom, eating pizza in a bubble bath and listening to Led
Zeppelin as loud as his stereo would play it. That was enough to
keep Jack away for a while.

Inside, only thin strips of sunlight shine onto the living room
furniture through the closed blinds. Jack smells a musty warmth as
he steps into the foyer, where he is surprised to see a good-looking
mountain bike, something he can't imagine Ralph ever using.
"Ralph!" he calls into the house, hears nothing in return.

Stepping up onto the living room rug, Jack hopes he doesn't
have to see Ralph naked in his tub again. A big couch dominates
the dark living room: a wrap-around sectional, situated in front of
an extra-large TV console, with a dark wood coffee table in the
middle. TV guides and magazines cover the top of the table, along
with some half-finished drinks in various non-matching mugs and
cups from various food chains. Jack notices a few magazines on the
couch, *Stuff* and *Maxim*, a *Penthouse*. He crosses the living room and
enters the kitchen: a small room with a brown linoleum floor and a
counter space cut into the wall, a pass-through connects it to the
living room. There's a pizza box open on the kitchen table, a single
pepperoni slice left in it.

"Ralph, I found your breakfast," Jack yells. "It's ready!"

He steps back into the living room and listens: no sound. He
waits, hoping to hear some movement upstairs, Ralph flushing the
toilet or walking across the floor. Nothing. No Zeppelin, no bath
water, no singing.

Next to the phone in the kitchen, Jack sees a small pad of note-
paper with a few names on it: the top one is Tony Vitelli, scratched
out; the next is Joe Buddha, an old friend of Jack and Ralph's from
the movie days back in Hollywood and the producer on *Shake 'Em
Down*. He'd been one of Jack's chief backers from the start, the guy
who took him from bartending on the party scene to movie scripts
and let him star in *Shake 'Em Down*. When it came down to the sequel, *Shake It Up*, Joe Buddha had never backed off; it was the other
producers who feared Jack was heading for an explosion, decided to
pull out. Joe Buddha's a good guy: short, funny, always smiling, big
belly. But his name is also scratched out.

The next and last name on the pad is Jack's. There's no line through it, but instead it's been underlined. Seeing his name here in Ralph's house, under these others, Jack gets a soft chill up his spine. He doesn't like the thought of these other names scratched out, his being left.

All the furniture and mess in the living room and kitchen are what Jack would have imagined he'd find in Ralph's house, but through the kitchen window he sees a pool. That's his second surprise: not because Ralph can't afford it, but because Jack can't imagine Ralph ever swimming. And the pool looks new; Jack can't remember it being here on his last visit. But it had been raining, and Jack never went out back. Maybe the point of the pool isn't exercise, Jack considers. Maybe Ralph's got it to show something.

Jack notices a shape outside that's strange, a dark mass under the patio table, something he can't discern: old, dark clothes or a folded-up rug. But it looks like it could be something else too.

Jack finds the sliding glass door off the living room open and moves slowly onto the patio, looking under the table. As he gets closer, he can see that it's not old clothes or a rug. Whatever it is is surrounded by a puddle of something dark. He pushes a chair out of the way and moves the table back. He still can't understand—or believe—what he's seeing. Then he gets the whole picture: dark fur.

With the table moved aside, it's clear that the dark shape on the concrete is a dog, was Ralph's dog: a chocolate lab. Now, lying on its side, its head rolled back so its neck and chin face up, it lies in a pool of its own blood.

"Shit," Jack says. He stumbles back a few steps and collides with one of the cheap plastic chairs that go with Ralph's table, almost falling backward. He catches himself on the chair, holding it underneath him, but then its legs buckle and he falls slow and sideways down onto the deck. Eventually, he's down, the chair wedged between his legs, suspending one of his feet up in the air.

He rolls himself off it and sits up on the concrete. From here he sees the dog's wet belly, too close, and he pushes back, moving onto his hands and feet, and stands into one of Ralph's hedges. It's just a big green guy, no prickers, but the small branches scratch at his skin through the sweat suit.

But he's on his feet.

Jack moves forward and, with the toe of his sneaker, rolls the dog over to see her other side. Completely wet, the fur matted in crimson, Jack can't see what happened, but the result is clear. He sets her back down, closes the dog's eyes. He pats her head a few times, hoping to send her some good wishes into the doggie after-life.

"Jesus," Jack says. He walks over to the house, puts his head through the patio door and calls out, "Ralph, what the fuck you been doing here this morning? You taking your fuck-up pills again?"

But now when he doesn't hear a response, part of Jack knows something's wrong. Back inside, he calls Ralph's name out loud into the house. No answer. "Ralph, I know you're tripping hardcore up there somewhere, but we're going to get you out of this. I know you've got some popsicles in the freezer, and when I find you we'll sit down and have some. They'll really calm you down."

Jack listens, unsure whether he's yelling for himself now, to calm his nerves, or if he really thinks he'll see Ralph on the stairs and hear him say, "Shit, Jack. I did a really fucked up thing to my dog this morning."

Jack knows that's not going to happen. Even if he's gone over the edge himself a few times, passed out in a bad way—needed a friend to pull him off his bedroom floor and shove him into a cold shower—he's never done anything like this. It's because of those times though, and those friends, that he feels an obligation to find Ralph and see what's going on.

Jack follows the carpeted stairs up to the second floor, to where Ralph's bedroom and bathroom are. He starts down the hall, calling Ralph's name into the quiet house as he moves. On his right, the first door opens onto Ralph's office: a bright room with a black computer and a flat screen monitor on the desk, bookshelves of plastic-jacketed comic books. Jack can see clearly that Ralph's not here.

The first door on the left is locked. From what Jack remembers, this is the bathroom where Ralph had his bubble bath. He knocks and re-tries the handle: still locked. At the end of the hall, Jack finds

Ralph's bedroom and a big waterbed, the sheets on it strewn about like a couple of Mavericks waves rolled in overnight. A skylight cut into the ceiling illuminates the room with sunlight, what probably woke Ralph this morning.

The place is a love-nest: Ralph has it all set up in here: big TV, DVD, surround-sound speakers mounted high up on the walls. The place even has zebra-print wallpaper and a thicker shag carpet to complete it. Jack would have to give Ralph a little credit if it weren't for another open pizza box—this pizza half-eaten—and a crumpled pair of tighty whities in the middle of the floor.

Then, when Jack walks into the bathroom, he forgets it all: everything that Ralph didn't clean and the drugs he took and everything good that happened last night. The first thing he notices is a red spray of blood against the wall, some kind of discolored mess in the center of it that Jack knows isn't vomit. Then he sees Ralph, fully clothed, lying face down in his Jacuzzi with a good chunk of his skull missing. And Jack knows Ralph won't be sleeping on that waterbed anymore.

Jack moves a little closer, sees the white of bone and something else, something gray that might be Ralph's brain, through the back of his head. The mess on the wall must be a spray of blood from where Ralph was standing when they—whoever it was—shot him. If he'd been facing the wall, then slipped down onto the bottom of the tub, he'd leave a trail down the wall and its side like Jack sees now, a big enough mess to cover what's here if they shot him from close range, held the gun to his head and told him whatever it was they wanted him to hear last in this life before they blew off the better part of his head.

7

Jack stumbles to the toilet and brings up this morning's corn flakes, holding himself up with one hand against the wall and one hand on the back of the john. He's seen enough; he stumbles out of the bathroom and into the bedroom, tripping over the thick rug and falling on the floor. He's got a feeling in his stomach like it's just been lined with metal. He can still taste the steel in his mouth. On the floor, he looks up, realizes he's got his hand on the underwear and throws them across the room. He sees the edge of the bed just inches from his head, is glad he didn't hit it and knock himself out—then they'd find two bodies here in the house and he'd be fucked.

"God damn," Jack says.

Jack looks up at Ralph's ceiling and the blue sky through the sky-light. He takes a few breaths. Mercifully, Ralph let the zebra wallpaper stop at the walls and left the ceiling plain white. Jack covers his eyes with the heels of his hands, presses against his face and irons his forehead smooth with his palms.

"What the fuck?" he asks. He can feel his heart pumping fast, faster than it does on the treadmill, faster than when he's lifting weights or jogging in the morning. It's racing too fast, and Jack breathes deep breaths, trying to slow it down. "Fuck," he says.

An image of Ralph's body in the bottom of the tub flashes across his mind's eye. He shakes his head, trying to clear it, sees the dog, its wet side. Then Jack struggles onto his feet, holding the bed for support, and tries to keep breathing deep breaths. He sits down on the edge of the waterbed, careful to keep his weight on the hard frame—not wanting to wash away—and holds his hand over his heart.

"Shit," he says, gasping for air. He's never had an asthma attack before, but he feels like people do in the descriptions he's heard: like he's breathing through a straw, only able to get small tastes of air. He feels his heartbeat in his fingers.

In a minute or two, when his heart stops racing, Jack sits up and looks around the bedroom. He knows he needs to leave, that whoever killed Ralph could come back or the cops might show up and find him in a crime scene, the house of a dead guy, but he can't move. The thick shag carpet is actually pretty nice, he decides. Sure, it's the kind of thing you can trip over and don't see anymore since the 70s, 80s at best, but when you're down on your hands and knees, it's good stuff. He looks around the edge of the room, past the TV and the chair piled with clothes. He looks past the bathroom, doesn't need to see more of Ralph.

From the fast look he already got, Jack knows Ralph had on a different Hawaiian from last night and tan shorts, short ones that look like he might have been planning a swim. It's a good way to cure a hangover, Jack's heard. Maybe that's why Ralph got the pool. But Jack knows Ralph hadn't planned on going out of the house in that outfit, not with those shorts.

He looks at the dresser and to the nightstand: there's a big bottle of ibuprofen, a roll of condoms hanging out of a drawer. The clock blinks 12:00. Ralph's wallet is next to the clock: a thick leather job that only Ralph could fit into his back pocket. Ralph's keys are on top of the dresser with a pile of change, next to a few credit cards, which seems odd. Why not keep these in his wallet? Jack gets up to look at the wallet, takes a few tissues from the night table and uses them to pick it up. It's full of cash. Ralph has a stack of papers, receipts that must date back to the 90s, and a wad of green that could finance strip club trips for a week, even at last night's pace. He looks through the rest of the wallet, but only finds more credit cards, so he's still not sure why the others are on top of the dresser. He pushes them apart so he can look: a Discover card and a

MasterCard are on top, both in the name Izzy B. Strong. Fucking Ralph.

With the tissues on his hands, he opens the dresser drawers, starting at the bottom. In it, with a few pairs of Ralph's underwear on top, Jack finds four clear plastic baggies of white powder. These are large bags, keys, Jack would guess, though he's never seen this much quantity before. They called them keys in his movie, in others he's seen, so he guesses they're keys. Without touching too much of what's here, Jack moves a few pairs of big, Hawaiian-print boxers to the side—what was it with this guy and Hawaiian prints?—and on the bottom of the drawer, to the side of the blow, finds a snub-nose .38 revolver, pearl handled, with a six-shot cylinder.

"Ralphie boy," Jack whispers, "What the fuck were you doing?" He takes the gun and tucks it into the back of his pants, thinks about taking the keys and decides against it. Protection he can use. Keys of coke he doesn't need right now. He closes the drawer gently with the tissues and with a quick look finds just clothes, T-shirts, socks and more swim trunks in the other two. As he closes the top drawer, he gets a chill like someone might be watching, and all of a sudden he doesn't feel like he's alone in the house.

On the way out of the bedroom, he drops his tissues in the garbage can, noticing a few porno DVDs on the bottom shelf of the TV stand next to it. There's a clump of what looks like Ralph's hair in the garbage, something that may be weird or could maybe also be just Ralph dealing with his normal life, cleaning out a brush.

The phone rings. Jack starts, actually jumps and does a half turn toward the bedside table. "Shit," he says. The ring comes again: loud and long in the empty house, shocking Jack into realizing that he should definitely get the hell out before someone finds him here with a dead man and his dead dog.

By the third ring, Jack's down the stairs, headed around the couch in the living room for the door. Then the machine picks up and there's a pause. Jack freezes. He hears Ralph say what he says, something with soft music playing in the background and low talking, something about how he's indisposed and will get back to you. Then a beep and a thick-accented voice comes on, says, "Ralphie. The meeting is this afternoon. At the wharfs, near the Bay. I will meet you there at three-thirty, but not if I do not hear from your call. Remember. Today is the day for you." The machine clicks off.

Jack stops for a second to look back around, making sure he hasn't left anything of his. He scans the living room again for anything that looks out of place, anything he'd notice and remember. Then he goes to the kitchen and rips off the top page of the notepad, the one with his name at the bottom. On the kitchen divider, he sees the phone and its Caller ID box with a phone number blinking on its screen. He writes it down on the paper in his hand. Just in case.

8

In his car, a few blocks away, Jack sits in the restored driver's seat with the motor running. "Shit," he says, running his hand across the top of his head. "Shit. Shit."

He gets out and paces on the hard, black asphalt of the street, then crouches, leaning against the car, and closes his eyes. In his head he sees the spray of Ralph's blood against the wall, the mess in the tub. He thinks of Ralph tripping out in the same Jacuzzi, holding a slice of pizza above the bubbles, and then Ralph's body lying face down on the bottom of the tub today, lying in his own blood. Jack rubs his eyelids with the pads of his fingers.

He's not sure what to do next.

Getting out and away from all this seems like the next logical step, but if Ralph's killers decide to track Jack to his house in Sausalito… Well, Jack's not sure what he would do if that happened. Maybe they saw his name on the pad and know he was working with Ralph, don't want this deal with the Czechs to go down. Either way, he's involved now, somebody knows his name and Ralph's dead, facedown waiting for the cops to show.

The cops.

Sgt. Hopkins is already after Jack about last night, for whatever reason, and now Ralph's dead, he'll want to find him even more. If he knows anything, he'll know Jack was with Ralph. If not, they'll find something when they turn Ralph's house into a crime scene, some way to connect Jack, and Hopkins will want to talk then.

Either way, he might as well head off the process, go in for a chat first thing.

He paces again, trying to get the image of the dead dog out of his head. Then Jack gets back into his car, drives for a few blocks, focusing on the road, the sound of the car's engine. What he really needs is a cigarette, some smoke to calm his nerves and slow this all down. He thinks about stopping at a gas station, smells his fingers from this morning's smoke, doesn't like the smell.

In his movie, the best friend got killed, but not until the end, just before the final showdown with the big drug dealer from Miami. That was all squibs then too, fake blood, the best friend just a character played by an actor. Here, Ralph wasn't anybody's best friend. Now he's dead before Jack even knows why or what's happening. Or who did it. There's the Colombian on Ralph's machine, the Czechs, two pieces of the puzzle that don't fit together yet, that need Jack to do the fitting.

He turns back out onto the main drag in El Cerrito, the street with the most stores and parking lots, turns back toward the highway entrance. With each gas station he passes, he thinks about going inside to buy some smokes.

He still sees the pictures: what he saw in Ralph's house, the pad with his name at the bottom. He imagines someone taking a pencil and crossing it out. Three blocks later, he stops, goes into a pharmacy and buys a pack of Parliaments. He lights up in the car and starts to feel better, nauseated. His heart finally slows.

As he drives toward the highway, he realizes he's going to head back toward I-80 and the Bay Bridge. The police might have more information he can use than anyone else does, at this point. And the sooner he comes clean about being at Ralph's the better. He hopes.

9

By twelve-thirty, Jack's at the police station downtown, a big, formidable-looking grey concrete building on Bryant with friezes of Blind Justice carved into the front. They call it The Hall of Justice, its official name, regardless of the fact that the Superfriends had a building by the same name in the cartoons Jack used to watch as a kid.

After a few long halls and some gum-chewing receptionists, Jack finds himself in an eighth-floor office sitting across the desk from a big, blunt-nosed cop and his nameplate: Sgt. Mills Hopkins. Behind the desk, a wall of tacked-on papers represents the latest of the cases and crimes Sgt. Hopkins has to deal with: lots of mug shots and bulletins.

Jack starts off asking about the Wonder Twins, but Hopkins doesn't crack even the beginning of a smile. So Jack starts in on the facts: what he saw at Ralph's. He may still wind up a suspect, but at least if he's cooperative they won't hold him, he hopes.

Hopkins sits at his big wooden desk, writing down on a yellow legal pad as Jack gives him the details. When Jack stops talking, he looks up.

"So you say Ralph Anderino was dead when you got to his house. He called you; you show up; you find him dead. That's what you're saying." He's nodding as he asks, still writing his notes.

"And his dog too," Jack says. "You don't want to forget that the person who killed Ralph also shot his dog. I think that's a very important detail."

"Right." He makes another note. The phone on Hopkins' desk springs to life, ringing loudly as only an old civil-service phone can. It's one of the early push button models, big and heavy with a little, domed light in one corner. Hopkins looks at the phone, turns his attention back to his pad.

"Let me ask *you* one question," Jack says.

Hopkins looks up from his writing and nods at Jack. The phone rings.

"Why'd you call this morning? What'd you want to ask?"

"We heard you were cruising downtown last night. I wanted to make sure the ladies were safe."

"That's nice," Jack says. He leans closer to the sergeant, putting his face over the desk. "You know Victoria's call was bullshit that night. But you let the papers run their wife beater story." The sergeant sits up straight, his back getting stiff. "Why'd those cameramen show up five minutes before you did, Mills? They just cruising? Nobody tipped them off?"

Hopkins puts the pad and pencil down and folds his hands on the desk. "So what you're saying, Jack, if I hear you correct, is *I* had to gain from telling the press that an S.F. celebrity, albeit a small, washed-up one, was about to go down for an assault on his woman?"

"Level with me. That way we get the past behind us, where it belongs."

"OK," Hopkins says, leaning forward. He looks serious, the space between his eyes turns into a crease. "I show up. You're junked out. She's throwing shit, carrying on. Yeah, it doesn't look like you been hitting her, but somebody's got to explain those bruises on her arms, right? And I thought drug bust or hits his wife, what's the difference? Both play good in the papers." He smiles, but then Jack stands up, and he stops. "Maybe that's my mistake. But who knew? We get you in and book you for possession. All I know, they went to press with the wife-beater story before you even hit your cell." Hopkins stands up, pushes his finger into the desk. "But you know what?"

"What?"

"Whatever came out that night didn't just happen in a minute. Whatever you had going on there had been building."

Jack shakes his head, partly to control himself, partly because he doesn't need this much *This is Your Life* at this point in his day. Getting into it with an officer won't put anything in his bank account or help him get out of the precinct while the day's still young either.

"So tell me how the papers get there?"

The sergeant frowns. "Drug bust? Home disturbance? I care? Things went wrong in your house and that is neither my problem nor the press'. You get what I'm saying?" He sits back down behind the desk, not lightly; his chair creaks like it's about to fall to pieces.

"Fine. You got my statement about Ralph's body and the state of his house. If you want to arrest me, go ahead." Jack holds out his hands for the cuffs. "If not, I have places to go."

"Sit down. I was just about to ask you about last night."

Jack keeps his hands up, his wrists tilted toward Hopkins. "Ask."

The sergeant opens one of his desk drawers, takes out a file. "If we say I owe you one about the papers, that I was wrong there, will you sit down and listen to me for a minute?"

"I might."

Hopkins points at the chair. "OK. I owe you. Now will you sit down?"

Jack sits down. "What?"

Hopkins puts the folder on his desk, spreads out a couple of group photos, black and white surveillance shots of the Czechs in some European city: Paris maybe, or Prague. "We heard you and Ralph were around town with some high rollers, spenders in from out of town. You know these tools?"

Jack shakes his head. "Not that I remember. They someone I should be aware of?"

Hopkins leans back, spreads his hands in front of him. "Our guys upstairs are hearing tips on some Eastern Europeans coming in, warlords or terrorists are the words they're hearing, and it's got them all in a bunch. I say it's bullshit, but orders from on high—" He points at the ceiling. "Dictate that we all have to follow up on this one like it's the Gospel. War on Terror and all."

"So?"

"So we follow all leads. What I'm saying: if you see these guys, you know what they're up to, drop me a dime." Hopkins takes a card out of his billfold and flips it onto the desk. "My cell phone's on the back."

Jack looks down at the card, at the picture of Vlade and the others. "These guys aren't terrorists."

"You know this?" Hopkins sits forward with a loud creak.

Jack shakes his head. "I'm saying your info, from wherever it comes, could be wrong."

They both look at the picture.

"This one," Hopkins taps Vlade. "And this one." He taps the quiet guy, Michal's pal. "We hear they've done a few violent acts on the other side of the world. Things no one we know would be proud of. Someone got worried about who they work for. Get me?"

Jack picks up Hopkins' card, reads it over. "That makes them terrorists?"

Hopkins lets out a long breath and looks to the side, then back at Jack. "Not my decision, Jack. Or my word. But you saying you're qualified to make that call?"

Jack stands up. "That all you wanted?"

"Just if you see these guys doing anything, if something starts to happen you're not sure of?"

"You want me to watch them."

"I'm just saying if you see them. If. And anything starts to look big, then you give me a call. OK?"

Jack reads the card again, slips it into the pocket of his sweat suit jacket. "OK," he says. "I see anything that screams War on Terror, I'll give you a call."

10

Outside, Jack takes the cigarettes out of his glove compartment, and taps the pack against his palm before he even realizes what he's doing. "Shit," he says, then he puts them away. He looks around, up at the bright blue sky ahead of him, out away from the city, and starts the engine. On his way to the Hotel Regis, Jack practices thinking about his breath, doing the kind of deep breathing he'd be doing if he was smoking—deep inhales and exhales—only doing it without the cigarettes.

Though the drive from the police station to the Regis Hotel is less than a mile, it takes more than twenty minutes with the lights. Getting to Market Street is the easy part. Below that, it's all wide avenues and four-lane traffic, but then around Market the cable cars and pedestrians, the streets coming in at all angles bring everything to a crawl. North of Market, the streets thin down to just one or two lanes, many still running one-way. Here the foot traffic's at its worst; the density of shops and what tourists consider "fine shopping" is higher here than anywhere else in the city. At each corner, Jack waits for large crowds toting big paper shopping bags to pass in front of his car.

When he finally pulls up at the hotel, the same valet from the day before smiles at him. Jack hands the kid a fiver for holding his door but still doesn't give up the keys. This time he tells the kid he won't be long.

In the elevator, going up to the penthouse, Jack checks himself out in the reflective doors: he's not exactly dressed for the top floor, wearing his blue sweat suit, but some guys can pull this off, he figures. As long as he acts the part. He could use a shave, he sees, and last night's left some luggage under his eyes, but his hair's tight and the sweat suit's new enough to look all right.

If he got this far, Jack considers, watching the floors hit forty-nine, then fifty, he must be doing something right. Then the doors open and the two handsome bodyguards, Michal and his pal, stand in front of Jack with their right hands tucked into their jackets, the silver handle of a revolver in each one's grip. He takes a step back, looks at the elevator attendant, a young kid from the lobby whose job is just to bring Jack up. The kid looks out into the penthouse and doesn't take his eyes off the floor to ceiling windows, the downtown-from-downtown views.

"Come in, Jack," Vlade says, standing between the two guards. He waves to Jack, nods.

"Thanks," Jack tells the kid, and steps out into the suite. As the doors close behind him, Jack says, "It's OK guys. Just me, Jack Palms. Remember all the fun we had together last night?"

The two guards don't speak, or move their hands to pull or release their weapons.

"What is going on, man?" Vlade says, stepping forward. He nods at the two guards just as they draw their weapons and aim them at Jack. Staring down the barrel of two guns, Jack hears Sgt. Hopkins' words "terrorist" and "warlord" and wonders if he shouldn't have just gone home to Sausalito. This is not turning out to be a good day.

"Whoa," Jack says, holding up his hands. As an actor, the number one thing he knows is to go with the scene, follow it through regardless. "What *is* going on? I come up here to see how you guys are doing, and you have Mike and the mechanic here pull their guns on me? What is that?"

"Oh, yes," Al says, suddenly appearing at the bar—though he could've been standing there already. "You want to check on *us*, see how *we're* doing. Well how are *you* doing, Mr. Palimas?"

"Palms," Jack says, losing it a little. He puts his hands down, points at Al. "First of all it's Palms. That's my name. You guys were

getting it wrong all last night, and now I need to tell you it's pronounced Palms. Like the *trees*."

"Whatever the fuck!" Al yells.

"Whoa!" Jack yells back. "Don't lose your temper with me, Ver-
sace."

Al looks confused at this, glances down at his clothes: a white
terry cloth robe, strictly hotel issue. Vlade frowns, as if he's thinking
it over, then says something softly to Al in Czech. Al turns back to
the bar shaking his head, starts to pour himself a drink.

Vlade regards Jack with interest. "No need to get angry, my
friend." He looks at Michal and then the other guard.

Jack re-raises his hands. "Guys," he says. "Can we put the guns
down and talk this through?" The two black holes of the barrels
stare at him.

Vlade doesn't budge when the two look at him for direction. He
angles his chin up toward Jack. "What happened to Ralph?"

"I don't know. I seriously don't." Jack watches the others to see
how they react.

"He is dead." Vlade folds his arms. Al turns back toward Jack, a
highball glass of something brown, scotch probably, in his hand.
"Someone has killed him this morning and when the boys go to
pick him up—" Vlade nods at Mike and the other guy. "They find
police crawling on his house like they are red ants. The biting kind."

"They told you he was dead?"

"You think they talk to the cops here? Crazy. They come back.
We see on the TV." David points to the flat screen model by the
couches. "The fucking TV show Ralph's body on the bed with
wheels, going out with the sheet over him! Fucking 'gang-related,'
they say."

Al nods in time to Vlade's statements, punctuating his anger.
"Fuck!" he adds.

Vlade gives him a quick look.

"It's true," Jack admits, holding his hands high. "I saw it myself
when I went over this morning." Jack shakes his head. "I guess I
was there before your boys, but I was not the one who did this. Tell
your guys to put their guns down. I'm the one who's trying to help
you."

Michal says, "You saw him? Ralph?"

Jack nods. "Fucking bathroom. Someone popped him in the back of the head and left him in a bloody tub. Even shot his dog."

Al frowns and tilts his head as if accepting this. "Probably barking," he says.

"Yeah, but you don't kill a fucking guy's dog!" And now Jack is upset and stomping on the expensive rug. "It's a fucking dog!"

"Freeze where you are," the two guards say to Jack together.

"I was not the one who killed him!" Jack says, and he walks right up to the guards, between them and directly to Vlade. He stands right in front of him when he says, "I can respect that you guys are concerned. But I was not the one who did Ralph. In fact, I think the guy who did it might be after me next. So let's drop the guns and find *him* together." He takes a good look at Al to make sure he hasn't moved, looks at first Michal and then the other guard, meeting their eyes, not looking down at their guns. "And this is fucked up; pulling these guns on me after all the shit we did last night."

Gauging from the look on the Czechs' faces—like he might be making a point, that or he's now the craziest one in the room—Jack goes on. "What we need to do is find out who did this. Hunt them down, kill *them*, and find out what happened."

Vlade nods to the guards and they lower their weapons.

"Thank you." Jack watches the guns go back inside the jackets. He takes a few deep breaths and then says what he has to say with his eyes closed.

"Vlade, guys. Don't *ever* point your guns at me again. Please. Because I'm telling all of you right now: if I have a gun pointed in my face again, I go home. End of story. I am the one on your side. I want to know what happened to Ralph." He looks around at the others. "Let me say it again: I did not shoot Ralph. No matter what we don't know, *that* we know."

Vlade frowns his acceptance and nods. He shows Jack his hands. Al walks over to the couches, puts his drink down and comes over to Jack, gives him a big, wide-armed hug. He holds Jack's head and kisses him hard on both cheeks. "We are sorry to you," he says. "You are the one is right. We are very sorry."

"Jesus," Jack says, pushing past Al and going over to the couches.

"How can we find out who did this?" Vlade asks.

Jack sits down, lets himself fall into one of the big, white leather couches. About a minute worth of air seeps out of it at the cushions settle around Jack. "First we have to look at all the information."

After explaining to the Czechs about everything he found in Ralph's house, the same basic story he gave Sgt. Hopkins, Jack waits for the three of them to suggest a next move. They're all sitting on the couches, speaking Czech, with the other two back on either side of the elevator doors. Jack's not the happiest that they're speaking a language he doesn't understand—especially since they're talking about him—but what can he do?

As far as his discussion with Sgt. Hopkins goes, Jack's not sure about his confidence in the Czechs anymore. Someone pulls a gun on you; that happens. But whether he'd drop a dime about where they are and what they're doing is something he hasn't decided. That much depends on what they do next. That and where he thinks he stands in relation to the people who killed Ralph.

Vlade looks away from the others, says to Jack, "You say you have the phone of the man who called Ralph to meet about the deal?"

Jack nods.

"What will it cost you to call him?"

"What?" Jack says. "Cost? I'm talking about going after the guys who shot him."

"I know." Vlade closes his eyes, nods. "We will pay you double what we would have paid Ralph now. I understand that the stakes have become higher. There is death."

Jack's already shaking his head. "I can give you the phone number and you guys—" Vlade shakes his head. "You don't need me. What we need is to—"

"Ten thousand dollars," Vlade says. "To make for us these deals. To help us. What do you say?"

"Ten?" That means they were going to give Ralph five at the start, *at least*, meaning he was only cutting Jack in for *less than half*.

But what's one thousand between friends? Jack can't hold it against him though: for one, he did all the legwork; two, the guy's dead.

"OK," Vlade says. "Fifteen. Three times."

"Fifteen?" Jack asks, nodding, not even sure what he's agreeing to, but sure about the number and sure about what that many reasons can set him up for. "Fifteen sounds good."

"OK," Vlade rubs his hands together like it's just gotten to be a cold winter's night in the penthouse. Jack starts thinking about what he can do with the fifteen grand, how long he'll be able to stay in his house, what legitimate ways of making money he can start up in that time. Vlade starts to talk, saying things that Jack doesn't hear. Jack comes back in at, "Set the meet for tomorrow."

"What?" Jack says.

"With this dealer. The man on the phone. Call him and set the meet."

"I'll call him, but we have to see what he says. He wanted Ralph."

"He will come," Vlade says, nodding. "For the kind of buy we are talking, he will meet."

"OK, but what about finding Ralph's killer?"

Vlade looks to the others before he speaks. Al nods and David gives a shrug. "We will track him down with you. We should. If this person doesn't want our meet to happen, we must neutralize them before it does."

Neutralize. Jack likes how that sounds. He nods and stands up. "OK. I'll make the call."

Jack steps away to the outside of the room, to the windows that look down on the rest of San Francisco. He can feel the Czechs watching him as he takes out his cell, finds the number from Ralph's caller ID on the folded up paper. Before he knows what he'll say, he's put in the numbers. The phone is ringing. Then the same voice from the message at Ralph's picks up. "Hola? Quién es?"

Jack hesitates. The voice comes again, "Hola?"

Above all else, Jack knows that fucking this up is not what he wants to do. "You called Ralph this morning," he says. "Wanted to set up a meet."

"Who is *this?*"

"I'm a friend calling to let you know I'll be there. I can meet you today."

"At the wharfs. Pier 39." Jack hears the guy on the phone say something to someone where he is, a muffled sound that doesn't sound like English. "Where is Ralph?"

Jack doesn't know how to play this, but figures it's better to keep Ralph's death on a *need-to-know* basis, unless everyone saw it on TV. "Ralph is indisposed at this point in time," he says.

"In-dis-po-sed?" the voice says slowly, breaking the word into its parts. "Ralph not coming to this meeting does not look so good for you, Mr. Friend. Do you understand what I am saying?"

"I'm bringing," Jack starts to say. He wants to tell this guy he's bringing the money, something to prove himself, but doesn't want to commit to anything he can't deliver. "I'm bringing Ralph's total confidence and permission to negotiate."

There is a short laugh at the other end of the line. "Ralph now has the confidence and he gives permissions? Ralph has grown in stature since we last spoke. Now he gets in-dis-pos-ed and cannot meet; he send his friend, The Negotiator. Well, I say OK to you Mr. Negotiator. We will meet today. Three o'clock. The Musee Mechanique." And then he hangs up.

"OK," Jack says into the dead phone for effect, not sure if the Czechs are listening to his end of the conversation. "OK. I'll meet you there." Jack looks around: he's come into a quiet corner of the penthouse, with window views on both sides. He puts his forehead up against the cold glass and looks down. He sees the huge bill-board of Tom Brady that stands on top of the S.F. Niketown: Tom Brady looking confident as ever, able to stand in the pocket all day and deliver every time in the fourth quarter, when the game's on the line. Jack can't even see the street below. He tucks the phone into his jacket, turns back to the room.

The two guards have gone back to their posts by the elevator, the quiet one smoking. David and Al cut lines from what blow they have left—exactly what Jack thinks they *don't* need—and Vlade leans back, his scotch on his lap and the remote control in one hand, watching the news on TV. He turns to look at Jack and shuts it off.

Jack comes back across the room to the white leather couches. He sits down next to Al. "The meet is on," he says. "I'm going to see the man this afternoon."

"You are good to do this for us," Vlade says. "You will be rewarded."

Jack wonders how he'll play it with the Colombian, his first acting job in a while, not counting last night and today. He decides to act like he belongs in all of this, keep with that as long as it works. Act like he's not just going one person to the next, trying to figure it out, even if he is.

"It'll be OK," Jack says, nodding to the others, hoping he hasn't just signed his own death warrant.

11

Driving up to Fisherman's Wharf, a short ride, the traffic is slow and it takes Jack even longer than driving to the hotel. It takes him ten minutes just to get around Union Square. It doesn't make sense, as he thinks about it, that the Colombian would be the one who had Ralph killed. If you're going to kill someone, you don't call them to make an appointment after.

There's the possible idea of the message being an alibi, but why would he bother? No one knew enough about this deal, even Jack, to ever make a strong connection to this guy if he did it, and if he wanted to, he could just vanish like Jack could have this morning. Now they're both in it, and the question is: why? For the Colombian, it's got to be the deal. Whether he knows about Ralph's death or not, he's not trying to make the deal happen because he *wanted* Ralph dead. At least not how Jack sees it.

As for Jack, maybe he's safer just going along with this, working with the Czechs instead of going home or running. If Ralph's killer is out there, why not stay one step ahead?

Stuck in Chinatown traffic, he flips open his cell phone. All around him people crowd the outdoor markets, sifting through bins of fruits, vegetables, every dried food, cured food, live food—anything one could imagine. It's his habit to talk on the phone in situations like this, places people might start talking to him or come up to the car. He looks at the phone, sees the slip of paper with last night's bartender's—Maxine's—phone number on it. She answers on the third ring, sounds groggy.

"You still sleeping?" Jack asks. "It's past two o'clock."

She makes a noise that is not quite a moan and may very well be the sound of her rolling over, sitting up, or getting out of bed. Jack likes hearing it, lets himself think about her bed; he imagines it high and soft, with a couple of big pillows. "Late night," she says.

"Aren't they all?"

"A few of us went out for drinks and then breakfast after we closed the club. I didn't get in until ten."

Jack gets through a light and starts moving again. He checks his watch. Up ahead he can see the Stockton tunnel and hopes it'll be a smooth ride from there.

"I didn't know there were bars that stayed open that late."

"There're places." She makes a soft sound again, like she's breathing her first waking breaths of the day. Jack imagines her walking across the bedroom floor in bare feet, just a T-shirt on, heading into the kitchen to start coffee.

"What'd you have?" He stops at a red light, has come almost ten yards. More people cross the narrow street in front of him.

"What?"

"For breakfast. What'd you have?"

"Steak and eggs," she says. "Juice."

"Nice." Jack likes a girl who's not afraid to eat steak and eggs after a night of drinking, but hell, this girl bartends topless at a strip club. What could be better than that?

"Who is this, by the way?" she asks, as if she's just started to make herself coffee and it's another normal part of the conversation.

Jack laughs. The light turns to green, and he inches the Fastback forward, heading further up the hill, then starts to open it up. "Jack Palms," he says. "From last night."

"Oh." She sounds surprised, then she laughs. "Sorry. That's good. That's good you're calling."

"Why?" He shifts up from first gear to second to third for the first time since the hotel, hears the welcome purr of the engine.

"Well, I had wanted to talk to you. I mean, I *want* to talk to you, but also we've got some things that we should talk about, you know?"

"I'd be up for some talking."

"No. I mean serious."

"Like what?"

"Things," she says. "Seeing you with Ralph last night and those suits made me wonder what's going on. Like maybe there are some things I can tell you. I know you wouldn't get into anything stupid, but I wonder how well you know Ralph."

"Thanks. I appreciate the compliment." On the other side of the short tunnel, he's in Fisherman's Wharf territory: more tourist foot traffic, even worse than Chinatown. And streets that wind through barricades, turn one-way without warning.

"No, for real," she says. "Seeing you in that movie, I know you've got to be the tough guy, but also kind of smart, right? I mean relatively."

Another compliment. Jack laughs. "That's actually just me acting. I'm really only tough."

"No," she says. "Really. I can tell you're smart."

"OK," Jack says, "I'm listening."

He cruises into the parking lot across from Pier 39 and the Musee Mechanique, sees a space on the outside, facing the museum, and pulls into what is the perfect place to leave the car: here he can watch the museum while he waits, then watch the Fastback while he meets.

"I should tell you in person," Maxine says. "Come by The Coast. I'll buy you a liquid dinner."

"OK," Jack says. "Drinks for dinner."

A well-tanned guy in a designer suit walks up to the museum and stands in front, looking around. He wears large, stylish glasses and has his hair combed straight back. It's just before 3 o'clock. This has to be his guy.

"Come before Tony gets there," Maxine says. She starts to say something else, but Jack cuts her off.

"I'll be there," he says, and hangs up.

12

Jack gets out of his car and looks around, checking for the Colombian's backup. He doesn't see any scouts, any rooftop snipers, but the Wharf is filled with enough crowds that anyone could be watching. And if the Colombian has someone with him, he's likely not to be wearing a designer suit that screams *drug dealer*.

There's a crowd of people standing around an ice cream booth not too far off, just one of the places down here that draws a crowd. Some wait in line and some eat their ice cream, looking at all the people and the fish shacks, the pigeons and the street performers. A seal barks somewhere. Just on the other side of the parking lot, a group of kids wearing helmets and funny hats tries head-spins on a linoleum mat. They've got a big, old school boom box playing loud music.

Jack locks the car, heads across the street to the museum.

He wishes he had some kind of briefcase to make himself look official, wishes he weren't wearing a sweat suit, that he had on nicer clothes, but there's nothing to be done about it now. In his trunk he has a clean change of clothes in his gym bag, but he's not changing now, not here. In his movie, he could imagine one of the guys wearing a sweat suit like his. So Jack just shakes it off, rolls his shoulders, and heads inside.

The first sound he hears from the museum is a loud laughing as he approaches, an ominous sound, as if he's entering a fun house. But when he gets inside he sees a large glass booth with a huge mechanical woman in it, a wooden puppet, and she's laughing: leaning forward and falling back, producing a howling cackle like she's just heard the funniest thing in the world. The interior of the museum isn't dark or scary: it features a row of big windows across the far wall, looking out on the water. The room is full of light and old-time arcade machines from way back before Pac Man was even an idea: big boxes made of wood, with real moving parts.

A sign in front of the laughing woman says that she's been here since the 1920s, and has been delighting and terrifying young children ever since. Hearing the laugh now, Jack's not surprised that kids get scared. He half expects the Colombian to jump out from behind a wall—or have one of his boys do it—and stab him with a long knife.

He goes farther into the museum, past machines that for twenty-five cents will show you pictures of the great earthquake of 1906 or of a woman from those times undressing, machines that let you sit in a vibrating chair, funny games where you try to get a ball to follow the path you want without falling into any of the holes, and machines that play music while little wooden characters dance around in circles on rotating disks. Around a turn, he comes to a large machine with a wrestler's upper body coming out of it. The wrestler wears a tight blue mask, like the WWF characters of Jack's childhood who always hailed from "parts unknown" and never revealed their real names. The wrestler has his arm extended for arm-wrestling. "Test your strength," the sign reads.

The Colombian, or the man with the nice suit and the slicked-back hair that Jack *thinks* is the Colombian, stands in front of this, looking as if he's deciding whether or not to try it. He looks at Jack and smiles. "Test your strength?" he says.

"You're supposed to arm-wrestle it."

The Colombian nods. "I would like to test it. But maybe you will go first?" He produces a quarter from a front pants pocket. "I will buy two tries."

A sign above the machine reads: *Warning: This machine exhibits super human strength. Be careful.*

"OK," Jack says, taking off his jacket and setting it on a nearby picture booth. The Colombian puts his quarter in the machine. It starts to hum, its tall back and sides vibrating. Jack turns the setting to Tough Guy and puts his elbow on the pad. Then he grips the plastic wrestler's hand. The whirring gets louder, and Jack realizes he's in a kind of awkward position: with his knees bent slightly and his body bent at the waist, he's not set up to be his strongest, but the machine wasn't built for people his height; it's low to the ground, its "table" not more than three feet up. When the arm starts to move, the hand pushing against Jack's, there's no time to think about it or do anything but push with all he can against the wrestler's white plastic arm. The Colombian stands behind and off to one side, where Jack can still see him. That part's good, less to worry about, but as Jack resists letting the hand push his back onto the mat, its pressure gets stronger and stronger. He shifts his weight lower to give himself more leverage, but finally can't hold the hand up anymore, and he lets it take his wrist back to the mat.

The Colombian laughs twice, in loud bursts, "Ha! Ha!" as if he is used to displaying his happiness in public places. "You are not so much the tough guy, then, I suppose. And maybe we both knew that?"

"Maybe," Jack says, picking up his jacket.

"Perhaps I should set the machine lower."

Jack steps back out of the other man's way and lets him move toward the wrestler, the dial above his arm. He lowers it to Pack Rat as the wrestler's arm slowly rises back up to its original position.

Now Jack laughs as, standing back, he watches the fine material of the designer suit fold at the knees and elbows as the Colombian bends down to his task.

"I'm Ralph's friend," Jack says.

"Of course," the Colombian answers, as the machine starts to whir. "And if I am lucky, I will be the Pack Rat." The machine gets louder and Jack can see him start to strain against its arm. He's shorter than Jack and so seems to have a better center of gravity for the task; he also shifts his feet around right away, to lean his weight against the arm. Slowly it starts to recede toward its own plastic mat, this one without the foam padding of the one that Jack's hand just fell against. The Colombian pushes harder, straightening his body as he leans against the arm, using his weight like a lever.

"I'm not sure that tactic is legal," Jack says.

The Colombian grunts. "Of course," he manages to say between locked teeth. Now the machine makes more noise; its hand moves back up to its original position, pushing back the Colombian's whole body—his feet slide a few inches across the floor.

"You had it," Jack says.

But the machine gets stronger again, as it had with Jack, and the Colombian starts to fall back, his whole arm moving toward the mat. Then, suddenly the whirring sound starts to decrease, and the Colombian makes forward progress. Again he puts his weight into the effort, and this time the hand continues to give. Gradually it slides back further and further until it comes all the way down to horizontal, touching its own mat. Lights go off and a bell rings inside the machine. The designation Pack Rat lights up above the wrestler's head. Music plays from deep inside the machine. More bells.

"Congratulations," Jack says, clapping. "What else can I say now?"

The Colombian stands up and rubs his hands together. His combed-back hair has come out of place around his temples with the effort, and he produces a comb from within his jacket. He runs it back over his scalp a few times, then puts it back in the pocket where it belongs.

"Pack Rat," he says, smoothing his sleeves, and then, offering his hand to Jack, "This is some distinction. I am Alex Castroneves."

They shake, and the guy has a good handshake: palm on palm and tight fingers, and Jack almost finds himself liking this guy until he remembers who he is and what they're here for.

"So here I am. I'm Jack. Sorry about Ralph not coming."

"That is all right." He straightens his tie, adjusting the knot closer to his neck. "I am not used to this—arm wrestling with machines." He opens his arms and gestures at all that surrounds them. "This place is quite strange." He leads Jack toward the doors that let out onto the pier, away from the shops and restaurants. This is a back or side door to the museum that Jack hadn't thought of, one that opens onto an empty pier, looking out toward the water. Jack can see the pay-telescopes lining the rail and then the water of the Bay, open and foggy, behind it.

"Let me try one more game," Jack says, heading toward the boxing robots, where a young Korean man and woman duke it out while two of their friends watch. "We can see who wins this time, when we're evenly matched."

Alex opens his hands and, as if to study his palms, moves them closer to his face. Seeming satisfied with their quality, he shows them to Jack. "That is all right," he says. "We have played a game. Now let us talk outside."

"OK." Jack stands where he is. Again, the Colombian turns to head toward the doors. Jack takes a step forward. "We're ready to proceed and go forward," he says, not loud. He doesn't want to spook Castroneves but doesn't want to go outside the protection of the museum, either; he doesn't see any people out on the boardwalk. Something tells him he's not supposed to be led into any places that might be a trap.

But another part of him wants to trust this guy, just follow what happens. The last thing he wants to do is to fuck this thing up.

Castroneves turns to look at Jack, unsure why he won't come outside. "You are the police?" he says.

"No. No." Jack straightens his arms, thinking he's fucking it up but not wanting to fuck it up. "I'm just a friend of Ralph's. We used to work together in L.A. I was an actor." Jack's not sure what else to say, so he goes with what he's feeling, just gives in to the moment, as his yoga instructor at the gym would say. "Now I'm here. A few people around town still know me from my movie and I can show our guys, *your buyers*, a good time."

A family of nice-looking Midwestern tourists walks past the vibrating chair and straight to the "3-D Pictures of the Great Quake" machine. The father wears a sweatshirt that reads simply, *Wisconsin*.

Too honest, Jack thinks. He wonders what he's doing telling this guy all about himself, doesn't want to be doing this wrong, losing his character, the deal, the Czechs' coke, their money. It occurs to him that he might mess up and be left with just a dead friend and the people who killed him.

"You made a movie?" Castroneves says.

Jack nods. "*Shake 'Em Down*. Late '90s."

Castroneves frowns and shakes his head. Then his face lights up and he looks right at Jack as if he's scrutinizing his face closely. "Yes. 'Shake Them Down.' I have seen that one. It is not bad, really." He frowns, ducks his head toward one shoulder and then the other. "It was nothing arty, but that is OK. I think I liked it, if I remember right. Who are you?"

"I'm Jack Palms. I played the ex-cop who's taking down the drug cartel to get back his daughter." Jack laughs, awkwardly. "No resemblance to the truth here."

Now the other man laughs. "Yes, the drug cartel movie. Now I recognize you." He tilts his head. "That was not an accurate portrayal of a cartel, you know?"

Jack shrugs. What can he say?

"You've put on some weight since then, no?" Castroneves hits Jack in the arm with his open hand, reaching his fingers around Jack's bicep. "It looks good. But you're still no Tough Guy." He turns toward the outside pier again, but this time offers Jack the door with an open hand. "I would like to smoke in the open air, is all. Nothing is to be afraid of, I can assure to you."

Jack steps through the open door and out into the windy sun of the Bay. Sometimes in life you have to trust people. In L.A. Jack made the mistake of trusting Victoria, which turned out to be a bad one. Now that he's pulled himself back, he doesn't want to choose wrong again, but he's got to take his shots sometimes.

Outside, it's cold and seagulls dance around in the air above the pier. To their left, a big WWII submarine is moored against the pier, a museum now for tourists to explore. The pier has a few places to tie a boat off, and beyond that it just drops off to the water. It's windy, even a little cold, though it's the middle of the afternoon. This is San Francisco.

Jack puts on his jacket. The Colombian steps to the edge of the pier and touches his neck. Is it a signal? Jack checks himself, tries to stop worrying so much.

"It is better here. Without people to listen." Castroneves opens his arms to the water. Jack looks out and doesn't see a sniper-mounted cigarette boat or a fancy South American yacht anchored and waiting anywhere. Fifteen feet from them, a young mother boosts her son up to one of the pay-telescopes and struggles to support him with one arm and her hip as she feeds in a quarter. Castroneves removes a pack of cigarettes from his breast pocket and offers one to Jack. He thinks, hesitates, and then the addict that remains in him wins out and he takes it. Castroneves puts another between his lips and lights Jack's with a fancy metal lighter. "Let us talk business," he says, lighting his own, and puffing smoke out the side of his mouth.

"OK. My guys want size." Jack takes a long inhale, feels guilty for smoking a third time today. But hell: it's been quite a day, so far. He hopes it'll calm his nerves, lubricate the situation. He sees the Colombian watching him and exhales faster than he would like, says, "I don't know the numbers, what you probably want to know, but they'll be there when we set up the meet. We'll get it done."

The Colombian takes his time exhaling smoke and touches his tongue to remove a small piece of paper. "That is no matter. Ralph has said that these friends of yours want ten. The cost is sixteen even. That is the best that I can do. Player's price, you understand. Best for this size. Tell that to your friends. Tell them we can go up to twenty keys, and not more."

"OK," Jack says, thinking that ten keys at that price means the deal's worth one hundred and sixty grand. He inhales a drag off his cigarette as he watches Castroneves look out over the water: his face serene, almost wistful.

"You know," he says, "The water does not look this color in my country." He shakes his head. "It is *more* blue."

"Atlantic or Pacific?"

"Ahh. Do you know where my country is? That is impressive if you do."

From something he's read, Jack thinks it's at the top of South America, with borders on both the Pacific and the Atlantic. But he could be wrong. He shrugs.

"Pacific, yes. Where I grew up is on the Pacific there." Castroneves nods. "Blue as the night sky."

Jack looks at the water. "Here I guess it's kind of green."

"Yes. And where is Ralph? When will I see him?"

Jack exhales. "Ralph is coming back later."

"Bullshit." The Colombian turns to face Jack, his lower lip covering part of his upper, as if he'd buttoned them closed. Jack feels his hands start to tingle; whether it's from the cigarettes or his own nervousness, he doesn't know. He takes another drag. Then Castroneves shakes his head. "Because Ralph is dead." He points at Jack with his cigarette hand. "If you do not know this, then you are worth less than nothing, Mr. Movie."

Jack steps back, then rethinks it and steps forward. "How do *you* know that?" He points at Castroneves for effect, thinking it's a good character move, but ultimately he's reaching; it feels like he's lost the moment, any momentum he had going. Maybe he should never have accepted the cigarette.

"I have people," Castroneves says. Then he laughs, looking at Jack's hand. "Put that down," he says. "I have people who watch TV. Your Ralph's death was on the TV news today. The fucking news. In truth, I was very surprised to get your call."

"Right," Jack says. He looks down at the concrete, his sneakers. "OK. It's OK." The Colombian drags off his cigarette, watching Jack through thin eyes. "I mean it's fucked up. Ralph got popped, and I want to find out who did this to him, but I'm also working with your buyers now, and we want to go ahead with this. I can make it run."

Castroneves holds the smoke inside for a few seconds and then exhales out one side of his smile. He laughs, then steps closer to Jack, pointing at Jack's face. "Do you even know who did that? Or if they wanted this deal to be stopped?"

Jack shakes his head, flicks his half-smoked cigarette into the Bay. "No, but—"

"You had better think, Mr. Palms. Because if someone does not want this to happen, then we had better know who they are. Do you understand?"

Jack nods. "I'm working on that already. Right after I leave here I'm going to talk to another contact about what they know. I will get to the bottom of it."

"I hope so. Because if you do not, then you are wasting my time." Castroneves' eyes narrow as he talks, but then he steps back, brings his hand down.

"And you don't like to have your time wasted," Jack says, finishing it for him, stepping forward to close the space that Castroneves has just left as he tries to take control. "Right. I'd imagine that. And I don't like meeting on docks and talking about drug deals that aren't going to happen, or the fact that my friend now has a bullet making a breezeway through his skull."

Jack watches as the Colombian steps back and flicks his cigarette into the Bay. He nods. "OK," he says. "Tomorrow then, Mr. Movie Friend. I will call you to set up the time and the place."

"And one more thing," Jack says, playing his part, taking another small step forward. "I choose the location."

The Colombian tilts his head to the side, as if he's sizing Jack up, waiting to see if Jack will laugh, apologize, or hold his ground. Jack waits him out. "We will see," Castroneves says, and then turns and walks away.

13

Back inside the museum and all the way to the car, Jack takes deep breaths. He can feel his pulse racing and knows that yes, he's found his way back to acting. Even as different as this is from being on the screen—the stakes are higher here, for one—he's back at it, doing the thing he loves.

When he's in the car, Jack sits watching people go in and out of the museum. He's not rattled, but he doesn't want to drive yet either. He's thinking about his next move: whether to go back to the Czechs' hotel or straight to The Coast to talk with Maxine. Then he sees a tough-looking guy in a white suit—slicked-back hair and a pretty good tan—walk out of the museum. The guy's talking on a cell phone. Then he closes his phone and heads toward Waterfront Park, left to right across the sidewalk in front of Jack's windshield, moving quickly through the heavy crowds, going the same direction as Castroneves had.

Something about him makes Jack uneasy. Maybe it's his look and the fact that he doesn't fit in with the tourist crowd, or maybe it's just that he's still thinking about what Castroneves said about someone wanting to stop this deal— Jack stands and closes the door of his car. He locks it and runs his hand over the hood, gives it a pat for good luck. Then he starts after the guy, just to watch, moving quickly so he doesn't lose him in the crowd.

The guy swings his arms as he walks, sees a woman holding a small child and goes right up to the kid to pinch his cheek. A family stops and walks around him. The mother laughs and the guy's all smiles as he keeps walking, almost bumping into a couple of kids, but then walking around them.

Jack jogs to the back of the sign about how to pay for the parking. What if he led the killer to Castroneves, right to the other side of his deal? But he could've led him to the Czechs too. He shakes his head; better to watch, not to worry. The guy walks with a calm self-assuredness, and Jack crosses the street to start after him, weaving through the people coming the other way. He watches the guy look up, checking around him to see if anyone might be watching. Who is this guy?

Jack follows him for most of a block, ducking through the crowds and trying not to walk at his full height so he can't be seen. That part's hard: trying to keep his knees bent and not looking too weird to the people around him. The guy carves out a wide path through the tourists. Then he turns sharply and goes to an ice cream stand, one of the many. Jack sits down on the closest bench. From what he can see, the guy just waits his turn in line, buys a cone and then, instead of heading the way he had been headed, he comes right back the same way, straight toward Jack. Jack loses him in a pack of people for a few tense moments, but then the line of sight opens up again and the guy's right there, ten feet away, looking at Jack and coming right over.

Jack tries to act like he's doing something else, waiting for someone—where is a newspaper when you need it?—and then he thinks about running, looking to duck into a shop or something, but there's nothing he can do now. He steels himself for the unknown, tightening his core and sitting up straight.

Jack crosses one leg and rests his ankle on the other knee. The guy walks around a last family and comes right up, holding the ice cream out as if to offer it to Jack. "You like vanilla?" he says. "Because I got this for you."

"No thanks."

The guy brings his eyebrows together. "It's a gift from us."

He leans down and puts the cone right into Jack's hand, so that Jack has no choice but to take it. Then the guy stays there, leaning down over Jack, his face too close. "That's good," he says. "This is the last gift we give to you. Do you understand what I am saying?"

Jack nods. In his movie, he'd kick this guy in the balls, then mop him all over the pavement as onlookers cheered. But here, they're surrounded by friendly tourists who'd be horrified to witness a street fight in San Francisco, on their sightseeing trip to a big city. Also, Jack's not sure about this guy, whether he's a real fighter or not. He's not sure about himself for that matter; it's been a long time. As if he anticipates Jack's thought, the guy taps Jack's sneaker and pushes it off the knee so that both of Jack's feet are on the ground.

"I'm just saying this to you," the guy says.

"OK. I hear you."

"That's good. Because you're lucky to get this word and not something else."

"Who *are* you?"

The guy shakes his head. "No," he says, simply. "No. This is the wrong question."

Jack doesn't know what to do next, what would be a good character move. "Do you know who killed Ralph?"

The guy squints his eyes and moves still closer, to where his face is right in front of Jack's. What pisses Jack off the most is when he says, "Go back to your Hollywood, you stupid pretty American."

And Jack head-butts him in the face, right across the bridge of his nose—a move that surprises them both about equally. The guy groans, stumbles back with both of his hands on his face. He juts his nose out over the ground, as far from his legs—and his white suit—as he can, and Jack can see blood dripping through his fingers.

"Wow," Jack says, more or less shocked at what he's done. As a kid, he did things like this sometimes, even in L.A. a couple of times, but his actions haven't taken control of him in a long time. He gets up and drops the ice cream into a garbage can next to the bench. In the movie, this is the part where he kicks the guy in the stomach, gives him a pretty good beating, but here he can already see that this guy's not used to fights. Everyone he runs into probably gives him what he wants, without many conflicts.

"You fuck," the guy says. "I kill you."

And Jack sees red: thinking about Ralph in the tub, the time in Sausalito, in rehab, the bad press and his dreams of being a full-blown movie star moving away from him, he moves in on the guy fast, punches him once in the side, then, as the guy's doubled over, almost backing into an unsuspecting group of tourists, Jack grabs him, holds the guy in place, breathing hard, feeling the air come in and out of his chest.

The tourists walk a wide circle around them. A woman says, "Oh, my God. What's happening here?"

"My friend just has a bloody nose," Jack says. "This happens to him all the time."

Someone else says, "Oh, that's awful!"

The guy's still holding his hands in front of his face, bleeding over the ground, not on his suit. "Oh, watch those shoes," Jack says, stepping on the toes of one tan suede loafer. "That's going to suck," Jack says. He can hear the guy's breathing: mannered and slow through his mouth. From out of the clean suit, he produces a white handkerchief and holds it over his nose. He stands to his full height, looks Jack in the eye.

"Fuck you," he says. "You fucking fuck." With his other hand, he reaches into his suit jacket and Jack, anticipating gun, backs him up against a big sign advertising the fares for the Alcatraz ferry, holding his arm where it is, the hand still inside his jacket.

"You know," Jack says, when he's got the guy's arm under control—all his time in the gym over the past two years is actually helping, he thinks—"I really hope you're not thinking about pulling a gun here." The guy tries to knee Jack, but his kneecap finds only Jack's quad—not his balls—and though it'll probably leave a good charley horse, Jack stays upright.

"OK," Jack says, pushing up against him harder. He reaches inside the jacket and feels the gun handle in the guy's hand. "Shit," Jack says, shaking his head. "Now *that's* just not right." He pulls the hand out with the gun and forces it low, down along the guy's side. Then he hits it against the sign enough times—it only takes three—for the gun to fall to the ground.

"That the gun you used to kill Ralph?"

"The fuck you talking about? Ralph?"

Jack pushes the guy away and stoops to pick up the gun, sliding it into a jacket pocket. "Now what?" Jack says.

The guy bends over, both hands over his face. "Who is Ralph? Anderino? He is our contact."

"Contact?"

"Yes. The man who we are supposed to make the deal. Who the fuck are you?"

"You're with Castroneves?"

The guy stands up to look at Jack. "You fuck," he says.

"Oh," Jack says, putting the nice suit and the slicked back hair together, something he should've done sooner. "I'm sorry about your nose."

The guy just looks at Jack, the handkerchief over most of his face. "Fuck you," he says.

"Oh." Jack knows this isn't the cool rejoinder that he should be able to come up with, but it's already escaped his lips. He holds his hands down by his sides, open and empty. "Now that's not nice," he says, knowing he's losing more cool points by the second. "What can we do here?" The guy doesn't answer, just stares at Jack; then he takes away the handkerchief and spits a big gob of blood onto the sidewalk.

"Castroneves is my boss," the guy says.

"Damn." Jack brushes off the guy's sleeve. "I hope you won't let this ruin our relationship. I really do." He looks at his watch; he first met with Castroneves less than a half-hour ago and already he's breaking ties, fucking up one of his associates. Jack takes out the gun and removes the clip. He thumbs out the bullets into his hand, dropping one handful into his pocket and then another before he's done emptying it. When he's replaced the clip, he offers the gun back to its owner. "Like I said, I'm really sorry about all this. I hope we can still be friends."

"I will fucking kill you," the guy says.

"I got to go, friend." Jack pats him on the shoulder. His suit is soft to the touch, definitely linen. "Nice suit. At least you didn't mess it up, right?"

The guy shakes his head. He takes away the handkerchief, looks at the blood in it. From what Jack can see, the bleeding has stopped, but the nose looks like it might be broken.

"Yeah. I'm sorry about that."

The guy makes like he's going to swing at Jack, and Jack pulls back, but the guy's hand doesn't go past his shoulder. He laughs. "No," he says. "Not right now. But soon, yes." As he starts walking back toward the way he'd been heading, he looks back at Jack once, shaking his head.

"Really," Jack calls after him. "Let's not let this interfere with what could be a profitable business."

The guy takes a few more steps looking back, then turns, walks away into the crowd.

14

Jack calls Castroneves from the Mustang, trying to head off any harm he's done as early as possible. But there's no answer at the number he used before, just a blank message that announces the phone number in a computer-generated female voice. Jack's on the spot to leave his message before he's ready, stumbles out something about being sorry and hoping that they'll still go ahead with their business despite the "unfortunate incident" that's just occurred, and hangs up.

"Fuck," he says. He hits the steering wheel a few times, trying to work through feeling like he's just ruined the whole deal, and then the phone rings in his hand. It's Castroneves' number.

"Hey," Jack says, leaning back, looking out at the museum.

"This is Jack?"

"Yeah. I just— I wanted to call and apologize. I just got a little carried away with an associate of yours. You have to understand I'm edgy about what happened to Ralph."

"Ahh." There are more sounds on the other end of the line, but Jack can't make them out. It sounds like someone else is having a conversation there. "Yes. He has just come in."

"So I just wanted to say I hope we can still do business."

"Yes, Mr. Palms. Oh. Well. We will have to see about that, I'm afraid. I have to say goodbye now." And the call ends.

"Shit," Jack says. He hits the steering wheel again, looks at the pack of cigarettes in the passenger's seat, and shakes his head. "Fuck, fuck, fuck," he says, starting the engine.

Inside of an hour, Jack sits at the bar in front of Maxine, a club soda with lime in his hand and a tall blonde dancing naked on the stage. He's come here because he didn't know where else to go. He couldn't face the prospect of going back to Sausalito, a night alone up there with his thoughts, the idea of whether he fucked up the deal the Czechs are paying him for, or the possibility that Ralph's killer might come looking. So he chose to take Maxine up on her offer. After all, it's The Coast where he's had the most fun in a while.

It's the first dance of the night, and the rest of the barstools stand empty. Just a few lonely guys from the after-work crowd have made their way in after hitting happy hours downtown.

Jack figures he'll get whatever background Maxine can give, and then head up to the Czechs' hotel to tell them about the meet with Alex, hoping they've come up with some ideas on who might have killed Ralph and that he can convince them things are still OK with the Colombian.

"I just lose my temper sometimes," he tells Maxine. "It's always been my problem when I end up in a situation I don't know how to control." Jack looks at his hands: plain and white, pink really; long thin fingers. A couple still have swollen knuckles from basketball and football injuries growing up. "It's not like I'm happy about hitting the guy or like it makes things any easier. I think it actually makes things worse."

She nods. They've already been over the fact that she's seen Ralph's death on the news and that she feels awful about it. She's cutting lemons for the night's drinks, looking up at Jack from time to time. Tonight she's got on a tight black tank top, plenty of cleavage, and Jack's not sure if she just doesn't feel up to taking it off, she's trying to make a different impression, or if that usually doesn't happen until the night picks up.

"Has this happened before?" she asks.

"One of my friends gets killed?"

"No, you've lost your temper like that."

Jack thinks about it for a second, decides that it hasn't happened since he did rehab, since he's been reclaiming his life. "Yeah, it used to happen time to time."

Maxine's brows come together and she looks up. "I guess I read about that in the papers."

"No," Jack says. "The papers made me out like I did this with Victoria but that never happened. I was so keyed out on H I couldn't have lifted my arm."

"And now?"

"I don't know. I thought I had the guy who killed Ralph."

"Yeah," she says. She stops her cutting, slides the lemon slices into a trough. She looks Jack in the eye. "So how much do you know about what happened to Ralph?"

"Not that much. Just the details."

"Right. Any clues on who would do that?"

Jack looks her over, tries to piece it all together: her calling, talking about Ralph, what she said he had to come to hear. "What do *you* know?"

"That's right, Jack. You want to be asking me questions, finding out what I can tell you."

"So?"

"So here's what you probably know: Ralph was dealing."

Jack nods. "That's where I came in."

"Yeah. But you don't know about Ralph and Tony, that Ralphie was dealing here until recently, when Tony told him to stop."

"And then Ralph became unwelcome, right? So why would he come in last night?"

"Good question." Maxine shakes her head. "Seems like an odd move to me."

"You know who those guys were that we were with?"

"Never seen them."

Jack leans back against the seat as he watches her move down the bar to help a few guys at the other end. He takes a deep breath, letting out all the anxiety about what's just happened, about the deal, about someone killing Ralph. He feels like he needs a drink to wash it all out of him. Seeing Ralph's body, the dog's, meeting with Alex, hitting the other Colombian, it's all taking a toll. He figures he's earned a shot of something strong, maybe a double, but he's been on the wagon too long to let that go. Jack presses his thumb and index finger into the corners of his eyes, across the bridge of his nose, squeezes his eyes shut.

He tells himself that he doesn't want to slip back on anything he's accomplished, all the days he could've had a drink or gotten his hands on some coke or weed or horse and found a way not to. He doesn't want to let that all go.

There's something else behind all the crap he's feeling: something inside him that feels *good*, like a part of him that's been bottled up has been let out, like his blood is flowing faster than in a while.

Maxine comes back. "Where're your friends tonight then?" she asks.

He shakes his head. "I don't know, eating dinner. Probably getting coked up."

She looks good, even better than Jack remembered. Even as much as he noticed her last night, he didn't notice her compared to how he sees her now. She has green eyes to go with her brown hair; her skin is just a touch darker than the rest of the girls', enough that she might be part Latina. She has a mole on her chest, on the inside of her cleavage, that Jack didn't notice last night, in a place that's as nice for any mole to land as Jack can think of. Her body is put together right, with all the curves in exactly the right places.

"Hello?" She smiles. Does she recognize how he's been looking at her? Jack decides that probably doesn't make him any different from anyone else in this place. He smiles back. She turns to look at the blonde, then down at her chest and does kind of a propping, a boob-fluff. "It's not a bad place, right?" She laughs. "Lots to see here."

"So what'd you want me to come down to hear?"

"Just this," she says. "What we're saying." She takes Jack's drink glass, swirls the remaining ice around the edges. "Let me get you that liquid dinner."

"What can you recommend? Something non-alcoholic." She's already got the good gin out of its rack. "Maybe just mix up an orange juice and a cranberry, will you?"

"Oh," she says. "The *virgin* madras. You don't like people to think you're a virgin, do you?"

Jack laughs. "That's usually not a problem." He looks her over again: the tight black pants stop a few inches below her belly button. He's glad it's not pierced, what's become the cliché of clichés at the gym and wherever else he goes. "If you want to think I'm a virgin, you can. If that'll make you any more friendly."

Maxine smiles and makes the drink. Jack looks her over, doing his best not to be too obvious—not too hard, considering there's a six-foot blonde in a white G-string behind her, humping a shiny metal pole.

"Here." She sets the drink on the counter. "Drink up, buttercup."

"Tell me what I need to hear."

Maxine's eyes are green, green and serious. A guy at the other end waves a twenty and calls for her but she tells him to hang on. She looks at Jack. "Ralph had made some enemies in here, around town," she says. "There's a guy who he was dealing for that you might want to watch out for. A guy named Junius Ponds."

The guy calls for Maxine again and she taps the bar, tells Jack to enjoy his drink. As she moves down the bar, Jack feels a hand descend on his shoulder. "Hello, friend." Jack turns, half-expecting to see Castroneves or his guy, but finds himself looking eye to eye, though he's sitting and Tony is standing, with Tony Vitelli, the owner of The Coast.

"Nice to see you, Jack," he says, sliding onto the next stool. "Buy you a drink?"

"Just got one." Jack holds up his madras.

Tony works his way onto the stool, then reaches behind his head and adjusts his ponytail, pulling it tight. Maxine comes back, pours out two fingers of Talisker scotch for the little man as he taps the bar with his knuckles. "Like a Virgin," by Madonna has just come on, as a girl with a lace maid's outfit on comes onto the stage. As she hears the song, Maxine gives Jack a wink and a big smile. Tony gives her the thumbs-up. "Why don't you go turn up the music for me, won't you dear?"

"Sure Tony." Maxine looks at Jack like she wants to laugh out loud, then heads off, ducks under the bar, and moves toward the entrance to the club.

When she's gone, Tony turns to face Jack. "Saw your boy got popped." He shakes his head. "That's a sorry thing there." He takes a long pull of the Talisker.

Jack fingers the side of his glass. "You know anything about it?"

Tony laughs. "Wish I didn't. I wish that bastard had never come into this place." As he talks, Jack notices new details about Tony's face: that he has lines along the sides of his mouth, a cleft chin, and that his brow wrinkles when he speaks. "Shit, Jack," he says. "That fuck was a loser. Had it coming for miles." He raises his glass and drinks, turns his attention to the stage. They watch as the maid finishes her dance and the song ends.

Now a woman with black hair and huge fake breasts comes out onto the stage. She wears a tight, leopard skin outfit. A voice announces her as "Brenda from Brazil."

Tony shakes his head, says, "Only a matter of time, really."

Jack leans forward, turns to look at Tony's face. It gets Tony's attention and Jack says, "Why don't you tell me some more about that."

Tony gets a serious look on his face. "You tell me, Jack. Tell me about his new boyfriends and their deal with the Colombian. Tell me about that."

Jack doesn't say anything, waits to hear what'll come next. After a few breaths, Tony shakes his head. "I can tell you about how he came in here for a while, always loaded and getting worse by the drink." He gestures to the room with his chin. "Touching the girls." Tony frowns, shrugs. "I could tell you about that."

Jack spreads his hands out on the bar. "But?" he says.

And Tony turns to clamp his hand onto Jack's shoulder. "But why should I bore you, Jack? You're a grown man. You knew Ralph on some level, had gotten to see the kind of slob asshole he was. You'd already know everything I'd say."

Jack holds up his arms, trying to shrug off Tony's hand, but Tony doesn't let go.

"Easy, Jack," Tony says.

"OK." Jack sits still. "But you don't kill someone for that, at least not where I come from."

Tony tightens his grip, brings his face closer to Jack's, "That's right," he says. "You'd have to start dealing behind someone's back to get killed like that, wouldn't you?"

"So that's why he wasn't welcome here anymore?"

Tony laughs. He shakes his head and then comes close again, says in a low growl, "Maybe you didn't hear me, Jack. I said he put his *hands* on my *girls*."

The music comes up in volume, Cameo's "Word Up" blowing out of the speakers and across the room. Tony turns toward the stage where Brenda from Brazil is down to a thong. She has just taken off her bikini-top and thrown it to a few guys in the front row, and now she gets down on her knees and starts crawling toward them. She stops a few feet from where they are and slides onto her back, raises herself up on her hands and knees and starts pumping her torso in front of them.

"You see this," Tony says, louder, showing Jack with his hands that he means to include the whole room. "This is my castle, my palace." He taps his finger on the bar. "I built this place up from just a SOMA shithole to a nice, respectable club. A *venue*." He shakes his head. "And nobody touches my girls here."

Maxine comes back to the bar, but instead of coming over to Jack and Tony, she starts washing glasses at a sink at the other end. She steals a look in their direction.

"Maxine's a nice girl, Jack. Don't you think?"

"Sure. Absolutely."

"Be a shame if anything happened to her, don't you think?"

Jack nods, not sure where this is headed. "Yeah. That'd be not good."

Tony laughs. "Not good. Right Jack. Nice talking. But you're right. That'd be not good. So you know what I mean." He leans back in his chair, relaxed.

"Right," Jack says. "But the question I'm asking you, is if you *know anything* about who would actually kill Ralph."

Tony tenses and sits up straight. He shakes his head slowly. "Maybe you don't hear so good, Jack. I just told you all I know.

And all you *need* to know about Ralph's involvement with this club." He reaches behind Jack, rests his arm on the back of Jack's chair. "Get me?"

"OK," Jack says. "But what I'm unclear on is what you mean about Maxine getting hurt. Are you trying to say—"

"No," Tony says. "I'm not trying to say anything. I'm trying to—" And before Jack can react, Tony pulls down on the back of Jack's chair. He pulls it hard, hard enough to pull it and Jack over, tipping backwards. Jack makes a grab for the bar but it's already out of his reach—he's falling backward, curling into a crunch so he doesn't hit his head, but heading toward the floor and then hitting it, his feet up over his head. He looks up and sees two of the big bouncers above him, looking down.

"So you want to know some shit, Jack?" Tony yells.

One bouncer stands above his right shoulder and another stands over his left. They both have their arms folded.

Tony hops out of his chair, stands above Jack, and kicks him in the side. "You want to know something, Jack? Do you? You want to know something about Ralph? To come in here and ask me questions?" Tony goes to kick Jack again, and Jack catches Tony's leg against his chest, and rolls over on top of it, bringing Tony down hard against the chairs at the bar. That's when Jack feels the bouncers' hands on his back and shoulders, pulling him up, and then something heavy hitting him in the back of the neck.

15

Through what looks like an indoor fog, Jack can see a strange apartment with paintings on the walls and, beyond his feet, windows letting in the sun. Outside he can hear branches scratching their leaves against the glass. He sits up, feels the pain ringing in his head like a bell in a cat toy.

"Don't get up yet."

A hand finds his shoulder, and Jack eases back down onto the couch. Something like a groan passes out of him. He touches his head, makes sure it's still attached. This is the part in the movie where he asks what happened to him, but Jack doesn't ask because he knows what happened, remembers the bouncers at The Coast kicking the shit out of him and how he couldn't do much about it from the floor. This is no movie; no stuntman came in to take any fake beating. When they were done, they dragged him out and left him in the alley. Jack remembers all of that and now he feels the tape on his face, the gauze along the side of his eye, and the hurt that runs all through him.

"Fuck," he says. "Where am I?" But he already knows that the only way he ended up in an apartment and not left in the alley for dead or frozen is Maxine, and that this must be her place. Her head comes into his sight from above, and he can see from the look on her face—she's got concern written all over it—that he must look pretty bad, which is more than he wants to know. She touches his forehead and, though her touch is soft, it starts the bell ringing in his head again and he closes his eyes.

When he wakes up, Maxine has him propped higher on the couch. He can see the plants now, set on the floor in a nice row along the windows. Very tasteful. She holds a bowl of soup up to his face so he can smell the chicken broth, feel the steam against his cheeks and in his nose. "Wow," he says. She touches the bowl to his lips and tips gently; he drinks, feels the heat in his throat. He drinks more and soon he can sit up on his own. The pain in his head lets him move now, doesn't increase to unbearable the instant he leaves the pillow.

"I guess Tony had a pretty bad hate for our Ralph," he says, when he can see Maxine sitting in a chair next to him.

She nods. "I'd say you touched a nerve."

"Then his boys touched a lot of mine." She laughs and he tries a smile, but it hurts to move his face like that.

She touches his brow again and this time it has more of the intended effect: it helps him lean back and relax for a minute, let himself feel the touch of a woman's fingers on his face. He hasn't felt this in a while and realizes he's missed it. He likes the feel, wishes he didn't have to get beat up first for it to happen.

"You're good to pull me out of that alley," he tells her. "And to bring me back here." He closes his eyes, feels her fingers smooth over his hair. "Thanks."

"That's OK," she says. "I was pretty much done with that job as it was."

"I guess you can't much go back now. Especially if you walked out."

She shakes her head. "No. Not so much." Jack looks now and sees that she has a sweatshirt on and her hair pulled back from her face in a bun. She looks good in clothes, more like the kind of person you could get to know and not just look at.

"You look good," Jack says. "I like you in clothes."

"Ha," she says, stone-faced. "These are my clothes. Remind me to put on something more revealing for you when you feel better."

"No," he says. "You're a lot less distracting this way. I can actually tell you have eyes and a face."

"That's funny, Jack. Almost." She puts on a big, fake smile.

"I mean it as a compliment. You have some really nice—" Jack stops; from the look on her face, he can tell she doesn't like where he's headed, any of what he might have to say about her look at the club. "Eyes?" he asks.

She fakes a laugh, then gets up from her chair and leaves the room. Jack hears her walking around in the rest of the apartment. He tries to sit up, to move his feet onto the floor, but even attempting that much motion brings back the bell. He lies back, closes his eyes.

It's dark outside the window when Jack finally gets up and turns to sit normally on the couch, even puts his feet onto the floor. He can see the bookshelves on the other side of the room, filled with books, too many for him to read the titles. He likes the way they look though, the sight of the shelves filled up. "Wow," he says, putting his hands on either side of him on the couch. He falls back into a prone position, with his head on the pillow.

"You already said, 'Wow.'" Maxine's back in her chair, looking a little more relaxed and less concerned. "How are you feeling?"

"Not that bad." There's no bell in his head, no sensation of his skull being a toy that an animal would play with. "I'll be all right soon. Just give me a few minutes to get up." Then Jack remembers that Castroneves was supposed to call to set up the meet, or that he was hoping Castroneves would call. "Have you seen my cell?"

Jack's wearing a T-shirt and there's a blanket over his legs. He feels underneath and realizes he's wearing only his boxers. Maxine points to a chair across the room where he can see his warm-up suit and under the chair his sneakers.

"Has anyone called?"

"It rang a few times. But I figured you weren't in any shape to talk." She gets up and sets down a steaming mug on the coffee table. Jack can see the string and the tag of a tea bag hanging down its side. She's got on shorts under her sweatshirt, and Jack sees her legs are thick and firm, good enough that she could've been one of the dancers at The Coast and not just a bartender. But he doesn't bring that up.

She starts to go through his things, pulls out his jacket and stops to look at him. "All right with you?"

He shrugs. "Of course. You're my nurse."

She smiles. In his inside pocket she finds the cell phone and brings it across the room. He flips it open, glad to find it still in one piece. The screen reads: 2 missed calls. One of them is Castroneves. The other Jack doesn't know. "You mind if I listen?" he says, holding up the phone.

She shakes her head. "Back to business."

"Yeah. That's me," Jack says. He calls into his voicemail. The first message is: *"Mr. Palms. Alex Castroneves. Thank you so much for calling to apologize about your incident with Juan José, though now of course he is very anxious to meet with you again. You understand. He is still very upset. But that is on the side. I would still like to meet with your friends tonight. Can you make that happen?"*

If the Colombian's guy wants to have another shot at Jack, he'll need to wait in line, Jack thinks, erasing the message. That or he'll have to deal with just these pieces, and not the whole Jack. Maybe that's more his speed.

The next message starts, *"Jack, my man."* He can recognize the sergeant's voice now. *"Just calling in to see what's up. Got a few items back from Ralph's house I want to discuss, get your feedback on. Know what I'm saying? Call my cell."* He leaves the number.

Jack hangs up and calls the Czechs, gets David. "Jack Palms," he says. "We have been waiting here to get your call."

"Good," Jack says. "I'm here. You ready to make this meet?"

In front of him, Maxine shakes her head like he's violating doctor's orders.

"Yes," he says. "Hold on."

Jack puts his hand over the receiver and Maxine says, "There's no way you're going out tonight!"

Then Vlade comes on the line. "Jack," he says. "What has happened? We thought we would hear from you before this."

"Sorry. I've been out of it. Nothing to worry though. I'm back. How about a meet with the Colombian?"

"Yes," he says. "We can do."

"Tonight. Get ready. I'll be back to you about location."

"That is good. Yes, we would like to go out, but we will do what you say."

Jack hangs up. He tries to pull it all together, quiet the buzz in his head and focus on the task at hand. Maxine sits across from him, holding her tea. "You're not seriously going to try and go out, are you?"

"Business. You know? If I can walk…"

She nods, blows on her tea. "You're fucking nuts."

Jack slides his feet back onto the floor, and feels a wave of pain and exhaustion run through him. "Shit," he says. "What hit me?"

She shakes her head. "You should stay on the couch, Jack."

He looks around the apartment, asks, "Where are we?"

"Inner Sunset," she says.

"Shit. Where's my car?"

"It's here. I drove us." She smiles, letting on any number of things from going into his pockets to get the keys, to driving the Mustang that no one else but Jack has driven in five years. But Jack doesn't mind. Despite the thought of someone else driving his car, there's no one he'd rather have doing it than a beautiful woman.

"How were you on the gears?"

"As nice as you could ever imagine." She nods.

"Thanks," he says. Then, dialing Castronves on his cell, "Thanks again. I guess it'd sound stupid to say you saved my life?"

Maxine nods her head. "You sound a little stupid, but I kind of like hearing it."

"No," Jack says. "I was just asking, not really—" But Maxine's already laughing at him and the phone starts to ring.

16

A few hours later, Jack pulls up outside a club in South Beach that Alex Castroneves decided on. He'd said he knows the owner, that they were OK with him spending a night partying and making a big trade. Business is business, Jack thinks, as he parks the car in the pay lot across the street, parking it himself instead of letting the valet get behind the wheel.

"That's OK," he tells the kid when he asks for the keys. "I'll be back out in a few minutes."

"Sir, we need your keys in case we have to move it to allow other cars to—"

"You won't," Jack says, palming a twenty into the kid's hand. He usually lets people have what they want, but a pimple-faced kid driving his Fastback, even around a parking lot, that's not going to happen.

Crossing the street to the club, he hears the blood pumping in his head, has a momentary relapse of the pain from the afternoon. Where his side still hurts he holds his ribs, thinking of the ways he'd like to repay Tony Vitelli. Maxine steps carefully down off the curb in tall heels, looking good in a black cocktail dress she threw on as Jack struggled to get up off the couch. When he finally did get up, he took a shower and it felt good: the hot water helping him to forget some of the pain and washing some of the dried blood away down the drain. He shaved with one of her disposables, soaked his face in a hot washcloth until the red from the heat took away some of the swelling, or at least made the rest of his face look red enough to match it. He changed the bandage, washed out the cut by his eye. In the mirror he saw the big bruise, the new dimension to his forehead, and the cut along the side of his swollen lips. The one by his eye, on the other side from the bruise, is probably good for about six or eight stitches, depending on when he gets himself to a hospital. Comparing it to the few serious fights he's been in, growing up and after, this is just worse than the norm. Except for the extra hurt around his body and shoulders, where he figures he took some kicking—that and the slight ringing in his head.

But washed up and wearing clean clothes—a button down shirt and crisp black jeans from the gym bag in his trunk—and with about five Advil kicking around in his bloodstream, he feels all right, good enough to drive and make sure things go according to plan at the club. He waits to cross the street with Maxine on his arm; she takes it as they leave the sidewalk and he looks over at how she's done her hair: still up but now wet-looking, with chopsticks holding it together in a tight bun. She wears her makeup like a pro—tasteful and not overdoing it, a bit less than when she worked behind the bar. Her dress is low-cut, showing off her assets even better than the tight top and the pants—more left to the imagination but the lines all clear, her smooth legs and her arms revealed; the tease and the want get Jack's mind racing.

At first Jack didn't think Maxine should come, but when she came out of her bedroom ready, looking like *this*, he couldn't argue. Her body slims in the middle, the dress accenting it, making her top and bottom individually stunning. As she walks ahead of him to the ropes and a bouncer, Jack notices that her calves look great, tight over her high heels: enough muscle that he knows she works out.

The bouncer waves them through a set of red velvet ropes toward a door under a sign that says "The Mirage." When he recognizes Jack, he smiles, claps him on the back, which hurts, and says, "My man. Nice to see you out tonight. Looking good."

"Good," Jack says, thinking the last time this guy probably saw him was a mug shot from the cover of a tabloid, his face gray from junk and taking Victoria's clubbing. "What's up?"

They shake as Maxine pulls Jack along, toward the open doors.

Inside, Jack follows her through a set of black curtains, to where she hands two red tickets to a blonde at a window who works the register. Next they walk down a hallway and come out into a huge, high-ceiling, wide-open two-level room with loud techno music and kids dancing all around them. When Jack's eyes adjust to the light, he sees there's a walkway leading up to a balcony, that the dance floor seems even bigger because its ceiling is so high. He points out the balcony to Maxine, leans closer to try and talk, wanting to say that Castroneves said to meet upstairs. Instead he just yells, "Upstairs."

As they make their way through the kids and across the dance floor, Jack takes Maxine's hand. He leads her up a set of stairs and then to the walkway above the main floor. At the entrance to the second level, there is another set of bouncers, and these two smile when they see Jack, say his name even, and let him by. "Good movie," it looks like one of them says, but Jack, reading lips in the loud techno cacophony, can't quite believe that's what the guy really meant. Still, he smiles back and touches the guy's bulky arm.

They walk up to where tables have been set up around the balcony so men in suits and women in dresses can sit in black chairs, drinking cocktails out of glasses, and look down on the dance floor below. The drinks of choice seem to be wine and martinis here, instead of the bottled water, drinks in plastic cups and chewing gum downstairs. This much is still like Jack remembers the clubs from his days on the scene, back when he and Victoria would make it out at least two nights every weekend, their days turning more and more into nights that became a push to see the sunrise, and then sleeping through the day.

Now Jack's life features order, exercise and calm, the view of the Bay in the morning, and knowing that he's doing the right thing. He thinks of the satisfaction he's supposed to feel, but he misses *this*: the music in his chest and the excitement of being in a place where there's energy in the air—a destination instead of a means to an end. He's slept through the day, still feels pain in his ribs, and knows he'll need extra sleep tomorrow, but for now he and all the other people here are doing something good, something that they *like*.

The feeling of Maxine's hand in his, for example, is something as good or even better than anything Jack's felt in a while.

They go over to the edge of the balcony, its rail, and look down onto the action just in time to see the Czechs walk in with Michal and his twin in tow. The five of them look ridiculous, so clearly out of place with their dark suits and serious faces, caught in the spin of young, small, American kids dancing to a techno beat. Al stands out from them even, a light blue blazer sticking out in the crowd, his silver shirt doing something in the flash of blue lights that is dazzling, mesmerizing to look at. The five move across the floor, pushing space in front and around them as they go, disrupting the rhythms of the dance, though Jack bets on the kids' ecstasy highs to help them recover.

It looks like David and Vlade both have briefcases; Jack can't imagine how they got these past the bouncers and metal detectors outside, especially if one (at least) is full of money. But then, showing a briefcase full of money is a very convincing mode of negotiation. That and saying you're there to meet with Alex Castroneves, a friend of the owner of the club, like Jack told them to.

Jack watches Al push a few club kids out of his way. They weren't really blocking his path, but he does it anyway.

He points out their pack to Maxine, who nods at the far part of the balcony where Alex and a few of his friends are sitting on black leather sofas around a low table. Jack can see the bottle of champagne chilling in a bucket of ice, and the unsuccessful bodyguard, Juan José, sitting at the end of a couch, with tape across the bridge of his nose. He sees Jack at that moment and raises his glass, smiles as if he wants to break every bone in Jack's body. He'll have a few less to break now, Jack thinks, feeling his ribs, testing to see if anything moves around. The right side hurts worse than the left, but both shoulders seem equally tight. What Jack needs is a long, hot bath.

With extra couches added to the Colombian's area, Jack and Maxine sit across the table from Alex. Jack sits next to Juan José, who leans in close and yells, "You broke my fucking nose. I hope to do the same to you."

He moves to shake Jack's hand, Jack thinks, but then slaps Jack on the chest, hard, feeling around his chest and arms to make sure he isn't wearing a wire or weapon, and, finally, slaps him once across the face. It's enough to make Jack wince.

Juan José smiles wide, nodding. "It looks like someone else may have beaten me to you. But I will still have the chance, no?"

Maxine pats Jack's knee and gets his attention. Her knees are close to his, one leg crossed over the other with her dress riding up to reveal the fleshy part of her thigh. Her legs look clean-shaven, smooth to the touch.

The Czechs make over-pronounced gestures of friendliness to the Colombians, ordering drinks all around, Jack still opting for club soda, though he feels more and more that he should just knock back a bourbon and Coke. He thinks this for a second, remembers Victoria drunk, the times she'd tear up their house. Just add another day of sobriety, he thinks. Even this one.

As the drinks come and the Czechs and the Colombians all start talking, Jack tries to look at their faces, but Al's shirt keeps drawing his eyes back like a magnet.

He wonders if any of them were the ones who killed Ralph and his dog. It's possible that one or two of the bodyguards, the Colombian's *or* the Czechs' could have done it, but Jack doesn't think so. Though Juan José couldn't have pulled it off, Michal would have done it. The other guy, the one who never talks, the one Hopkins pointed out in the picture, he could have done something. Who knows what *he* could have done?

Jack reaches into his inside pocket to check his cell phone and, bringing it out, sees he has a missed call from Sgt. Hopkins, nothing else. He looks at Maxine and she smiles at him, nods back toward a friend of Castroneves' who's talking at her. Jack leans close to her to whisper, "Do you think one of these guys killed Ralph?"

She shakes her head.

Then she leans closer, and here the music's reasonable enough that he can hear. "I wish I knew," she says. "Maybe I'd feel better right now."

Jack can feel her breath against his neck. "It wasn't Tony," she says. "He just got pissed off that Ralph didn't pay his—" Jack can't tell whether the last word is "bills" or "girls" but figures it's pretty much the same thing either way.

Then Jack's phone lights up, and he sees he's *received one text message*, something that's never happened before. But the phone has a button clearly marked "Show" and he pushes it: the text is from Mills Hopkins's number. "Know you're at Mirage. Need to talk."

"Fuck," Jack says, though in the noise he hopes no one else can hear him. But Alex catches his eye. "Jack," he says. He comes over to where Jack sits and crouches in front of him. "I am not angry over what happened with Juan José. He can be difficult, I know." Castroneves raises a finger. "He is, of course, angry, but I will let the two of you sort through that."

Jack leans forward to try and speak, opens his hands.

Seeing the bandage on Jack's temple, Castroneves winces. He reaches to touch it. "I guess someone has beaten Juan José to your acquaintance," he says. "Who did this?"

"A friend." Jack holds up a finger, "Excuse me." He gets up and sees Maxine's look of concern—part *Where are you going?* and part *Don't leave me with this guy!* He points to the bathrooms, hoping that will be enough of an answer for her.

17

In a polished-metal stall, Jack leans his head against the cold side and takes a deep breath. His ribcage feels like it's on fire as the constant thump of the bass rattles his chest. It's less loud inside the tiled walls of the john, but the pumping beat still comes through loud and clear.

Jack stands up, listening to his own breathing, trying to gauge whether any parts of his ribs might be poking his lungs. He calls Sgt. Hopkins on his cell, thinks about sitting down, but knows that's not a good idea. He leans up against the metal side of the stall. Then he thinks he hears his own name come through the phone.

"Mills," he says. "What the fuck?"

"This is your favor, asshole. Get your ass out of that club."

"Whatever you're thinking of doing, Mills, don't."

"Oh, we are, Jack. Sorry, but the S.F.P.D. is about to crash that party *hard*. Nothing I can do about it now."

That's when Jack hears a pop that's louder than any of the beats he's heard all night: a sound that comes through the walls loud and sharp instead of muffled and raw. A gunshot. Then another: *pop, pop.*

"Shit," Jack says into the phone. "Fuck is this?"

"What's happening, Jack?"

He flips the phone closed and rushes out of the stall. But before he can get to the bathroom door, he bumps into a guy in a black suit and his woman racing in, pupils like big black dimes. The woman screams.

Jack pushes past them.

Outside the bathroom, people run in panic, kids on ecstasy scream, and the music pumps on. Some still dance and drink like nothing's happened, but the ones who've lost their shit are running wild in the club, crashing into each other, knocking people over, flailing for the exits.

In the midst of this, around the couches, two guys stand over the Czechs and Castroneves with guns. One has a handgun and the other holds an automatic with two hands—something with a big clip. They both wear black suits, the first with dark glasses and a shaved head, pale face and scalp—he looks like a cue ball on black felt—and the second with a flattop, brown hair and wraparound shades.

Jack stands still for a moment, a breath, and then starts toward them, pushing his way through the crowd. His friend from the wharf stands up and goes after Flattop, but the Cueball knocks him down with a backslap of gunstock. Juan José falls back onto a couch and the Cueball opens up at him: two shots, both to the chest.

For just an instant, a tiny part of Jack is relieved, thinking that there's at least one less person in the world that wants to break his bones. But this relief is short lived: he's looking at two new guys busting up what was supposed to be *his* deal, putting bullet holes in the couch he was just sitting on.

Castroneves rolls Juan José off him and starts moving to the side. Cueball points his handgun at him, but Michal jumps up and starts shooting at both of the guys, first Cueball and then Flattop. He hits the Cueball—some of him sprays out his back, but Flattop gets down behind a couch. Jack's ten feet away and closing. The running hurts in his ribs and neck, but he keeps going.

Then Flattop pops up and rips through Michal with a spray of bullets that assures the whole club something is going on. Abruptly, as if the power were pulled, the music stops. Everyone on the balcony who hasn't already panicked panics, loses it: some head for the bathrooms and fire exits, some for the ramp and the main floor.

From the dance floor some drugged-up club kids begin screaming like they're four-year-olds, maybe because they're on acid, whatever stops them from seeing with any remove; they blindly freak out, lose all control, the sound awful: naked terror without a soundtrack.

Jack keeps moving forward, toward his group, knocking suits out of his way as he moves. The other Czech guard starts shooting, tearing up the couch, but Flattop stays behind it. Castroneves and his friends start to crawl toward the main floor. When they clear the couches, they get up and run, heading down the walkway into the crush. Jack sees one of them carrying a silver case.

Almost at the couches, a panicked clubber runs into Jack at full speed, hits him from the side like an end rush on the quarterback, knocks him into the rail and almost over the edge. Jack holds on, closes his eyes and feels the bell ring in his head again, the pain coming from his ribs start all over. When he opens his eyes, he sees a few of the club's bigger bouncers coming up the ramp, and below him, at the far end of the dance floor, Jack notices Mills Hopkins and a few of his boys in blue trying to get in past the throng of panicked club kids who are trying their best to push themselves out of the club. Mills and the others have their guns drawn, but they still can't get anywhere through all the kids. They try to fight their way through the crowd but can't get far. It's like the running of the bulls down there. He has about a minute before they start shooting in the air to clear a path, Jack guesses.

Now the rest of the Czechs start to rush the couch with Flattop behind it, but the guy raises his gun, and lets off a spray that gets everyone down, mostly knocks out a few lights above their heads. Still, it's enough to make the Czechs, except for Al, think twice about moving on him. Al starts over the back of the couch, and the gun sprays again before Vlade and David pull him back, unharmed somehow, and drag him away in the other direction. They start to head the same way as Alex and his friends, carrying their briefcases over their chests.

The guard who doesn't talk opens up with his *and* Michal's guns now, shooting up the couch, but in a heartbeat, the club bouncers reach the scene and they shout at him to stop. As he looks their way, the shooter with the automatic stands and opens up again.

Jack, the Czech, and the bouncers all get down fast. Maxine emerges from the other side of the couches, in a crouch, moving toward the bathrooms. By the way she's moving—long and swift fluid movements, no pauses—Jack can see she's all right.

In all of it, Jack has a moment of indecision, a point where he doesn't know which way to turn. He's moving toward the guns and realizes that's not the best direction but isn't sure of the best way to go or what to do. The main entrance has the cops, and the ramp leads to the panicked crowd. There's got to be another way out. Maxine starts pointing at something behind him, and he looks, sees a red "Exit" sign off down a hall beyond the bathrooms, and starts to go back that way as he hears the automatic open up again and more glass breaking. He looks back to see Maxine cutting down a different hall, standing and running full out now, her heels left behind. There's no time to go after her when he hears shouting and someone, probably Sgt. Hopkins, shoot a gun from the dance floor below and shout, "Everybody stay put! This is the police!"

Jack breaks through the exit door and into the emergency stairwell just in time to hear more shooting. He hopes Maxine will get out fine; she looked like she knew where she was going, but he stops before he gets to the stairs and knows he's got to go back. Ahead of him suits and women in dresses go for the flights of stairs that lead to some exit, but back there behind him are the Czechs who are paying him and a serious mess; maybe Maxine is also stuck in it. "Shit," he says. "Shit." Before anything else goes through his head, he's turning back to go find out.

Jack pushes his way past the suits coming at him heading for the door, and starts toward the shooter. Flattop's behind the same couch, but now it's pushed back all the way to the wall, and the club bouncers are holding him there. One of them is hitting him with the back end of his own gun, they've knocked the wraparounds into oblivion, and it's starting to get bloody. Maxine is nowhere to be seen. Jack looks where she'd last been heading and sees a long corridor with another exit sign at the end. She's probably gone, he hopes.

But Al, in all of his wild suit attention-grabbing glory, is standing at the balcony rail, waving a gun around and aiming it toward the dance floor. The balcony is still full of people, club kids *and* the suits now, as some of the scared clubbers have run up the ramp to get away from the cops. What was once a nice bar with backlit glass shelves behind it is shot up: destroyed, broken bottles, booze, and glass everywhere. Jack closes on Al as he starts aiming again and, thinking there's no way this bastard is even worth it, Jack tackles him to the floor. He gets a hold of his gun and, holding Al's face in front of his, he says, "We have to get out of here."

With wide eyes, Al speaks in Czech.

"Listen to me," Jack says. He gives him a light slap on the face.

Al's eyes focus. "Show me."

Jack gets up, pulls Al to his feet. The ribs hurt, his leg's bothering him, he wants to vomit. But he can see the door. Cops are coming up the walkway from below, battering their way through the crowd. "Come on," Jack says, pulling Al toward the bathrooms. Al's got one of the briefcases and it slows him down, but they make it to the bathroom and down the corridor, to the emergency stairs before any further orders come from the police.

18

The exit stairs come out onto a back alley: dumpsters, a chain link fence and the city's hot clubbers running off into the night. Jack holds Al's arm. He lets him go, and Al stands still, more confused than ever. "What was happening there?" he says. "Who was that guy?"

Jack puts his hands on his knees and notices they're covered in blood. He wipes them off, realizes it's not his blood, might even be wine and other drinks, and that now he's a mess. The whole night is something worse than he could've imagined. He can hear the bell starting to ring in his head again.

"Who *was* that?" Al yells. "Fucking who? They killed Michal!"

"Calm down," Jack says. "You're all right?" He looks Al up and down: his suit seems to be in worse condition, wrinkled and messy around the knees, sweat showing through his silver shirt, but that's no loss to the world. "We have to get out of here," Jack says.

"Who! Who!"

"Stop." Jack grabs Al by the shoulders and yells in his face. "Listen to me! I don't know who did that, but we will find out. Right now we have to go!"

Al brings his arms down, finally stops shouting.

"Go!" Jack says, pointing to the other end of the alley. "Find your car."

He turns to head toward his Mustang, goes a few steps, and when he looks back, Al has disappeared into the crowd.

At the front of the club, Jack sees the street packed with club-bers and police cars with lights flashing. He ducks around the barri-cade, crosses the street and makes his way to the parking lot, straight back to the Mustang. The valet kid is gone and people's keys are locked up inside his little booth. No one's going anywhere. Jack sees Maxine leaning against his car, still looking hot in her dress, smoking a cigarette.

"What took you?" she asks.

He opens her door and lets her in, walks back around to his side of the car. He sees her reach across the front seat and unlock his door—she's his kind of woman, he decides now, if he was ever un-sure. When they've both got their doors closed and the roar of the engine has calmed, he says, "I guess it took a while because I went back for you."

She laughs. "Get us out of here, hero."

Jack backs up to fit between the cars parked in front of him, a tight squeeze, then slowly rolls up the concrete embankment, onto the sidewalk, first the front wheels and then the back bumping over the rise. Then down off the curb, two more bumps, and they're on the road, leaving the police cars and tripped-out crowds behind as they head north toward Market. In his rear-view, Jack sees the kids spilling out of the police barricade, some of them running and get-ting away into the night.

He slows down to make the turn toward Market and later, as he shifts up to third gear heading onto Van Ness, Maxine puts her hand over his.

19

They wake late the next morning, make love slowly, gingerly, Jack trying to protect his bruises and delicate ribs, Maxine as beautiful naked as Jack imagined, her bare skin practically glowing in the morning sun. She reacts to every touch; her skin soft under Jack's fingers, her body so real, so sweet.

They share a cigarette after, give in to the cliché, but enjoy it: the soft exchange of the sharing, the slow inhales watching sun rays seep into the bedroom, the slow opposition to their hunger, the body's desire to eat.

By 11:30 they're in Jack's kitchen making coffee, wearing robes, Jack in pajama bottoms. He sees he has four messages on the machine. Mills Hopkins, he guesses, and the Czechs, but who else? Castroneves? He starts the coffee. Maxine's found herself a seat on one of the high bar stools Victoria bought to go next to the kitchen island. She has on one of Jack's old robes, a green plaid, and it looks good with her dark hair and green eyes. He can see a light spray of freckles on her skin at its neck.

"What is this?" Maxine asks, gesturing toward a six-inch gold statue of Bruce Lee on a small black pedestal. Jack looks at it, something he hasn't thought about in a while.

"That's my Action Movie Guild award for Best New Actor. You didn't know?"

"Right," she says, smiling, holding back a laugh. "That's a nice place for it, right next to your bowl of fake fruit."

"Victoria," Jack says, nodding at the plastic produce. "What can I say?"

He picks up the statue, looks it over. He'd forgotten about this thing, can't remember the last time he noticed it. "It's funny," he says, running his finger over the stern features of Bruce Lee's face. "You can get used to things and then completely forget them sometimes; you get so focused on everything else." He puts it back down, thinking about the time when Victoria threw everything on the mantle at him, piece by piece. "I'm not even sure how this got here."

"It's real nice," she says.

Jack nods. "Did those guys last night say anything before they started shooting?"

"Not in English. They said something to your friends, but it wasn't English. Sounded different from that stuff they were spitting at The Coast the other night, too."

"Did anyone say anything back?"

Maxine shakes her head, no. "But the guy you were supposed to trade with? He didn't like it at all. He started calling them motherfuckers, saying he would kill their families."

"Nice. So they shot him."

"They shot his guy. The one who wanted to kill you."

Jack laughs. "Right. Lots of that lately."

"But that's basically how it went. They were looking at the Czechs when they first walked in. Then the other guy spoke up."

"You ever seen them before?"

"I feel like I have," she says. "But I can't say. Maybe they came into The Coast?"

"Think they know Tony?"

Maxine frowns. "I can't say. Probably not though. I don't think they're Tony's kind of style. Too exciting, too—and I say this without any offense to your current bruises—too *actually making something happen.*"

"Right." Jack's not convinced that hanging with a few shooters is beyond Tony, but he leaves it for now. "But let's acknowledge." He waves his hands along the sides of his torso, putting some of Tony's work on display. "Tony can make some things happen. He's a bit of a psycho."

"You're not the first one to say that."

"Not that he won't see something coming back for this."

"Forget it, Jack. Let's move forward."

They make eye contact, and Jack thinks it over. He gives it up for now.

Jack hits the button on his answering machine. The thing rewinds, then beeps. *"Yo, Jack,"* Ralph says. *"Where the fuck are you man? A couple of guys are here parked outside and banging the door. I may have to split. Wanted to make sure you knew I tried to call you if I do. Take care of Arthur, will you? That's my dog. She's here. If anything goes wacky with the Czechs, talk to Joe Buddha, from Paramount. He's here now in SF. Pacific Heights. Shit."*

And then that's all. The machine beeps again and the voice from the bank comes on, the guy starting to say something about the mortgage payment, and Jack stops it. He rewinds the tape back to Ralph's message and plays it again. "When did you last check this thing?" Maxine asks.

Jack waits for Ralph to finish. "I checked it Thursday morning, before I left."

She moves around the counter to pour her coffee. As she walks, Jack sees the robe part and gets a good view of her leg, most of her thigh. He pulls her toward him and kisses her hard, running his hand down inside her robe.

"Hey," she says. She turns and pushes him back. Then she kisses him on the lips. "Stay with me," she says. "Pay attention."

Jack nods, puts a good-boy look on his face. "OK."

"I guess Ralph called you when he knew something was going to happen."

"And then he got popped."

Maxine makes a face at this. "OK. So who's Joe Buddha?"

"He's a guy from Hollywood who helped me get my start. One of the producers on *Shake 'Em Down.* The funny thing is his name was above mine on the list in Ralph's house. But I didn't know he was up here, didn't think of it until now."

The machine beeps again and Sgt. Hopkins' voice comes on, *"Jack Palms. Trying to get you out of some trouble tonight. Call me before you go to The Mirage, fuckhead. OK?"*

"Nice," Jack says. "Very professional police work."

"Who is this guy?"

"He's an old friend on the force. The question is how did he know about The Mirage? Seems like a lot of people got clued in on our meet."

The machine beeps and Vlade's voice comes on, says, *"Jack Palmas. We are at the hotel and Al is not with us. Michal is no more. What the fuck was that happening? Call us. We want to talk."*

"Fuck," Jack says. He pours his coffee, looks back down the hall toward the bedroom—he knows his cigarettes are on the table by the bed—and raises the mug. "Here's to working," he says. "Looks like I have to follow this through the whole way."

She looks at him long and hard, gestures to the room around them: the high ceilings and skylights. "You sure you want to leave all this to deal with these people? There's two dead at least now, people you knew. Plus three, four with that shooter. You want to be part of all that?"

Jack nods, thinking about the money, Sgt. Hopkins' words about terrorists and warlords, Jack not knowing what he was into. He shrugs. "It's a good fucking question. I could tell you I need the money, but you'd think that's bullshit."

"So why else?" Maxine's eyes get narrow, like this is the moment she's really going to figure Jack out.

"Right," he says. "Why?" He knows this has gone beyond the zero-sum game part of his involvement, that if it hasn't, he's in it now for the positives: the chance to act again, be somebody he's not, even if this is real world with real guns. He has to admit it, to himself at least: he's been enjoying parts of it, the challenge of acting like he knows what he's doing, feeling like he has a part in something, a role to play. Like part of him that hasn't felt in a while is starting to feel again. But he's not ready to say this out loud.

"What's going on up there?" Maxine asks, reaching for Jack's temple. "I can practically hear the gears."

"Right," Jack says. "So I'll tell you two things." He holds up his hand, first one finger. "One, I'm not happy about this shit with Tony." He gestures at his face and his ribs. "And I still think if I follow through I'll find out why this happened and maybe get a chance to do something about it."

Maxine's starting to look more and more serious. She has her hands on her hips, everything about her telling Jack she's evaluating him. "He's a fuck. Why else you doing this? What's two?"

Jack's about to explain how he feels when he's acting, that he hasn't felt good like this in a while and how he enjoys that part, but there's something in her face, her narrowed eyes, that tells him she'll think it's bull. He shrugs. "The second part is my name was on a pad at Ralph's house and I want to find out who killed him before those same people come up here and try to get to me."

She puts her coffee mug on the counter, and pushes her finger up underneath each of her eyes, wiping off last night's makeup. "Yeah," she says. "That plan did real well for us last night."

Jack takes her in his arms, runs a hand across her back. "That was bad," he says. "But what if I stay up here? Who's to say they won't come after me?"

He can already feel his eagerness to go back out there, down into the city: it's in the way he feels in the robe, a tingle running across his skin, the way he's already checked the clock behind Maxine and thought about what time he can get to Sgt. Hopkins' office to talk this over with the cop. He hasn't even had his coffee yet and he's already got that bump: a reason to get going like he hasn't had in a long time, maybe as long as he can remember.

She shakes her head, her arms around Jack now. "Well count me out. This girl's had enough getting shot at."

20

After Jack's driven Maxine back to her apartment and dropped her off, he heads to the Hall of Justice, like any good super hero would. But the secretary for Sgt. Hopkins' section of the precinct won't let Jack back to see him. "The whole task force does not take visitors without an appointment," she says, stonewalls him until he finally has to go outside and call Hopkins from his cell phone.

"Mills," Jack says, when the cop finally answers. "Tell your girl at the front desk to let me back there. She's got this place like Fort Knox."

"Palms. Glad you're here. We need to talk."

"I'm here. I've just been *trying* to get back to you."

"We might've had to get a warrant for your arrest this morning."

"Like I said, Mills, I'm here in your fucking precinct wanting to meet with you. Let me back."

"Right. Actually let's meet outside. I'll buy you a coffee across the street. Blue Diner." Hopkins hangs up.

"Shit," Jack says into the phone. Only a cop with something fucked up going on wants to meet you outside of the station, away from his desk. But Jack needs to see him, talk it through a little and find out what Hopkins knows. He has no choice.

Jack finds the Blue Diner right across the street from the Hall of Justice in the middle of a row of bail bonds offices that come in every ethnic denomination: Aladdin Bail Bonds, De Soto (Sé Habla Español), Al Graf, and Puccinelli (24 hours). The diner may as well be called the Justice Diner; the place is crawling with cops in blue uniforms, walking out with coffee and donuts or just coffee. The counter is lined with them from end to end.

Hopkins claps Jack on the back as he's standing outside, taking it all in. "Nice place here, Sergeant. This would be a great theme bar for the Castro."

"Good one," Hopkins says. "I'll have to remember that for later." He starts to head into the diner and then stops short. "Ho! What happened to your face?"

Jack shakes his head.

"You look like you got hit with a truck. A small truck, maybe, but still."

"Right," Jack says, touching the fresh bandage along the side of his eye. "I'll be happy to talk about that if you tell me why we can't meet in the Hall of Justice. What's up? Has Wonder Woman commandeered the whole place to vacuum out her Invisible Jet? It got lost?"

"I guess you've been through some tough times," Sgt. Hopkins says. He pats Jack on the back. "Must have been hard on you running out the back of The Mirage last night. Next time save yourself the trouble and call me when I leave you a message."

"Why not, Mills? Aquaman's upset because the fish won't listen to him anymore? The Wonder Twins having separation anxiety?"

Hopkins looks nonplussed, folds his arms. Twenty years of working in a place called the Hall of Justice and the humor must get old. He shakes his head. "The Hall of Justice is nothing to fuck with, Jack."

"Let me guess. You've heard these before?"

Hopkins nods, so Jack changes the subject. "Why the fuck did you want to meet outside? They bug your office?"

Hopkins directs Jack toward the diner with his chin. "Not quite." Inside, he points to a booth by the wall, away from the windows. As they're walking over, he winks at a waitress, orders two coffees.

"Seriously, Jack. Who knocked hell out of your face? Is it these Czech bastards? Did they interrogate you?" They're just starting to sit down.

Jack looks at the sergeant. He's got a tweed jacket on today and a blue button-down shirt stretched tight across his belly. The look's an improvement, but he still looks like a human being posing as a cantaloupe, or the other way around. Above his pockmarked face, he's wearing an old-fashioned panama hat. He takes it off, puts it next to him on the table.

"What's up with the hat, Mills? You trying to get some fashion?"

Hopkins shakes his head. "Cut it. We're here to talk."

"I'll talk, but I've got some questions too. We need to share."

Hopkins frowns. "OK."

"First off, tell me what you know about who killed Ralph."

"We have some suspects, but nothing's panning out. Truth is we don't know much about that yet."

The waitress brings two pots of coffee and pours Sgt. Hopkins' to the brim. Jack asks her for the decaf; he's already had enough caffeinated with Maxine.

The sergeant takes a sip of coffee. "You don't drink real coffee?" he asks.

Jack pushes the cup aside. "Listen. I didn't come down here to have you jerk my chain. You wanted to meet in this place. We're meeting. I don't want coffee or to talk about coffee. Stop acting like you get paid by the hour."

Hopkins looks at Jack, but Jack waits him out. Then Hopkins says, "Last night. Club owner gets a call from Alex Castroneves, a friend, but he doesn't want the place to get the wrong kind of reputation. Also, he's convinced there are a lot of young guys coming in, selling ecstasy. He wants that stopped. Figures he'll call us before we move on our own, get him in some real trouble. Then I find out Castroneves was Ralph's man, put two and two together, and I figure out it's your thing. You had called me back, we could've both saved each other a lot of trouble."

"You mean you could've saved me the trouble of going ahead with my deal."

Hopkins shrugs. "Or you just move the location, we get a big bust of kids dealing x at the club of some asshole who'll turn over his friends. If your boys are only in it for the drugs, I don't much care." He leans forward. "This is all off the fucking record."

Jack looks at his coffee. "You're a dirty cop, Mills. You know that?"

He shrugs. "Twenty-three years on the force, two more to go till retirement. So sometimes I'm more concerned with keeping my friends than with every fucking arrest. Is that the worst thing in the world?"

"Maybe not." Jack sits back. "But friends can get you killed, too."

Hopkins laughs, sits back in the booth. "What're you trying to say, Jack? You talking for you, or for me?"

Jack shakes his head. Though he gets Hopkins' point: that he might be the one with the friends who'll get him into trouble.

Hopkins taps his knuckles on the table. "Other thing is your boys can lead me to the serious weight in this town. You get me to that, I don't care how much these out-of-towners want. Show me the supply line, Jack. That's what I need."

"You saying I give you a name, you stay off my back?"

Hopkins nods, waits for Jack to say something else.

"What?"

"Go ahead. Tell me a name."

Jack shakes his head. "I need more time. Right now I don't have anything bigger than Castroneves. You know him. Let me find out who else is there, who took down Ralph."

"Done. But—" Hopkins holds his head rigid, his eyes fixed on Jack's. "There's one more thing: we're getting more tips on the Eastern European mobsters coming in, guys who pack serious fire and don't worry about civilian presence. It's still the terrorist line. Your guys aren't them, they can go and do whatever. Your guys are these warlords—and that's the word we've been hearing, Jack, 'warlords'—then they're going down."

"Sounds like you found your boys last night," Jack says. "Two punks come in shooting up the place. That sound like they fit your description? Did you get them?"

Hopkins shakes his head. "That's another part of the problem. One's dead. That we know. We're still trying to find out who he was. The other one we had in custody until six this morning when one of the city's finest, and by that I mean most expensive, lawyers comes down to spring him. You don't get those fuckers out of bed in the morning without some *heavy* cash flow, maybe even political pull."

Jack slides his coffee cup back within easy reach, adds some sugar and milk.

Hopkins drinks, sets his cup down on the table. "Now *you're* waiting, Jack. What's the next question?"

"Someone tipped *them* off about our meet. Say they popped Ralph, now someone's looking to sour his deal, hit his supplier and take him out of the picture. Why?"

Hopkins shrugs. "The way these things go? My guess is we follow this long enough, we find someone's trying to take over the action in this town. *That's* the supply line we want, because that's the one who's going to be big. Castroneves? He doesn't give a shit about San Francisco. He'll be gone in a week. We want the local line."

"*Someone* had to tell them about our meet." Jack makes sure he's looking Hopkins in the eye when he asks, "You know who dropped that tip?"

Hopkins shakes his head. "I'm with you. Either we got a hole somewhere in our force, or this club owner, guy who owns The Mirage, wants a raid *and* a shooting in his place in one night." He shakes his head. "I'm not banking on that one. He wants bad elements out, he calls us. He's not looking to call in a murder."

"Agreed." Jack looks across the room at a few of the other cops. "So you think there's something wrong within your hallowed halls?"

Hopkins shakes his head. "There may be, but these blue-suits ain't it. Something's up in my task force. That's why we're here."

"Ahh," Jack says. "Some truth finally comes out."

"OK." Hopkins holds his hands in front of him, pushing down air. "But be quiet about it."

An officer from a booth across the aisle gets up, comes over to Jack's side of the table. "You Jack Palms?" he asks, extending his hand with a pen in it and pushing a beverage napkin across the table toward Jack. "My kids loved your movie."

Hopkins laughs. Jack signs the napkin, shakes the guy's hand and thanks him. Then Hopkins tells the guy to get out and make some arrests for a change.

Jack excuses himself, stands up. "I got to go too, Mills. You have any other questions?"

Hopkins shakes his head. "But next time you call me back. After this little talk, I think you're the one who owes me."

Thinking about the press he got for the bust at his house, the pictures of him handcuffed in the newspaper and Hopkins laughing in the front seat of the squad car, Jack drops a dollar on the table for his coffee.

"Oh, no," he says. "We're not even close to square."

21

Walking back to the car, Jack thinks over who knew they were meeting at The Mirage: Castroneves, the Czechs, the club owner, a few cops on the force, it turns out, and *Maxine*. It's a small part of him, but there's a nag inside that he's got to get to the bottom of.

She wasn't away for long, just his time in the shower, but she was away. Part of him hates that he's even thinking it, but Jack's never had good experiences with trust and women. He thinks of Victoria, remembers Ralph lying on the bottom of his tub.

Once he's in the car, he heads for her apartment.

Maxine's home, buzzes him up as soon as she hears his voice through the speaker. When he comes up the stairs, he sees her door open and she leans into the hallway, her hair wet, wearing a thin Kimono that only comes down to the middle of her thighs. "Hey," he says to her.

"I didn't think you'd be back so fast."

Jack gets to the top of the stairs, and she kisses him once, long and wet, her skin still warm from the shower and her mouth hot. She smells like apples.

Inside her apartment, he can smell the steam of the shower and the sweet smell of her shampoo. Her hair hangs wet to her shoulders, stringy instead of full, and Jack remembers the soft feel of it on his face last night. She sits down, her robe showing off more of her legs.

Jack puts his hands in his pockets, then takes them out.

"What's the matter?"

He rubs his hands together, not sure where to start. "Tell me everything you know about Tony. Start with how you got work in his club."

"Well, Jack." She crosses her legs and sits up very straight, as if it's an interview. "I met Tony when I applied for a job as a bartender. I've wanted to tend bar for a while, went to some dumbass bartending school, and when I got out, there were no jobs. I saw one opening at a bar in the Oakland airport and then I tried Tony's because a friend of mine used to dance there and she said he'd put me on. Then he did. Does that answer satisfy your curiosity?"

"What's Tony like?"

She shrugs, relaxes her posture. "Tony's mostly OK. He can be an asshole, but mostly he takes care of his girls. Sure, he tries to put his hands on once in a while, but he's not that bad. At least he wasn't with me." She nods at Jack's fresh bandage, points to his torso. "Wish I could say the same about you."

Jack walks over to her bookcase, starts reading the spines. She has some good books—Hemingway, Flannery O'Connor, Raymond Carver, Jayne Ann Phillips—things Jack's started to read in his downtime.

"I just want to know that you don't give a fuck about this guy, that you wouldn't tell him what's going on if he called."

"You know, Jack?" She raises a finger, points at the front door. "I almost want to ask you to leave right now. What are you really asking me here?"

"Someone called someone and let them know where our meet was last night. I know the club owner called the police, but those shooters didn't just happen by."

She stands up. "And you think it's *me*? You're going to fucking stand here in the room where I cleaned your cuts and say this shit?" Her chin crinkles as she says this, but she doesn't cry. "What is wrong with you, Jack Palms?" She comes over to him, stands close, and slaps him across the face.

Jack turns away, feeling the sting of her slap. Luckily she hit his good side. He tastes blood; then touches his lip and looks at his finger: red. "I just have to know," he says.

"If you don't already, then there's nothing I can do." She moves toward the bedroom, then looks back once, tells him to fuck himself, and goes inside, slamming the door.

Jack waits a few breaths, tapping his finger against her shelves. He knows she's not coming back out. He finds a pad on her kitchen table and writes a note, *Sorry I had to ask. I shouldn't have, but I did. You're right, I'm an ass. Call me.*

Then he leaves.

22

Jack's not sure about his next move, so he heads to the Hotel Regis, figuring he owes the Czechs a visit. He's prepared for anything when the elevator door opens, so when the bodyguard has his gun raised at Jack's head, he's not surprised. Jack looks right at him, raises his hand to point at the guy's face. "Now what did I tell you about that?"

A moment passes where Jack's eyes and the guard's eyes meet. Then the guard blinks, and lowers his weapon. Jack looks around the suite. "Can somebody tell me this guy's name?"

From one of the couches, David salutes Jack with a thick glass of scotch and then turns his attention back to the TV. He's wearing a while hotel robe, has his white-socked feet up on the glass coffee table. "That is Niki," he says.

"OK, guys," Jack calls out to the room. "It's me. I'm still not the one fucking you, but we got to start working together on this thing."

Al comes out of a bedroom, holding a handgun of his own, a semi-automatic Beretta. He's wearing jeans now and a too-tight yellow polo shirt, tucked in. "No, fuck this, Jack. Why we need this trouble?" He frowns. "We want coke, we can get. Do not need all the shit in this town, people shooting, people dying. If we need that shit, we need to be the ones doing it." He holds up the gun. "*We* kill. *We* shoot."

Jack can hear Vlade call from somewhere in the suite. "People die here." He comes out to the main room. "We come here to have fun. In America we plan big drive, big fun: San Francisco, L.A., Vegas, Phoenix, Dallas, New Orleans. Who knows?" He raises his shoulders toward his face, holds his hands out. "Maybe keep going. All the way to New York. We don't know."

"New York is good," Al says. He waves his gun around the room as he talks. "New York we don't have this shit. Why in San Francisco we have? Why this trouble?" He comes closer, stops when he sees Jack's face. "Jack Palms," he says. "What happened to your face?"

"Come on guys!"

"No," Al says. "What happened? Did that occur last night?"

Jack shakes his head. "It was dark. You may not have seen it. This was yesterday, day before. It happened at The Coast."

"The Coast!" Al yells. "We will demolish that place to the ground. I go in there and burn that place gone. I will kill Tony Vitelli! We stop everything else right now." He's pointing his gun around the suite.

Jack looks at the others; Niki and Vlade appear serious, like they want to do what Al's saying, like they're mad enough to go after Tony and whomever else they can find, take out all of their anger on somebody. David looks drunk, like he's not going anywhere.

"Guys," Jack says. "Relax. We've got work to do."

"Fuck the deal," Al says. "I want to start we should shoot back."

Jack shakes his head. "You want to find out what happened to Michal, right? And to Ralph." He raises his hands. "That's not going away if we leave it."

Al walks over to the bar. "Oh, this is fucked up, Jack."

"What can we do?" Vlade asks. "Now we have no coke. Our friend is gone. Let us repay the fucks who did this to you."

"OK. OK." Jack opens his hand toward the couch. "All right if I sit down?"

Vlade nods to Jack and comes over to sit on one of the couches himself. He waves to Niki that he can come sit down too. "Niki did good job last night. So did your Maxine." David and Niki both nod. "Without her, we get arrested. She showed us way out."

Al comes all the way out into the center of the room, stands be-hind the couches. "Thank you Jack," he says. "You helped me there." He's got his lower lip buttoned up over his upper one, looks like nothing could be worse than how he feels. "Can I make you drink?"

"Sure," Jack says. "Club soda."

Vlade laughs. "This has not made you to drink yet?" Al walks to the bar as David drains off the rest of his scotch and holds his glass up, clinking the ice against its side. "Yes David," Al says. "I hear you."

In a half-hour, Jack's got the Czechs telling stories about where they're from and how they made their money. They explain that they have an importing business in the Ukraine that brings in fish for the fancy sushi restaurants that've started popping up in the former Soviet Bloc. It's doing well enough that they can take a few months off and come to tour America. But not so well that they aren't thinking about staying on if they can score enough blow to start dealing a little. First they want to rent motorcycles and drive across the plains and around the whole US, stopping at the major cities. Their bikes won't be ready for another few days, and getting the coke they want for the trip is causing problems—problems they'd like to see end.

Jack wonders whether he should tell them it's not a good idea to be driving across the U.S. with guns and a big supply of coke, but he figures that's their problem, not his. The coke they started with came from Ralph—he gave them a key when they arrived—then he was supposed to connect them directly to his supplier, a guy named Junius. The one Maxine mentioned. Then, Ralph being Ralph, he decided he thought he could get a better deal from Castroneves.

They never got to meet Ralph's original connection.

"What the hell kind of name is Junius?" Jack asks.

They all frown, then shrug. "We do not know," David answers. "We just know Junius. That his name."

This is when Jack remembers Ralph's message from his machine that morning, telling him to contact Joe Buddha. It's not a lead to Junius but it's someone else Jack needs to follow up with.

"Let me get one thing straight," he says, unable to leave it alone. "You guys want to take ten keys across the country with you on motorcycles?"

Vlade laughs, shakes his head. "Ten is too much. We will take just enough and leave the rest here in San Francisco. They have lockers here, no? We leave and then sell what we can for ourselves, to our own community here."

"Yes," David says. "Part we sell, part we keep."

"OK." Jack raises his glass and the others follow. They're all drinking scotch except for him and Niki. "We put this thing back together. Find out what's happening with the guns, get in touch with Junius if that's what needs to happen, and find out who did Ralph and Michal. We get you your coke."

Jack looks at his watch: it's a little after three in the afternoon.

"It is now Saturday. If you give me until this time tomorrow, we will get these things done." Jack holds his glass over the coffee table and waits while the others exchange glances. Finally, they lean forward and touch glasses with his, Niki using his bare fist.

"You are on, Jack Palms," Vlade says.

"But first we go to The Coast and burn down the motherfucks who have attacked you. About last night, we do not know who. But this," Al gestures toward Jack's face. "This we know."

Vlade picks up his gun off the table and sights down the barrel. Then he holds it back and looks at the gun's side. "We have business there with Mr. Tony Vitelli."

23

Jack finds Joe Buddha listed in the phonebook under his real name, John Wesley Taraval, with an address in Noe Valley.

Driving down Market, Jack tries Maxine at home to apologize and gets her machine. "Sorry about before, Max. I just found out you helped the Czechs get out last night. Thanks for that. I guess I owe you in more ways than one."

He hopes he hasn't pissed her off completely but thinks she'll be OK once she settles down and has some time to unwind. If he has time, he decides, he'll stop by her place again before meeting the Czechs at The Coast.

But that's after Joe Buddha's, where he pulls up in front of a white row house on Church Street, at Chavez. As he gets out of the car and walks closer, Jack notices a little altar mounted high up beside the front door, that it's a small shelf screwed right onto the side of the house. It holds a bowl of pears, a small collection of incense sticks, and a ribbon, what looks like the prize from a horse-riding contest, but with Japanese characters on it.

Jack rings the bell and in a little while hears feet in the hall, then a small Asian woman opens the interior wooden door, regards him through a thin metal grate.

"Joe Buddha?" he says, and when that brings no response, "John Wesley Taraval?"

"Oh," she says. "You are here to see John? Come right in." She opens the metal grated door and leads Jack inside a dark, carpeted hallway that smells like incense. At the end of the hall, Jack can make out a kitchen in the light of the room's windows. Inside, at a small table, a small, wide man sits on a chair, eating in silhouette. Jack can tell it's Joe Buddha even without seeing his face; nobody else has the body, the round paunch like Joe—the reason for the nickname Buddha. The woman leads Jack down the hall, and before she can announce him he bellows, "Old Joe Buddha!"

Buddha turns fast, surprised, and stands up. Jack comes into the kitchen and sees him in the full light: before him stands his old friend, only smaller, older, more wrinkled, and with an even more pronounced middle. He's always had one of those bellies that look like someone stretched the skin over a watermelon: tight looking, but large.

"Holy shit," Jack says. "You look even more like the old man now than ever."

Buddha nods, spreads his arms. "As it has turned out to be."

Jack fakes a punch at the paunch. "Don't tell me you've finally gone Asian in your old age, turned religious on us."

"This?" Buddha raises his short arms. "No," he says, waving at it all with both hands. "This is all her. You just met my wife, Yuko." He puts his arm around her and she smiles. They both laugh.

"Joe Buddha," she says, rubbing his belly. "My little religious icon."

Buddha runs his hand over his scalp and then around to the sides of his head, where he still has a bar of hair behind his ears and around the back. Otherwise, he's shining bald. "Old Buddha," he says. "Haven't been called that in a while. You heard from Ralph then?"

Jack nods. "Before he passed."

Buddha shakes his head. "Yeah. We saw that one on the news. Not good." He shrugs. "But what can you do? He got popped."

"He told me to come find you."

"He would. It was only a matter of time." Buddha tucks in his chair at the table, carries the bowl of cereal he was eating over to the sink. He turns to look at Jack. "How *are* you?" he asks, all serious concern.

Jack nods. "I'm all right. Getting by."

Yuko leans against the counter and looks at Jack sideways, regarding him. Buddha shakes his head. "We were worried about you, Jack. Really worried."

Jack sits down at the table. "Yeah, well. I'm OK now. How long have you been up here in S.F.?"

Buddha shrugs. "Two years." He moves to the table and puts his hands on the back of a chair. "I'm sorry we didn't get in touch with you. I wanted to. I was concerned about how you'd be doing."

"So you saw what happened?"

"Who didn't? I'm still so sorry about Victoria, about what happened to the second picture." Buddha was like that: he liked to call movies "pictures." He'd been involved with Jack's sequel, *Shake It Up*, as one of the producers. When it came down to it, though, the others all pulled out around the time of Sgt. Hopkins' arrest. "The thing is, Jack, we could all see that coming for miles."

"And you tried to warn me," Jack says. "I know."

"Victoria, Jack. She was fire."

Jack nods. "But it was me too. I wanted some of that. I got into the coke myself, I guess H was just a matter of time. What did I know?"

Buddha shakes his head. He pulls out the chair and sits across from Jack at the table. "You know, Jack, we knew. We could see it all happening too slow. I'm just sorry I couldn't help you."

"I don't know." Jack shrugs. "Maybe it had to happen."

Buddha nods. Then he shakes his head as if he's considered it and decided that it did not have to happen. "No Jack," he says. "We could've helped you more, gotten you out of that mess, helped you clean up. I have to believe that now."

Jack nods, feels the soft tablecloth under his fingers. He knows what he's come back from, that he's in the middle of something crazy now, something he's only hoping he can control.

"Can I have some cereal, Joe?" Jack says, realizing he hasn't eaten breakfast, that all he's had is the coffee with Maxine and no food.

Buddha laughs. "Yuko, will you bring my friend here a bowl of our finest?"

Yuko looks at Jack, then back at Buddha. "No," she says. Without hesitation, she walks out of the room. Jack can hear her feet padding on the rug in the small, quiet house as she moves back down the front hall and then up a flight of stairs.

"Did I say something wrong?" Jack asks.

"No. I did. I guess I'll be getting that for you."

Buddha gets up and moves around the kitchen, placing items on the table in front of Jack: the box of cereal, milk, a spoon and a bowl. Jack pours out the cereal for himself, adds the milk. He hasn't had any cereal in a few days and misses something about it, about the routine of eating from the round bowl, the cold milk.

"Routine is what makes us who we are," Buddha says, as Jack starts eating. "It's how we find our true self." He nods. "Once you read this Zen business, it's actually not that bad." He rubs his own stomach. "I actually used to hate that nickname for a while, but now it seems I've really grown into it."

Jack tastes the corn flakes, still crunchy, and counts his chews. He won't have another cigarette today, not for a while, and he's been doing well by avoiding all of the drinks he's been offered. He's still on the wagon. And he's turned down the blow—all of it. He's been out of the hills and his routine for three days now, and he's still getting by. But it's nice, in the small bowl of cereal and milk, to go back to routine even just a little. "I had a hard time coming back from the drugs and shit," Jack says.

Buddha nods. "No one ever said that part was easy."

Jack looks up, regards the lines around Buddha's mouth, as he says, "You know I never hit Victoria, right? Any woman."

Buddha puts his hand over Jack's, then withdraws it. "I know," he says. "I knew from the first time I heard it, never believed those stories. But you know how they are down there. Still small and you get some bad pub, no one will touch you. You're big and the bad pub works *for* you. The whole system is fucked.

"You got through though. That's what's important. Those battles have been fought. The newspapers fucked you, and now you're here. The question is, how you going to move on?"

Jack sits back. "You really have turned into a little buddha! You fuck."

He nods. "It's true, as they say. Sometimes life imitates itself or gives some indication of where you're going. I met Yuko when I got into Zen, and we moved up here." He waves his hand dismissively across the table. "Fuck L.A.!"

"Fuck L.A." Jack holds up his bowl of cereal to toast to that— it's all milk now—and drains it off with one swallow. "I was at Ralph's house the other day, the day he got killed. I found him." Jack shakes his head, pushing away the image. "I saw a pad by his phone with both of our names on it, yours just above mine. It was crossed out. Any idea why?"

Buddha shakes his head. "He called me about helping him out with some drug deal and I turned him down. Let me guess: he came and asked you next?"

Jack nods. "That's how I got into all this: I guess I was a second option."

Buddha laughs, his small compact frame bouncing from the middle as he lets out the sounds. "Figures. Then he'd tell you to come find me and we'd talk about it. That sounds like Ralph."

"I was trying to help him, you know? He seemed like he could use it. And I can use the money. But things got weird. The deal went sour. What can I say?"

Buddha nods, he stands up and leads Jack into a room off the kitchen that, sure enough, has a few meditation pillows set up around a low table and incense burning in a burner on the wall.

"Come on," he says, walking in ahead of Jack and sitting down on one of the small pillows. "Let's sit zazen for a little."

24

When they've both been on the cushions for a couple of minutes, Buddha starts to laugh. "What the fuck, Jack. Welcome over here. It's good to see you." He jumps off his cushion and slaps Jack on the knee. "We were pretty worried about you for a little while." Then he tackles Jack off of his cushion, knocking him back onto the floor. Jack laughs, pushes the smaller man off him like he was doing a bench press. Buddha rolls over and sits up.

"You're lucky you guys got these soft pads down, little man."

Buddha laughs, climbs back onto one of the pillows, and tucks his feet into the lotus position. "So let's talk Jack. You're back now, out from your self-imposed exile at your house in Sausalito."

"I'm out, man. I'm riding this crazy thing that Ralph got me started on, trying to make sure I'm safe when it's all over, that I don't end up dead. And you know what? This is better than living in the hills by myself. This kind of feels like acting again. It's a rush."

Buddha holds up one finger like he's a less-wrinkled Yoda. "But you don't want to get hooked on that rush, Jack. This time you have to remember: be careful. It'll get you hurt. This is real shit here."

"No, man," Jack says. "It's not like that. I'm still clean off drugs *and* alcohol, and it's just— I don't know, it just feels like this takes me back to living again, like I'm acting, having fun that I haven't had in a while."

"I hear you." Buddha slaps Jack's knee. "That's why we were getting worried about you up there. No news is bad news, you know?"

Jack nods. "But now I need you. I need to find out what happened to Ralph: who shot him, who he was dealing with."

Buddha closes his eyes, furrows his brow. He brings his hands together over his chest in a prayer position. "You'll figure it out and do what you have to. I can see that in your future. But you must beware of…" He opens his eyes. "What do I know. I'm just a little bald guy who has a bunch of pillows." He folds his hands on his stomach and laughs.

"You're fucked, little man," Jack says. "I got a message from Ralph, from before he got killed, saying that if I got confused I should come to you. So I'm here. Unconfuse me."

Buddha nods. "So you are. And I should tell you about Ralph: that he was into coke for a while, and then started dealing. He'd go around to a couple of clubs where he had deals with the owners. He basically sold for them, would try to find high rollers who wanted a supply of good product. He'd occasionally find some guys who wanted to make a big score. That's where these boys come in. They showed up as Ralph's dream clients. He thought this would be the last deal he'd ever need."

"You got that right," Jack says. "That's exactly what he told me."

"Problem is, sometimes Ralph got ahead of himself. And being Ralph, he got to pissing people off. He'd get pushed out of one club, thrown out of another. My guess is somewhere along the way, he pissed off too many people."

"So who was his supply?"

"Some guy," Buddha says. "I don't know much about him. He lives up in North Beach or Pacific Heights. Some kind of name like a body of water. Something like Marsh. Julius or Junius."

"Yeah," Jack says. "That's the name the Czechs used. Who Ralph told them: Junius."

"OK, yeah." Buddha starts nodding. "Last name is Lake or something like that." He snaps his fingers. "That's this guy's name: Ponds. Fucking Junius Ponds."

"Junius Ponds."

"Yeah. That's it. He was Ralph's guy. Bald, pretty serious. I only met him once, but he's hard-core. Junius Ponds."

"If I need to get a deal done for Ralph, he's the guy?"

"He's *definitely* the guy. Wouldn't want you to go anywhere else."

"Is he Russian?"

"Shit." Buddha shakes his head. "Big black guy. Earring in both ears, likes to wear nice suits. That kind of tough."

"Junius Ponds," Jack says, nodding, starting to wonder what Ralph was thinking when he went to Castroneves. "Would this guy kill Ralph?"

"That I have no idea. I mean, we both know Ralph was mostly an asshole, but who'd want to kill him? That one I can't answer."

Jack gets himself onto one of the pillows, doesn't bother trying to tuck in his feet. "You know a Colombian named Alex Castroneves?"

Buddha shakes his head. "Nope. Who's that?"

"How about Tony Vitelli?"

"No. Not personally. I've read about his clubs in the papers, but never met the man. From what I've heard, though, he's getting to be big-time in this town, starting to run some serious shit south of Market."

"He's the owner of The Coast, this place Ralph got pushed out of, from what I can gather."

Yuko pokes her head into the room through a door off the hallway. "John, you know we have our yoga class soon."

"I know, babe. We'll get there. Just visiting with an old friend from the movie days."

Yuko comes all the way into the room. "Was John good in those days? Or did he run around like crazy?"

Jack has to laugh: Buddha got his name for his big belly and the fact that he always seemed calm, even in a room filled with strippers and people partying all around him, with all the drugs they could get their hands on. He never got too bent though, no matter what kind of partying he did.

Jack shakes his head. "Not this guy. He was a strong, upstanding citizen."

Yuko laughs. "In L.A.? I know what that means." She looks at Buddha and tilts her head. "But I still love him. He was a good producer and made some good pictures. Now that's over." She pats the top of his head. "Fifteen minutes, OK?"

Buddha nods. He takes her hand from his head and kisses it. "We'll be done in a bit, hon."

She leaves the two of them alone.

"She's all right," Buddha says. "Marriage has been good to me."

"Mine was one of the worst things I've ever done."

"Victoria was difficult, to say the least. She'd been through it when you met her, and she had a ways to go to get out. She took you through some hard times."

"What about now?" Jack asks. "How's she doing in L.A.?"

"Like I said Jack, Fuck L.A. I haven't heard anything from down there." Then he smiles. "Time to move on, Jack. You'll do better the next time."

"Next time?" Jack works his way up to standing. From a cushion on the floor, it's not that easy.

"Here's the thing about Ralph: we both know he was going to get himself into the shit. I don't know how he got things fucked up so far he got popped, but he did. Now you should be careful. We've only got a few of the old crew around, and I don't want to lose any others. OK?" Buddha reaches out his hand, and Jack takes it.

"I'll be all right." Jack points at Buddha's chest. "We'll see each other again. Just answer one more question: if Ralph went to another dealer, say this guy Castroneves, a Colombian, would that get Junius pissed off enough to kill him?"

Buddha frowns. "A Colombian?" he says in a thick accent. "I fucking hate Colombians, man." He gives Jack a hard, tough look, holds it. "Who do I trust? Who do I trust? Me that's who!"

Jack looks around and sees Yuko's still gone. "What's that?"

"That's Tony Montana, Jack. *Scarface*."

Jack shrugs. "OK."

Buddha slaps him on the thigh. "Sorry. Movie moment. Would Junius want to pop Ralphie. That I don't know."

"What do you think?"

He turns his hands up, places one on each knee. "That *sounds* like something that could happen, but who's to say, really. Junius would be a better one to tell you. Why don't you go ask him?"

"Just ask him?"

"You're ready to meet the man. Somebody has to find out what happened to Ralph."

Buddha fakes a punch at Jack's groin, laughs when Jack flinches back.

Jack laughs. Sometimes you have to give it up for the little man. "So where can I find Ponds?"

Buddha frowns like he's thinking it over. "Well, I can tell you where I've seen him, which is in Japantown. Ralph said he spends a lot of time in SOMA, but he has a place in Japantown where he eats—it's the *only* place he eats. My guess is that you go around dinnertime any night, he's probably having dinner. You'll find the place right across from the Peace Tower. Big round window on the front. Can't miss it."

"Thanks. I owe you."

Buddha holds up his hand, shakes his head. "If you see Junius, you'll think he's big. But he's not that bad. He isn't half the size of his bodyguard: a big guy named Freeman. Guy has a chest like the hood of a car." Buddha holds both hands out to his sides. "He used to play for the Jets. Now *he's* big. But they'll talk to you."

"Freeman *Jones*?" Jack says. "Jets lineman? Pro-bowl?"

"That's the one. Give him my best."

25

Jack tries Maxine's cell *and* her house phone on the way to The Coast, but can't get her on either one. He leaves a new message on her cell, apologizing, but doesn't add a second at her apartment.

He's sure letting the Czechs talk him into a repeat visit to The Coast isn't right, that he should probably stay away for a while, but they're probably already there. Part of him wants to see them try and take the place down piece by piece, see Tony Vitelli made to eat it.

And besides, it'll be nice to see his old friends in the tight black shirts again, this time with some friends of his own watching his back. But he knows it's the wrong move. Still, whatever it'd take to stop it, Jack's not making those moves.

When he pulls up outside, he sees the Czechs' sedan, a Mercedes, and Vlade standing next to it with his arms folded. Jack pulls up in the spot next to theirs in the parking lot, lets the car idle.

"What's happening?"

"They do not let us inside. They say the club closed to us now."

"What?" Jack puts the car in park, shuts it down, and gets out. When his sneakers hit the ground, he feels good standing, like it's the first time in a while that he's been on solid ground; he's ready to go in there and break heads. Niki gets out of the Mercedes, followed by Al and David. Jack can see the bulge in Niki's jacket that covers his gun. Al already has his in his hand. This is ready to get serious, fast.

"OK," Jack says. "Hold up for a second. You trying to shoot his place up or are we going in talking?" For a second he hears his own version of Sgt. Hopkins' voice in his head, saying, "These are my mob guys, Jack. The warlords I was telling you about."

Al waves his hand in front of him. "Fuck yes," he says. "We get to them and then we go after the guys who shot Michal?"

Jack shakes his head. "Whoa," he says. "Wait with the guns and we'll talk this thing through first. Let's see if these are even the guys who did it."

Vlade puts his hand on Al's shoulder. "Al," he says. "Put the gun away."

"But," Al says.

Vlade shakes his head. Al puts the gun into his jacket and turns toward the door. "It does not matter, Jack Palms. They did this to you?" He looks Jack up and down, lingers on Jack's face. "They did this, they need to pay."

"OK. But we need to see who we're dealing with first. There are different guys who work here."

Jack walks around the corner of the building, away from the parking lot and toward the front door, where the bouncers hang out. Two big guys have been here checking IDs the two other times Jack's come. Now it's no different. One of the guys is the one who recognized Jack the first time they all came, when they got into the V.I.P. room that impressed the Czechs so much—the one where Maxine used to work. He has another tight black shirt on, the tight short afro. Now the bouncer looks at Jack and stands up. The other guy, the one with the clipboard, puts it aside and stands, folding his arms. This guy has a wide mustache that touches both cheeks, the mark of a definite asshole. A third guy, smaller than the other two, maybe the talker of the group, runs back into the club.

"Can we help you?" asks the one who first recognized Jack, the Afro. These guys don't wear nametags, just tight-fitting black shirts and jeans. Both of them spend a lot of time in the gym, it's clear, probably more than Jack.

Jack walks up to where the two bouncers stand, close enough that he has their full attention. "We're here to see your boss."

They shake their heads, almost in unison. Now it's Mustache's turn to talk: "You and your friends ain't allowed inside The Coast no more." He turns to the side and spits on the ground. "Anyway, he's not even here."

Jack touches the bandage on his face, the new one that Maxine put on this morning. Maybe it isn't worth it, he thinks. Maybe Junius is the man to go see. "What about Junius," he says. "You seen him?"

"Junius?" The bouncers look confused. "Shit man, he ain't here. Motherfucker don't come around here no more."

"Fuck *Junius*," Mustache says.

Jack takes a step back. What he wants to do is rush both of them, knock them down and walk in over their bodies, find Tony Vitelli. With a glance at the Czechs, he sees that they want the same; Niki and the others look ready, waiting for something to happen so they can make a move. But Vlade stands in front of Al, holding him back.

Jack rocks back on his heels, thinking for a second. Here is where the indecision creeps in and he doesn't know what to do, what separates him as an actor from the others around him, the ones who will act. When it comes down to it, looking at the bouncers and rushing them seems like a leap across a bridge that he's not willing to take. Sure, he got violent with the Colombian's guy, Juan José, and where did that get him? He's not even sure where it came from. Uncertainty grips Jack, gets him second-guessing whether coming to The Coast was the right move. He folds his arms.

Now the little guy comes back out and he's got another bouncer with him: the white guy from Jack's last visit and untimely departure, one of the guys who Jack remembers looking up at from the floor. This guy touches the side of his face where Jack has the bandage. "What happened to your face, bro?" he asks, all surfer accent, raising his chin at Jack.

"I will fucking kill you!" Al shouts from behind Vlade. He starts to point at the Surfer, who jumps toward him. At the same time as Vlade holds back Al, the other bouncers hold back the Surfer. Vlade turns Al around, starts walking him back the other way.

Now Jack really doesn't like where this is all going, but he likes the numbers a whole lot better than the last time he was here. But with Al on the loose, Vlade holding him back, and David an unknown, he doesn't like the prospect of the immediate violence. Also, if Tony Vitelli's not even here, what's the point? He raises his hands. "We don't want any trouble here, guys. We're just looking for Tony, is all. Just want to ask him a few questions about our friend."

Now the little guy, the Talker, comes forward. "Mr. Vitelli doesn't want to see you today."

"Oh?" Jack says.

"No. He told me that *you* were not allowed in *here* any more."

Afro steps forward; unfolding his arms, he reaches out to Jack. "I did like your movie, though, man. You have to understand though. This is business here."

"But we're still not allowed inside The Coast?"

"Huh unh." He shakes his head. "You don't come in no more. And Tony don't come in Saturdays because he be at the other club."

David and Niki are looking at Jack like they don't know where this is going, why he's talking so much. But now that Jack knows Tony's not here, he wants to leave; there's nothing else in it for them. Vlade tilts his head toward the cars. "Maybe we go," he says.

Jack steps forward toward the bouncers. Maybe he can buy the Czechs and himself some insurance for the next time. "Guys," he says. "Part of why I came down here today is that I just finished talking with Joe Buddha. You guys know him?"

Afro nods; the other bouncers look uncertain, and then nod just slightly.

"He's the Hollywood producer who made *Shake 'Em Down*. We were talking about a new movie, a sequel, and he's pitching me a script." Jack shrugs. "I think I like it, and Joe's excited about the project. But he wants to make it up here in San Francisco. He's just asking me if I know any local talent with muscle." Jack shrugs again. "But I told them I don't know." He turns to look at the Czechs as if sizing them up for the parts. Then he turns back to the club.

"You guys don't do any acting, do you? I'm only asking you because this is what I was going to ask Tony."

"You don't have to talk with Tony about putting us in no movie. He don't own us."

"That's right. I guess he doesn't." Jack strokes his chin. "But if you guys are interested— Would you be interested in that?"

The three nod agreeably. They try to look cool, still insouciant, but part of them wants to be on the screen so bad they lose their normal role of instigator, leader, and man-in-charge—they have to nod. Part of them believes they're *that good*. They've spent so much time looking at themselves in the mirror that they believe it's a sight everyone should appreciate.

"That'd be cool," the Surfer says.

Jack nods. "That's good. I'll let Joe Buddha know I've got some possibilities. But you may have to take some time off from work here, so I just want to ask Tony. You know how that goes, right?"

Again they nod. "He be here. Later then." Afro shrugs. "Just come back. He be here to talk with you."

"Don't tell me you guys believe this shit," the Talker says.

The bouncers look at him like he just appeared. "Man, shut up."

But he keeps talking. "Joe Buddha? Who the fuck has a name like Joe Buddha? This motherfucker is totally lying to you guys. You think he's going to put you in a movie?"

"Check *Shake 'Em Down*," Jack says. "John Taraval's the producer. People call him Joe Buddha. That's his name."

"We look," Afro says. "And you better not be fucking lying, either."

Jack looks at the Czechs, then back to the bouncers. "You believe these guys? I just ask them one thing about the movie, they think I'm lying." He shrugs. "I just want to know, do you want to act or not?"

Again they all nod. "Yeah, we do. We do."

"OK," Jack says. "That's good. I'll tell Joe Buddha we may have found some of our muscle."

On the way back to the car, Niki walks close to Jack and tells him softly that he'd like to be in a movie too. "Whoa!" Jack stops walking. "You talk?"

Niki nods. Jack looks around at the others. They all look surprised, too, but more at him than at Niki.

David says, "Of course he talks. Niki's just quiet."

"OK, OK," Jack says. He claps Niki on the back, assures him that he can be in the picture.

26

The Czechs want to know their next move, but Jack's not sure. He wants to find Junius and talk with him, doesn't want a posse of Czechs to go when he does. The backup could be good, but it could also not be. He tells them to follow him back uptown, toward their hotel. So he's driving slow, letting them hang behind in their rented Mercedes as he makes his way uptown, knowing he doesn't have much time to figure out what to tell them before they get back to Market.

When he gets to Market, Jack takes a left, doesn't look back at the Czechs to see if they know this leads away from the hotel. He's heading across downtown now, on a diagonal through the city, away from the water.

He tries Maxine again, doubtful that she'll know anything about where to find Junius, but running out of ideas. She's still not answering her phone though, or at least not his calls.

So Jack calls Castroneves.

He picks up on the third ring. "Hola?"

"Yeah. This is Jack. I'm glad to hear you're all right."

"What the fuck, 'This is Jack!' The fuck was that last night?"

"That's the question, my man." Jack slows down at a light and watches the pedestrians cross Market. In his rear view, he looks back to make sure the Czechs are still there, still relaxed in their car, which they are. "We got to talk about this and my guys still want to make the trade. You up for that?"

"Oh, no, Mr. Palms friend. Fuck you. What the fuck *was* that? Now my Juan José is no more, the club get shot up and we almost get arrested! What the fuck is that, my man?"

"Do you still have your product?" Castroneves is quiet on the other end of the line. "Do you?"

"Yes. We have. And we are very lucky to get out with that."

"Then let's do this right now. We got the money and we'll meet, before any other shit." Jack looks back at the Czechs again to see whether they're looking doubtful. Al's sitting in the front seat, smoking a cigarette and looking away from the others. Niki is driving, both hands on the top of the wheel. "Right now at the wharf," Jack says.

Castroneves sounds like he's walking somewhere and talking to someone else at the other end. He comes back on. "We do that. Give us two hours. Then we meet at Pier 39. You bring one of your friends only, not all. And their money. We trade only. No party."

"OK," Jack says. "Alex, my man. You're my man."

Jack puts the phone away and turns off of Market, onto Van Ness, pulls over to tell the Czechs what's next.

"You guys have the money?" Jack asks, leaning in the passenger-side window of the Mercedes. Both cars are pulled over and Jack stands on the sidewalk, his Mustang still running. The Czechs are speaking to each other in another language, and David starts actually yelling at the others. This is the first time Jack's seen him get mad, the first he's seen David get anything other than drunk or high. Jack steps back from the car and goes back to the Mustang to get his cigarettes. As he leans in the window, he turns off the ignition, figuring they'll be here for a little while.

By the time the Czechs stop arguing, Jack's half-through a smoke, getting that nausea in his stomach that he likes for how it slows down his world. Sure, it makes him want to sit down and breathe slowly, but that's usually a good relaxer. It all goes away soon.

Vlade gets out of the car and walks over to Jack. "We do not know about going through with this idea of having the trade still with the Colombian. Some of us yes, some of us no." He opens his arms, shows Jack his palms.

"I hear you, man." Jack drops his cigarette, scuffs it out with the toe of his sneaker. In the car, David looks straight ahead, chewing on the inside of his lips. In the back seat, Al punches the side of the car. He looks beside himself. "Seems like that last meet was enough to fuck up anything," Jack says. "I were you, I'd be halfway to Vegas by now, maybe. But—" Jack waits to see if Vlade is with him, acts like he's thinking it all over.

Vlade stops watching the cars drive by to look at Jack. "Yes?" he says.

"But what the fuck?" Jack shrugs. "You know these guys weren't the ones who did the shooting. They were the ones who got shot. That seems safe to say. Plus, they don't have time to set anything up. We go meet them right now, get this thing done, and then whatever happens, you guys'll have your blow to take on the trip when you leave. How's that sound?"

Vlade nods, thinks it over. Al slides across the back seat to put his head out the window closest to Jack. He yells, "We should do this. Jack is right."

Vlade acts as if he's heard nothing, nods again. In the car, David still stares straight forward, stays quiet. Vlade says, "That might not be bad, though."

Jack goes for broke, puts it all out on the table: "Then we get to the bottom of this mess about Ralph and Michal, deal with Tony and Junius, get this whole thing figured out and wrapped up, and you guys are off for fun in the sun, my man." He claps Vlade's shoulder to wrap it up.

"Whoa, whoa, Mr. Palms," Vlade says, his hands up. "Now you go too fast. But it is good, I think." He smiles. "You feel good, no? That's good. Let me talk with others for one minute."

As Vlade goes back over to the car, Jack checks his watch for the time. It's true: he does feel good, better than he has in a while, though the fact that Maxine still won't answer his calls has him concerned. But damn, the sun's shining, there's less fog and, standing outside in the sun, Jack even feels warm enough to take off his jacket. He leans down to put it into the back seat of the Mustang. Just as he's bending over to do this, he sees a car coming up Van Ness going way too fast and then realizes there's a man in the passenger's seat hanging half-way out the window with a gun. Then next thing Jack hears is gunshots as he drops into a crouch beside the passenger door of his car. "What the fuck?" he hears himself say, and looks over at the Czechs. They're down inside of their car and Vlade's crouched on the sidewalk. The guy in the car fires more shots, and Jack can hear bullets hitting the side of the Czechs' Mercedes and breaking glass in the car. At that, his heart freezes up at the anticipation of what might come next; he starts to repeat the word, "No," under his breath as the world slows down and then— *chunk, chunk, chunk*—he hears bullets punch against the other side of his Mustang, ripping through its pristine, mint-condition body panels and—though he hopes not—doing untold damage to its interior. "Fuck!" Jack yells, over the shots.

Al scrambles out the sidewalk side of the Mercedes, a large handgun drawn in front of him, and pushes Vlade out of the way as he moves to the hood of the car, leans over it, and starts to fire. He lets off two shots and then Jack's up and running. Trying to stay low, he makes it to the Mercedes in three strides and knocks Al back behind the car. The sidewalk behind them is empty of people and fronted by a brick wall, but across the street Jack has no ideas if there're people behind where Al is shooting or who's in what buildings he might hit. With Al under him and Vlade beside them, wide-eyed, Jack asks if anyone's been hit.

Vlade shakes his head.

Jack stands in time to see the car that shot at them pulling away, up Van Ness, and turning around to come back. "Motherfucker," he says, then yells at Al and the Czechs to stay down. Vlade slaps Al across the face. He takes his gun away and holds him down behind the car. As the other car starts to come back toward them, Jack can see now it's a Ford, and the guy from The Mirage, Mr. Automatic Weapon with the bad flattop and the fancy lawyer, now wearing a bandage over the center of his face, and a stabilizer for his nose, pushes his head and arms up over the roof, holding the same silver handgun that he shot at them on the last pass.

"You motherfuck," Jack says, wishing for probably the first time in his life that he had a gun in his hand to shoot at someone.

He can't tell if Flattop sees him or not, but can only watch as the guy lets off a few more shots toward the Mustang, has to hear them punch through the fine metal—hoping and praying that nothing hits the engine—and then Jack hears the pop as one hits the Mustang's back tire and he gets down low behind the Mercedes. He can already hear the air hissing out of his tire.

Again Jack hears the bastard shoot at the Mercedes, but only twice, probably his last two bullets. If he were better at this, he would've counted the shots, it occurs to Jack. Niki fires two shots out of the Mercedes' window at the Ford, though Jack can't see if he hits anything from where he is on the sidewalk, on his hands and knees.

Now Vlade jumps up and shoots twice at the Ford. As Jack stands, he's just in time to see its rear window shatter. He runs over to the Mustang and around to its other side. There he sees the damage: three holes in the door and two along the side of the trunk. They're small silver welts, just like you'd expect them to be, with little holes that Jack can just get the tip of his finger into. "Fuck," he yells, kicking at the asphalt. He can already see the rear tire going down.

"Jack," Vlade yells, waving at him to come.

Jack runs his hand over the smooth metal curve of the Mustang's roof and leans in the window to grab his keys. Then he takes a step back to look at his car again, the anger welling up inside him like he hasn't felt it since he was still with Victoria. He shakes his head as Vlade calls his name again. Niki's pulling the Mercedes away from the curb, turning to go after the Ford, with Vlade climbing into the back seat and David already out on the sidewalk. Al starts toward the car, but Vlade yells at him to stay. For a second, Jack's caught in the street, watching Niki and Vlade in the Mercedes, and seeing it turn to go after the Ford. But then Niki pulls up to where Jack stands and pushes the front door open at him. Jack meets his eyes across the seat for a heartbeat, then gets in as Niki nods, says something to Vlade in Czech.

"What are we doing?" Jack says, looking at David and Al standing on the sidewalk, Al waving his hand, yelling for them to go. "What are we doing?"

Vlade says something to Niki in Czech, and Niki honks the horn, starts waving his arm out the window for the traffic beside them to stop. To Jack he just says, "We go."

"Watch my car," Jack yells to Al and David, throwing them his keys, as Niki peels out into a hard U-turn across the four lanes of traffic, cars braking wildly to get out of their way, horns blaring as they accelerate going downtown toward Market and after the Ford.

27

On Market, Niki slows down in the traffic when he sees the Ford obeying traffic laws, driving normally about seven cars up. They stop at a red light and Jack says, "Shit, I can get out and run those bastards down."

"No," Niki says. "I drive." He pulls out into the Muni lane just ahead of a bus that blows its horn at them. Then he drives the Mercedes up alongside the traffic and smashes into the side of the Ford. Jack can see Flattop from The Mirage inside and another guy driving, someone new with big bushy eyebrows and a head shaved bald. What is it with these guys and baldies, Jack wonders. People along the sidewalks start yelling and pointing, stopping to watch. Other cars start honking at the Ford as it swerves through traffic. The Flattop aims a gun at them and Niki pushes the Ford over to the other side of the road, riding it hard, metal scraping, but then the driver sees an opening and floors it to get through some cars and turns onto 10th Street.

Now, with the Mercedes behind him, Flattop turns around in his seat, aims at them through where the back window once was and shoots through their windshield just as Jack ducks down in his seat. Niki has slid way down so that he can barely see over the steering wheel, and Jack feels an impact on his side of the car as they crunch through two cars—one parked—to follow the Ford onto 10th. Now Vlade takes a shot from the back seat. The sound of the shot rings through the car like a bomb going off and Jack's world goes quiet.

They hit the back of the Ford, and Niki takes a shot over the dashboard blindly, then hands his gun to Jack and puts both his hands on the wheel. Jack looks at Niki: still driving, he gestures with his chin ahead of them and at the gun, and Jack gets the message that he's supposed to do some shooting. He hears a ringing in his ears that's unlike anything he can remember. Everything moves in slow motion around him with the ringing setting the world in relief.

Jack looks out over the dashboard and sees the Flattop and the back of the driver's bald head in the Ford. They're swerving all over the street and so is the Mercedes. He raises his gun even as he can't believe that he's doing it. Part of him is thinking that this is absolutely *not* a movie and that in real life people have to pay huge consequences for taking actions like these, for shooting a gun on city streets, possibly even shooting someone. He can see that 10th Street. is wide open ahead of them: no one on the sidewalks, a green light up ahead. Then he remembers that these guys shot up his Mustang, and he's filled with rage in places he didn't even know were empty. Just as he's about to shoot, Vlade lets off another shot from the back seat, right next to Jack's head, and the sound breaks through Jack's silence, leaving an even louder, deafening ringing. Jack's ears hurt so bad that he drops down below the dash, puts his hands up over his ears. The cat-toy bell feeling starts in his head again. He sees Vlade's arm and gun above him, realizes that Vlade's leaning forward and trying to shoot through the windshield himself.

"Get out of here," Jack tries to say, but it sounds like he's underwater, trying to yell in the pool like he did when he was a kid. He gets himself up and looks out through where the windshield should be in time to see the Ford turn onto Mission. Now the wind in his face takes away some of the ringing; the underwater feeling is gone. He pushes himself further up, holding the gun, and at the same time feels Niki push the Mercedes faster. They hit the curb going around the turn, and Jack braces himself against the door. He tries raising the gun again to shoot but can't get into a steady enough position to aim. Then the Flattop rises up in the front of the Ford, shooting at them, and Jack ducks down.

Vlade lets off another two shots, and the Ford spins out, hits an oncoming car, and Jack just has time to brace his knees against the

dash before they hit the Ford broadside and send it skidding back
into another oncoming car swerving to avoid it.

Jack feels the crashes echo through his body, his knees wracked
against the dash with each one, and as the Mercedes turns, he's
thrown against the door, glad to know that Mercedes makes a
strong interior passenger cage. Finally both cars come to a stop with
the hood of the Mercedes crushed and the two cars smashed side
by side. Steam or smoke rises out of both engines. Jack's knees hurt
bad but he looks at them and doesn't see any blood, realizes he can
still move his toes. To his left he sees Niki smiling and removing his
seat belt—he was probably the only one wearing one—and then
Niki kicks open his door to get out of the car. Behind him the rear
door opens, and Vlade steps out and stumbles around the car leaning on it as he moves to the hood. Jack looks out over his door and
only sees the Ford, its steering wheel but not the driver. It is locked
in place, sandwiched between their Mercedes and the two small
Japanese imports that it ran into. Then Jack sits up a little more and
he sees the Ford's driver slumped against the wheel of his car,
blood running down his forehead. The back of his head is a mess
where Vlade's bullet went in.

"Jesus," Jack says, looking at all the blood, the hole in the back
of the man's skull, thinking that that had to be one damn lucky
shot. He sees Niki jump up onto the hood of the Ford and go over
to pull the Flattop, already half-hanging out of his door, all the way
out of the car and onto the hood.

In the distance, Jack hears the ringing in his head, and then it
comes back in full and it's all he can bear. He closes his eyes.

When he looks again, Niki has the Flattop up off the hood and
backhands him hard across the face once, then twice, followed by a
stiff cross to the nose. Jack sees a stream of blood slap across the
car's fractured windshield. Vlade says something to Jack, reaching
across the driver's seat, jostling his shoulder. At least in some re-
spects his hearing is still there, he can hear rough sounds, but not
words—more of the underwater effect. Then Vlade waves his hand
at Jack to get out of the car, and he crawls out across the driver's
seat, onto the asphalt on his hands and knees. Realizing there's glass
all around him, he tries to stand and, by putting his hands against

the car, is able to brace himself and get up. Vlade picks up Niki's gun off the floor of the car and hands it back to him as Niki comes around to where they are. There's not much left of the Flattop: Jack can see where his head broke the Ford's windshield as it crashed, and there's a lot of blood pooling around him on the hood.

Vlade grabs Jack by the shirt-front and starts to pull him away from the cars, toward the sidewalk. Jack wonders if they should head north, thinking that if they can get onto BART or the Muni, that maybe they can disappear into the crowds and get far away from this whole scene, but Vlade pulls him toward an adult video and porn shop on the other side of Mission. Niki follows. On the sidewalk, the few witnesses look at them awestruck, their mouths open. Jack's sure he looks like hell, maybe worse. The drivers of the other cars that hit the Ford seem to be calling something out to them, their cell phones to their ears, no doubt calling the police, but Vlade doesn't stop. He leads them into an auto detailing and repair shop next to the porn store, where some Asian guys in blue jumpsuits look on, horrified. Then Vlade says something they can understand in a language that Jack can tell isn't English. He makes wide arm motions and talks at them fast. Even though Jack's still underwater, the sounds are shorter and faster than how he thinks English would sound.

The guys in jumpsuits take Jack and the Czechs to the back of the repair shop, and there Vlade pays off a guy at a desk by peeling off fifteen crisp hundred dollar bills and dropping them in front of him. The guy's face gets brighter and brighter with each one. Finally, he nods and another guy in an oil-stained jumpsuit shows them a back exit and leads Jack and Niki out to a dirty white van. He opens its sliding side door and motions for Jack and Niki to get inside. Then he goes around to the driver's side and lets himself in. They're in an alley parallel to Mission, removed from any other cars. With what works of Jack's hearing, he can make out police sirens calling from not far off.

Another guy in a jumpsuit comes out the back door of the shop with Vlade, shows him to the back door of the van, and closes it behind him when they're all inside. This guy gets into the passenger seat, and then the driver starts the engine and pulls away.

Jack can't see out the back of the van because it has no windows and, from where he's sitting on the floor, all he can see out the front windshield is some tall buildings and blue skies. He sees a few street lights pass over him, but can't tell where they're going.

Gradually, the sound of the van comes through his ears and he starts to hear the rudimentary elements of life: the rumble of the van, the sound of wind blowing in through the windows, the sound of people talking—Vlade on his cell phone and the two guys in the front seats arguing—and the occasional car that has a huge bass system banging outside on the streets. Somehow the thumping of these sounds gets through.

28

The van drops them off at another Asian auto repair shop, this one somewhere in the Tenderloin. The two guys let them out without saying anything else.

Vlade walks up to the front window, says something to the passenger and hands him a few bills. The guy reaches behind him and pulls the side door shut as the van drives off. Jack can see the Mustang right away, a new tire on the back wheel, and hopes that Al and David didn't drive her here on the flat, knowing that they probably drove her here on the flat.

He walks over to his car, looking at the bullet holes, and counts them again, three in the door and two on the side of the trunk. He runs his hand across the door, feeling the welts, rests his head on the top. "Fuck," he whispers. He gets down low and crouches to see the holes, looks at each one to see if it went through. In the back seat, it looks like a bullet went through the door, but he can't see any damage inside.

He opens the door, and slumps down into the driver's seat tired and somewhat defeated. The pristine body of a '66 Mustang Fastback does not come into one's life often. And now Jack's is gone. His hearing is still partly wrecked too, and now the Czechs and he are probably wanted by the police. Or they will be. He closes the door behind him to sit in the quiet of the car's interior by himself. Outside, the Czechs are talking, gesturing with their arms. After a few breaths, Jack takes the cell phone out of his jacket: no calls and they have less than an hour to get to where they're supposed to meet the Colombian. He figures he'll probably be hearing from Sgt. Hopkins about what just happened before the hour's up, if not sooner.

Vlade comes over to the car and taps on the passenger window, so Jack reaches over and unlocks the door. Vlade gets in, sits down and starts talking to Jack.

Jack looks at his face, trying to get a sense about what Vlade's saying.

"What? My hearing's fucking fucked." Jack points to his ears. "They shot up my car."

Vlade holds up his hand and rubs his thumb against his first two fingers: money. "You want to go back to the hotel and get the money for the meet?" Jack asks. Vlade nods. "Good," Jack says. "Something should come out of this." Vlade nods again. Then he reaches across the seat and takes Jack's face in both hands, pulling him forward. Normally, Jack wouldn't be comfortable with this, but right about now, with the world a quiet ringing place, a little human contact seems to narrow his spectrum in a good way. Vlade's face looks serious, but his eyes are calm, relaxed.

"Jack," he says. He may be shouting. By the look of his face, he probably is. But Jack can just barely hear him, make out what he's saying by reading his lips.

"You are OK?"

Jack nods.

"Good," Vlade says. "We need you." He lets Jack go.

Jack nods again. He gives Vlade the thumbs up.

Outside the car, the other Czechs are looking in at Jack. He gives *them* the thumbs up, and they seem to look relieved: their faces soften into smiles. Then Vlade takes out his wallet and shows Jack some kind of official-looking I.D. card. He points out the letters K.G.B. to Jack, then points to himself and Niki.

"You're K.G.B.?" Jack shakes his head, does his best to speak, but he realizes it's difficult when you can't really hear.

"No," Vlade shouts. He makes an X with his arms. "We are ex-KGB. No more."

"I don't know," Jack says, shaking his head. "Explain to me later."

Vlade nods. "OK, but let me tell you. These men, the ones we left back there, in their car. These are K.G.B. too. These are not happy because we leave. We left. Now they see us here and they do not like. There is also... there is also something that they are doing here."

He says something else to Niki out of the car, then shuts the door. Niki walks over to a new rental, a too-big white Escalade that Al probably picked out. Niki and David and Al get into it. It's nice looking, but large, a brand new American-made SUV.

Jack looks over at Vlade, and the Czech nods. "I'm riding with you," Jack thinks he says.

When Jack starts the Mustang engine, it breaks through his world of silence and ringing with the roar of its 289 cc V8. The sound washes over him in waves of relief because he can hear it and also because it still sounds like it should; he can tell right away it didn't catch any bullets. It's not the biggest engine around, but it makes enough noise for you to know it's alive. And alive is how he wants it. The body of the car he can fix, maybe, but the engine, that's a much more serious job. He closes his eyes, living in the sound that he can hear, revs up the engine louder and then still louder, enjoying the noise until Vlade taps him on the arm. He opens his eyes, then pulls out behind Niki and the Escalade, following them out onto Polk, heading downtown.

They make a quick stop at the Regis, long enough for the Czechs to go up and get a briefcase of money.

Jack washes his face a few times in the brass-sink bathroom off the lobby. He doesn't look good, but the water helps bring him back to his senses and, pushing his fingers into his ears, he starts to feel the hearing come back. It's been returning since the accident and as he started driving, but he's still a little cloudy. The downtime in the bathroom, his face in a sink full of water, definitely helped.

Next they head north toward the waterfront and the meeting with Alex Castroneves. In the car, Jack drives with the windows open so he can hear the air rushing past. It sounds like a vortex, but at least it *sounds*. Vlade motions for Jack to roll up the window, and Jack does. "I guess you must want to say something," Jack says.

When he gets the window up, Vlade says, "I want to say something." Jack nods. He's watching the road but steals a glance at Vlade and sees he's serious. "Niki and I used to be KGB, Jack. I want you should know. We can make that problem back there go away."

Jack shakes his head. "I don't know about in your country, man, but here shit like that doesn't just disappear. That was a big fucking mess back there. Fingerprints, witnesses—"

Vlade nods. "That is why I tell you." He opens his hands on his lap. "We are sorry. I am sorry. We did not want to get you involved in all of this, but now it is too late."

"Too late? Now we're driving around in a car with bullet holes in it, *my car*, the '66 Fastback K-code. Bullet holes. Fuck."

"Yes. We are sorry, I can tell you."

"Fuck. Fucking holes Vlade, five of them in my car."

Vlade puts his hand on Jack's knee and yells, "We will pay you for the damages, Jack. We will pay!"

"I can hear you," Jack says, shaking Vlade's hand off his knee. "You don't have to yell anymore."

Vlade turns to Jack, surprised. "Good. It is good you can hear again. You should be normal soon."

"It's OK," Jack says. "I'm just upset about the car."

"Then OK. But let me tell you what I was saying to you, Jack." Vlade waits a second, then continues. "Niki and I have been agents for the KGB. We know other agents come here and to work in drug industry. They do not like that we have left, moved to Czech. That man, the one who shoot at us in the car and at the club last, he was also K.G.B. A Russian. That is why this is serious. There will be others here too. His friends. These Russians."

Jack watches the road; he's doing his best to make out everything that Vlade's saying, put all of the pieces together. "What about Al and David?"

"These others, David? *Al?*" He waves his hand dismissively. "Pfft. This is all fun and games for them. They want to have good time and explore American country. But to *us* this is serious. This is about life and dealing."

"And what about Michal?"

"Yes," Vlade says. "He was ex-KGB too. That is why we are so upset when he got killed. Why we have to revenge him."

Jack's getting closer to the piers; he looks back in the rear view and sees that Niki and the others are right there behind him. "And now you did?"

"Yes. But there will be others."

"OK, but my guess is that that mess back there is going to come after us, even if it takes a little while. Our prints were all over that car." Jack takes his cell phone out of his jacket pocket. "You see this? When it starts ringing and it's a policeman on the other end, he's going to want some answers. And if he doesn't get them, he's going to bring our asses in."

Vlade shakes his head, pointing to the Bay and the bridge, and beyond that the roads that lead east. "It does not matter," he says. "We will be gone."

29

They park near the piers in one of the expensive pay lots for tourists. Normally Jack would want to spend some time looking for a parking lot that had an easy way out, but they're late enough, and he doesn't want to miss Castroneves. It's a Saturday afternoon and the piers are jammed full of tourists—more than crowded, they're packed almost wall-to-wall with people wanting to see the seals, go to the aquarium, take boats out around the Bay, to Angel Island and Alcatraz. Jack and the Czechs have to go all the way up to the top level to find open parking spaces. From here, they can look down on Pier 39, where they'll be having the meet. Jack leads the Czechs to the edge of the lot and then points down to where Alex will be. There are a lot of tourists walking around, watching the street performers and shopping. Almost everything below them is a restaurant or some kind of boat trip into the bay. And all of them are crowded. At the meet, Jack will be surrounded by the crowds, which is good: no one will have an open shot if anything goes wrong. Jack turns back toward the parking lot to face the Czechs. "He only wants one of you this time," Jack says, and then, knowing who it'll be, "Who's going to come?"

Vlade steps forward.

Jack nods. "The rest of you can watch us from up here. When you see us coming out from behind that building," he points to the Hard Rock Café, the first of the shops on the pier. "Bring this rental SUV piece of shit down there and get us. We don't need to be out there with this kind of product for too long."

Niki steps to the edge of the parking lot, acts like he's holding a rifle and sighting down onto the pier; he points into the crowd. There's no way he's going to get a clear shot: they'll be less than fifty feet away from the crowd, but with so many people all milling around, he'll never get a fix on one person. But maybe that's not Niki's goal. If shots are fired, most of the tourists will either panic or hit the deck, maybe both. He nods and gives Jack the thumbs up.

"Right," Jack says. "If something, anything, goes bad, get your asses down there in the car. Fast."

Vlade says something else to them in Czech that David and Al respond to. This leads the three of them into a heated discussion, Al pointing at David and Vlade and yelling, then David chiming in. Jack watches for a minute and then interrupts. "Guys. Guys." He taps on his watch. "Time to go."

They cut it short, and David gives the briefcase to Vlade.

"Listen," Jack says. "This is good. I told you tomorrow we'd have this stash for you and now we'll have it today, Saturday. We're way ahead of schedule. Great, right?"

The Czechs look less enthused than Jack would have hoped. Part of it is the fact that they got shot at out of nowhere, and that they're giving up their money to Jack and Vlade while they have to wait and cross their fingers, but really, it's not all that bad. Jack reminds them, "Soon you guys will be out on the open road, having good times and laughing about all of this. OK?"

They nod. "OK," David says.

Al looks like he just wants to shoot up the whole pier *and* Castroneves, like he won't be happy with anything less.

"Fuck." Jack nods to Vlade. "Let's go then."

From the foot of the parking lot stairs, it's a short walk across the street and over a small stand of damp, bumpy grass onto the Waterfront Park area, where the crowds begin: tourists walk around wide-eyed, and the Navy and Marines have set up stands for recruiting. The Saturday afternoon crowds are dense, watching all of the Wharf events happen around them. On a stage outside of the Hard Rock Café, a band of four female singers and an all-male backup band plays to whoever will listen—mostly tourists from out of town and families with matching sweatshirts that say "SF" on them somewhere, most of which get bought because people don't expect the weather to be cold here in sunny California and then need another layer. Some of the people have on T-shirts and shorts, some have jeans and sweatshirts. It all depends on whether you're in the sun or not. Jack's gotten used to the weather, but he still gets cold all the time. Now he's got his leather jacket on and checks his phone: still no call from Maxine.

"Task at hand," Jack whispers to himself, repeats it like a mantra. "Task at hand."

Vlade starts tapping his ring against the handle of the briefcase, and Jack's glad he can hear it—it's a small sound in all of the crowd noise and the music—though Vlade's tension puts him on edge. Now would be the perfect time for a cigarette, but Jack pats himself down. They're back in the car somewhere, not in his pockets. With this many people around them, it could be hard to smoke though; they have to weave through the crowd to get anywhere, go wide around the gathering at the front of the bandstand. Groups stand around talking, some browse at the restaurant windows looking at menus, others walk quickly to the escalator entrance for the San Francisco Aquarium. Further out Jack can see a huge NFL shop and more restaurants advertising as many kinds of seafood as you can imagine. Kids are running everywhere.

"So you were KGB?"

Vlade nods.

"What're you doing here then, partying it up and buying cocaine? How's that fit?"

The two walk closer together. A kid runs right at them and only realizes at the last moment that Jack and Vlade aren't going to part and let him through; he almost crashes into Jack's legs but manages to turn himself at the last second.

"David and Al are our friends," Vlade says. "Al is just a businessman but he thinks he is K.G.B."

"He's fucking crazy," Jack says.

Vlade laughs. "He is not all bad. A little hot-headed, yes. But good in business."

They pass a small ice cream stand similar to the one where Juan José bought Jack a cone the last time he was here. There's still no sign of Castroneves; Jack looks at his watch: they're ten or fifteen minutes later than he planned, just over the two-hour mark. He hopes Castroneves hasn't left, understands he'd be spooked given what happened at The Mirage and might disappear if anything didn't feel right. They walk around the line of people waiting to get ice cream.

"We were agents in Czech Republic," Vlade says. "Undercover. They set us up in business there to watch, report to K.G.B., and then, when the countries break up, we stay. We leave our duties and make business and now are friends. Now that we have money, we want the good times."

Jack looks over at Vlade. "Did you speak Chinese to those guys at the body shop?"

Vlade nods. "Yes. I speak some Chinese, some German, Russian, Czech of course. The English."

"That's good. No Spanish?" Vlade shakes his head. "Then those aren't going to help us now." Jack stops walking, looks around for Castroneves. "What was that back there downtown?" he asks Vlade. "You guys went apeshit."

"No," Vlade says. "We cause mess, yes. But it will go all right, as I tell you. That man in the car, he see us in club and start shooting. He shoot at us from his car. We know that he is Russian. How does he find us?" Vlade shrugs. "So we have to shoot back. When his papers come through, they see he is non-person, already dead in our country. Your police won't know what to do."

Jack starts to say something, but Vlade cuts him off. "We don't have time to guess, Jack. We know. We act."

"No," Jack says. "But now there's a block of downtown with cars and blood all over the place. How's that shit not going to come after us?"

"Yes," Vlade says, shaking his head. "This is not good." He spits on the ground. "Now we have to finish and move on. Our time is more important now."

"Damn right." Jack starts to take out his cell phone to make the point again about Sgt. Hopkins calling him at any time, but he sees

Castroneves up ahead in the crowd, toward the end of the pier. Jack points toward him with his chin and they start to move. "The guys in the Ford might not have been K.G.B. And I don't know if it's better or worse for us if they weren't. Shit." Jack shakes his head, trying to clear out the fog and what's left of the ringing. "Someone else could have sent them, too."

"No," Vlade says. "This I tell you: this is reason why."

Castroneves notices them and raises his right hand above his shoulder, gives a slight wave. He's with another guy, someone Jack doesn't recognize from The Mirage, probably his new Juan José. They both have nice suits on, Castroneves' a light blue. He starts to move across the pier to the far side, coming slightly toward Jack and Vlade, but moving away from them as well. Then he turns toward a row of shops and a small coffee shop set into the rest of the restaurants. Jack and Vlade start to head for the same shop. Castroneves stops at its glass window, sets down a large, white shopping bag on the ground.

Jack and Vlade have to move through the crowd to get there, and it takes them a little while. Mothers with strollers, a large woman wearing a wide-collar T-shirt that reveals too much pale skin, another woman who looks just like her and must be related. Inside the coffee shop, several boys stand around in a circle, watching one of them play a hand-held video game of some kind while they wait for their parents to stand in the line.

"We are glad to see you," Vlade says, looking at the shopping bag.

"Yes," Castroneves says, scanning the crowd behind them. "You came alone?"

Jack nods. "The product?"

"Right here." Castroneves looks at Vlade. "It is the amount we decided at the club. To be truthful, I was lucky to get it out before the police."

Jack laughs. "You can thank your boy for that, as it turns out."

Castroneves spits on the ground, wipes his mouth. He says something to his friend in Spanish. This new guy is wearing a dark suit and a silky black shirt, tucked in. He's got big silver cufflinks at the end of his sleeves, his hair slicked back. Castroneves points his chin at Jack, says, "What is this now?"

"Your friend. The owner of The Mirage. He's the one who called the police."

"Motherfucker." Castroneves spits again onto the ground. This time he doesn't wipe his face. He says something else in Spanish to his guy. The guy makes a fist and wraps his other hand around it. He regards Jack like he's ready to hurt someone. "How do you know this? This about Vitelli?" Castroneves asks.

"Vitelli?" Jack says. "How's *he* in this?"

"He is my friend who owns the club Mirage."

"*Fuck*," Jack says, feeling like a few of the pieces just slammed together. "So that bastard knew the whole time."

Castroneves looks disgusted. "How do you know this?"

"I have a friend on the force," Jack says. "I heard it from the inside this morning."

Castroneves tightens his lips into a pucker, then makes a noise from the back of his mouth. He looks like he might spit again, but doesn't. "How do I know you are telling me the truth? That *you* did not tell the cops?"

"Come on," Jack says. He gives Castroneves a few slaps on the shoulder. "Who's here now with you, with a trunk of money and a crazy fucking Czech K.G.B. assassin buying your blow?"

The Colombian nods. He laughs. "In truth," he says, "I know you are trustworthy, Jack. Even when you lie, you tell the truth."

Jack turns to Vlade. "That motherfuck from The Coast is the one who called the police last night."

"Yes," Vlade says, nods. "So it seems." He takes Castroneves' arm. "The other, the one at the club who killed our friends. He is no more." He cuts across the air in front of him with his hand, holding it parallel to the ground. "We have taken care of."

This makes Castroneves smile. "Yes?" He says. Vlade nods. "That is good. That is very good." He takes out a cigarette and lights it with a windproof butane lighter. "Today holds some good news, then, to go with the bad."

"So, gentlemen." Jack points to the bags. "What do we have here?"

Vlade places the briefcase down next to him. Inside the store, one of the boys' mothers starts yelling at them.

The Colombian and his friend start to move down the board-walk, toward other stores, but not before the friend bends to lift the briefcase. Vlade lifts the white shopping bag and he and Jack follow. Jack sees the bag is topped with light blue tissue paper that matches Castroneves' suit. "That's nice paper," he says.

Castroneves laughs. "My wife," he says. "She likes me in the colors. What can I do?"

He says something to his guy in Spanish that makes them both laugh.

"You like this?" he says, handing his lighter to Jack. It has a motorcycle on it and lights that flash when you open the top. "You need these here. With this wind." He gestures around him, and out to the water. "Keep it."

In the distance, Jack sees a vintage cigarette boat out on the water among the sailboats, a hundred yards beyond the piers. It's the kind that has cabins below the decks, room for sleeping and who knows what else. Jack points to the boats on the water. "Is one of those yours?"

Castroneves nods. "We are not here for long. You know?" He frowns. "Here it is cold. Soon we leave." He lifts the briefcase as if testing its weight. "Gentlemen," he says. "If it is all here, you will not hear from me again."

"And us," Jack says. "It's all here?"

Castroneves laughs. "Have a look." He gestures around them at all the people.

But Vlade moves the tissue papers and looks into the bag. He reaches in and feels around, then slips a knife into the bag and brings his finger out with white on its tip. He rubs the powder along his gums. Then he looks at Jack, smiling. "We are good," he says.

"Alex," Jack says, reaching out to shake the Colombian's hand. "If we're lucky, you and I won't ever see each other again."

30

At the top of the parking structure, in the SUV with the Czechs, Jack feels his cell phone vibrate. At first it gives him a start, but when he checks and sees it's Maxine, a wave of relief passes through him. He excuses himself to go outside, but before he can, Al gives him the thumbs up. He's rubbing the white powder onto his gums and smiling, grinning like a kid on Christmas morning.

"Hold on," Jack says. "I'll be right back."

Outside the Escalade, Jack walks over to the Mustang and flips open his phone. His eyes go right to the holes along the driver's side.

Maxine's talking before he can even say hello. "Jack. You're still an asshole, but I have something to tell you. Something you can shove into your theory hole."

Jack feels along the door of the car, touching the holes. He pulls his hand away. "It's good to hear your voice again," he says.

"Anyway."

"No. I mean it. I've been trying to call. You were right. I'm sorry."

"I got your message," Maxine says. "But shut the fuck up and let me be mad for a little while."

"OK," Jack says. "You're due." He switches the phone to his other ear, his left, but realizes that he still can't hear as well on that side, the side that was closer to Vlade's gun. He switches back. "What?"

"The other club. The Mirage. Tony's the fucking owner. I just went down to The Coast to get my last check and when I started talking to one of the girls, she told me he was there. I said, why? She said because he owns it. That one, and one other in SOMA. *He's* the one who called the cops."

"I know," Jack says. He looks away from the parking lot, sees the fog starting to roll in over the northern part of the city, across the Golden Gate.

"*You know?*"

"Yeah. The Colombian just told me. I guess he's friends with Tony, or *was*. He's pretty pissed off now."

"Yeah. Have a friend drop the cops on you and I'd be." Maxine laughs. "What's he plan to do?"

Jack looks out at the harbor, at the boats, and sees that the cigarette boat is already gone. "My guess is Tony will hear from him." Maxine laughs or coughs, Jack can't quite tell which. "So when will I see you?"

"You'll see me. Don't worry."

"No, but—"

"Bye, Jack." She hangs up.

Jack flips his phone closed hard, mad that he didn't apologize more or get her to come around. But she's melting; soon she'll be all right.

Jack looks at the Czechs' car, the SUV, and walks over slowly. Inside, the Czechs are enjoying themselves, snorting little bumps of the product.

"Jack, my man," Vlade says through the open window. "Come back to the hotel and we'll give you your cut."

Jack takes a step toward the SUV but doesn't go farther, even when Vlade swings the door open.

"You come back with us and we show you a good time in this city, Jack. Even better than before. And we also give you your money. Come!" The others are nodding to the car's music, oblivious to Jack.

"The party's right here," Jack says.

"Ah, but our clothes and your money are back at the hotel."

Jack's phone starts to vibrate. "Hold on," he says. On the screen he sees it's the call he's been dreading. Jack steps away from the SUV, opens the door of the Mustang, and sits down.

"Hello, Sgt. Hopkins," Jack says, pulling both legs into the car and closing the door.

"Jack, you know what I'm going to say first, don't you?"

Jack closes his eyes, kneads the bridge of his nose with his thumb and first finger. "What's that, Mills?"

"What the fuck, Jack? That's what I'm saying to you. It looks like you and your buddies started fucking World War fucking Three out there in SOMA today."

Jack starts to respond, but Sgt. Hopkins keeps talking. "Do you know that I'm calling you from my home today? My fucking home? I tell them to call me if anything looks like you, and I get *this* called to me, *explained* in full detail at my fucking house. I'm in my back yard right now, hearing about how your fucking pals just shot up downtown!"

Jack reaches for the glove compartment, hoping to find his cigarettes. "I can see you're pretty mad there, sergeant."

"You're fucking right mad. You try going home on a Saturday afternoon and see what kind of shit comes after you. You ever worked a Saturday morning in your life, Palms? Matter of fact, how about if you took off a few *years* instead, you and your friends, *in the cooler?*"

Jack finds the pack and flips a cigarette into his lips. "Shit, Mills. You know that guy was your shooter from The Mirage. Why not just consider it a case solved?"

"Because there's a four car crash on a downtown street and five witnesses saw shots fired and some guy beat this poor bastard's head against the hood of his car."

Knowing he can't argue with that, Jack lights the cigarette with Castroneves' lighter. He looks it over and then pitches it out the window into the garage. "So what are we talking about, Mills? What can we say here?"

"I don't know, Jack. Right now I'm listening, is what I'm doing. I send your ass out— No, I *let* you out there to tell me about some Europeans, and since last night I got bodies all over town. Three shot up at a club and two dead in broad daylight today downtown. Now tell me how I feel about that!"

Jack starts to fumble for an answer, but Hopkins goes on. "No, wait. Don't answer yet, because it gets better: I've got *you* at the scene of each one! But tell me that the guys you're with aren't the terrorists I been looking for."

"They're not."

Jack hears silence on the other end of the phone, and then a quiet clicking that's probably Hopkins chewing his gum. "You better tell me a good story, Jack."

"OK, sergeant. Here's what I think: I think the ones you turned up dead today are the mob you want. They came at us, tried to shoot at us from a moving car on Van fucking Ness, and then my boys went after them. And you're right, that was fucked up, but I still think you've got this on wrong. Someone had to tell them where we were, right? There's some crazy K.G.B. tie-in to all this shit."

"I'm listening."

It takes Jack about a full second to put together the fact that he and the Czechs were coming from The Coast when they got shot at and the name Tony Vitelli. "I think these were the guys who killed Ralph, but I don't think they're alone in it. I think someone sent them on that hit, someone who wants to take over the drug action in this town."

"I'm hearing you, Jack."

"My guess is I can lead you to more of these mob boys if you give me some time."

Sgt. Hopkins is quiet. Then, softly, he says, "Make me an offer."

"How about this: you give me a day, the rest of tonight and tomorrow, and I'll give you the major drug player in this town right now. I'm not talking about a couple of out-of-towners and a washed up actor, I'm talking about the guy who knocked off Ralph because he wanted his action and wants control of these streets. I think whoever that is, he'll bring us to your Europeans."

Sgt. Hopkins laughs. "Now, Jacky. Now you're starting to talk my language. You understand me. I'm talking about you save your ass by helping me out. One ass washes the other, right? Do you want to see yourself in court, maybe even going to jail? That'd play pretty nasty in the papers, don't you think?"

"Yes, Mills. Fuck you, Mills."

"But you get what I'm saying."

"I'll call you," Jack says, "When I have something." He flips the phone closed and takes a drag from his cigarette. It's burned half-way down in the time he's been talking to the cop. Maybe he's going back to smoking, but he'll worry about that when his life returns to regular. Right now, he's conning police officers to keep himself out of jail, making deals that involve putting his own ass out on the line by going after mobsters and drug dealers, and he's past the point of no return. For now, he leans back in the Mustang's large, comfortable American seating, reclines a little, and takes a long drag, looking out at the water.

The sun has started setting, and already the pier is darker than when he and Vlade met with Alex. Soon the street lights will come on above the tourists, enabling them to stay out on the pier for another few hours, until the wind makes it too cold. But for now, they're all right: maybe having another cotton candy or buying their kids an ice cream, waiting for later when they can have a beer back at the hotel, put the kids to bed and get in some love time and really enjoy their vacations.

Beyond the pier, out on the Bay, a ferry boat makes its way under the bridge, headed toward Oakland where bright lights have come on at the port, isolated strings of bulbs that make the big freight cranes look like overgrown, industrial monsters. They'll stay busy until well into the night, unloading the large metal shipping containers off the boats and putting them onto trains and trucks. Behind the port, Oakland's downtown glows red in the lights of the buildings and farther off the hills stand dark under the sky.

On Jack's side of the water, off to his right, the San Francisco downtown stands monumental above him, the buildings too close and too large, looming over the piers and the parking garage, to where he can't see their tops from the inside of the Mustang.

31

It takes some convincing, but Jack finally gets the Czechs to understand that he won't be going *right* back to their hotel to start the
party. Vlade's eager to give him his fifteen grand and the others just
want to get back. Jack explains that there are other problems like
trying to find Ralph's killer, and dealing with Tony Vitelli and what
happened to Michal. He'll tell them anything but what he's just dis-
cussed with Sgt. Hopkins. But Al shakes his head. He's in the back
seat of the Escalade and Jack's standing outside, hands on the win-
dowsill.

"We have iced those murderers," Al says.

Jack shakes his head. He doesn't want to get into his deal or the
fact that Hopkins wants European terrorists, but whether it's his
gut or his head, he knows there's more to what's going on, more to
this than just a couple of ex-KGB going after each other. That
might be part of it, but he still needs to know what happened to
Ralph, wants to know who put him at the bottom of his Jacuzzi.

Vlade motions for Jack to come around to his side of the car.
"You are going after Tony Vitelli?" he asks.

"No. I want to talk with Junius Ponds. That's the man I need to
see."

Vlade sits back into the car. "Then you won't need us?"

"No," Jack says, taking his hands off the car. Might as well let
them have some fun for a while and collect his money later. They'll
be around.

Niki gets out of the Escalade and walks Jack away from the car with his arm around Jack's shoulders. "You go to find who killed Ralph?" he asks.

"I was going to try," Jack says. "See what I can find out."

Niki nods. He takes a card out of the inside of his suit and hands it to Jack. "Call if you need help from me. I do not party with them. I will be ready."

"OK." Jack nods. He looks at the card in his hand. It has a San Francisco cell phone number printed on the back. "Thanks." He pats Niki on the shoulder as he heads over to the Mustang.

Vlade, grinning wide, some white powder left in his moustache, pokes his head out of the SUV's back window. "You will join us later, Jack?" Jack waves and nods. "No, Palms. I am serious." He points right at Jack. "You will come to our hotel. We have business to settle."

"Yes," Jack says. "*Trust me.* I'll be there after I handle a few things."

"Good," Vlade says. "Good." He slaps the side of the Escalade as they're starting to back out, and from inside Jack can hear the techno music double in volume.

32

In Japantown, it's not hard to locate the restaurant Joe Buddha was talking about: the Peace Tower is the kind of thing there's only one of, a tall concrete column with increasingly small horizontal platforms set along its height. Jack parks close to it, walks around into the park space that surrounds the tower—a concrete stretch that might be grass somewhere else, but here in the heart of Japantown is very much gray concrete with a few jutting shapes and round constructions to sit on. Jack sits down to catch his breath for a moment, his hands on his knees. He takes a deep breath through his diaphragm, lets it out slowly, counting to seven. He thinks about doing any of the half-dozen relaxation exercises that he used to do before scenes, the ones that got him ready to work. And now, just over five years out of actually doing any acting, he'd almost rather just smoke a cigarette. But isn't that the most common breathing exercise of them all?

He thinks it all through, taking stock of what's happened. Now he's not only lost a friend, but someone shot up his Mustang. Just thinking about it turns his stomach. Now the idea of going home, even if he could and not have Sgt. Hopkins come after him for what happened downtown, feels like it would be a failure. But it's no longer even a choice. Now he has to work with Hopkins, and he *gets* to find who shot up his car, who sent the dead K.G.B. fucks who did it.

He's here in Japantown because he has to know who that is, because Junius Ponds is the only lead he has left, the only road that's not Tony Vitelli. For all he knows, Tony V. will be at the bottom of this eventually, that's the feeling Jack has in his bones—the bruised ribs especially—but right now he's got a few more questions to ask.

Across the street Jack sees a big restaurant, one of the area's larger and nicer ones, with a round window covering a large part of the first and second floors. He can see tables through the window, lined up against the glass on the second floor for what must be a decent view, people eating at them, and, below that, the floor beneath and a big classy chandelier that must hang above the main lobby. The front entrance to the place is two big wooden doors, guarded by twin concrete lions.

Jack takes a last deep breath, gets up and crosses the street, makes his way up the steps and through the big double doors into the front vestibule of the restaurant. Here two guys stand at the far ends of the room, one on either side of a tall maitre d' stand and a snappy-dressed host at its helm. "Sir," he says, looking Jack up and down. He frowns disdainfully. "I'm afraid we have a strict dress code here."

"Right," Jack says. "But I'm here to see Junius Ponds."

"Ponds?" the maitre d' says.

"Yes. The guy that always comes here. Big black guy. You know him."

"Ahh," the man says, raising a finger. He drops it onto his chart and starts consulting his table arrangements. Jack looks over the front of the podium to see how the place is laid out: a lot of round tables across the first floor, with a few private rooms in the back. The two thugs on either side of the door start to nudge closer to Jack.

"Let me guess," Jack says, pointing to the rooms behind the main dining floor. "Junius is back here in one of these?"

"No, I—"

Jack raises his hands to ward off the bouncers, showing them he means peace. He only hopes to slow them down, but when they actually stop coming, he has to fight off a look of surprise. "I'll just go on back, if that's OK," he says, then, without waiting for an answer, walks past the host and into the main dining room. He passes the first few tables and looks back to see that, sure enough, one of the guys from out front is following him.

"Sir," the suit says. Jack weaves through the tables, cutting and zigzagging so it's hard for the other man to follow, heading for the back. In a flash, he wonders if this was really the best way to come in, if he couldn't have talked it up a little smoother, but now he can't change and go back. He keeps making his way toward the rooms at the back of the restaurant.

On the chart at the host stand, Jack had seen that of the three private rooms, only the two on the left were in use. He can see them now, the kind with rice paper walls and dark wood framing, sliding doors. He has a fifty-fifty chance of getting Junius Ponds' room on the first try, knows that'll probably be the one chance he gets before they have him escorted out, or at least he has to deal with the suit that's following him. Jack chooses the room on the end, the far left.

He climbs two stairs to reach the private rooms, slides open the rice paper door to find a number of people sitting around a low table, the kind where you take your shoes off and there's a space for your feet sunk into the floor. At one end of the table is a large black man, bald, wearing a white shirt open at the collar. He's got women on either side of him, nice-looking Asian girls in silk dresses.

"Jun—" And that's all that Jack can get out before he's flattened to the floor by something he didn't even see, something from back against the wall beside the door. He feels the weight of something heavy on top of him, something that knocks his wind out and, looking up, it seems to have gone fully dark in the room. Then the weight is gone and he starts to raise himself with his hands. The people at the table look nonplussed; they watch him struggle to breathe with only moderate interest. One woman lifts a piece of sushi with her chopsticks and offers it up to the large man at the head of the table. He takes it in his mouth and, chewing, holds up one hand.

"I'm a friend of Ralph's," Jack manages to get out. Suddenly he is dragged up off the floor and held partly off the ground. He's face to face with one of the biggest Samoans, probably the biggest *person* he's ever met. The guy has a tattoo over half of his face, and long black hair hanging down below his shoulders. He's holding Jack above the ground with Jack's toes just brushing the floor.

"Damn," Jack says.

The restaurant's bouncer comes in, and Jack hears a deep voice say, "It's all right, thank you. We will take care of this." The suit nods, takes a short bow with his hands pressed together over his chest, and leaves, sliding the door closed behind him.

The same voice, Jack realizes it belongs to the man at the head of the table, says, "Freeman, he's OK."

The big Samoan puts Jack down, and Jack takes a step back to get a complete look at him: he's got on jeans and a big short-sleeve button-up, a more tasteful print than the Hawaiians Ralph used to wear, something in blue with a samurai on its right half, standing holding a sword. The shirt has to be 3XL at least. The guy's arms bulk out of the sleeve-holes and his chest, really what looks like two huge muscles that could make up the hood of a car, fills it out to the point where it looks like it might split.

Resisting the urge to put his hands on his knees and cough something up, Jack stands tall, holds his hand out and introduces himself.

The guy nods, doesn't take Jack's hand. "I've seen you in a movie," he says.

"Right." Without turning his back on the big guy completely, Jack turns to where he can see the rest of the room. It's just Junius and the two ladies at their end of the table, two guys at the other end: a black guy with sunglasses and a black Kangol hat turned backwards, and another guy with a dark blue suit on.

Junius says, "When's the funeral?"

Jack doesn't get it for a moment, thinks it's a comment on his clothes—but he's not wearing black—and just looks at the man he assumes is Junius Ponds.

"Ralph's," he says.

"Oh. Good question. Soon, I would guess." Jack straightens his shirt, does his best to get his breathing back to normal.

Junius Ponds finishes off a shot of sake, and one of the girls next to him refills his glass. "Jack Palms," he says, as though he's introducing Jack to the room. "Friend of Ralph Anderino's. The former friend and acquaintance of ours. This guy was in a movie. He's a actor." He says this last word with a noticeable disdain in his mouth, his lips turned down. "A little tall today, aren't you?"

"Huh?" Jack says, just as the big guy, Freeman, hits him in the back of the knees. Suddenly Jack finds himself kneeling on the floor.

Junius nods. "That's better. No offense, but we don't like looking up while we talk."

Jack looks up and sees Freeman looming over him. "Right," he says.

Junius tilts his chin in Jack's direction. "You're lucky that you arrived after we finished eating. It would be rude of you to show up during dinner, don't you think?"

"Sure," Jack says. "It's not my aim to be rude here. I just want to talk."

"You talk numbers, man?" the guy at the other end of the table, the one with the sunglasses and the Kangol, says to Jack.

Junius holds up his hand for him to keep quiet. "Turner. You see we're talking here?"

The guy raises his hands in front of his chest. "Apologies, Mr. Ponds."

Junius pushes his plate away and turns to Jack. "So what'd you need to say with such urgency that you had to barge in here and disturb us?"

"I just wanted to talk about Ralph."

"Oh." He shakes his head. "You just wanted to talk about a dead friend of ours and you came down here during dinner?" He exchanges a look with Freeman that Jack hopes doesn't mean more punishment. Junius clicks his tongue, scolding. "That was not a good idea."

Jack tries to explain. "This is the only place where I knew to find you."

"That's a shame. I'm afraid there's not much to say either. I would like to talk with you, Jack, seeing how I'm a fan of your movie and all, but I don't know what I can tell you. Ralph's dead, my man. That's the final word." He holds up his hands, then stands and offers them to the two women, who rise with his assistance.

Jack starts to get up, but Freeman puts a hand on his shoulder, holding him in place. "I mean, can't we just talk about how you knew him? What kind of relationship you two had?"

Junius frowns. "That wouldn't be so good right now," he says. "You can see I'm entertaining, and when I'm entertaining I don't talk about business." The men at the other end of the table stand up and start over to where their shoes are lined against a wall. Junius slips into a pair of brown loafers. One of the women removes his suit jacket from the coat rack. She holds it up for him to put his arms into.

"Perhaps we should talk first before our next meeting," Junius says. He shakes his head, slipping his arms into his jacket. "I'm not that interested in sudden meetings or this kind of surprise. I prefer to *plan* my discussions." He waves the back of his hand at Jack.

The women start to head toward the door, followed by the other guy in the suit. The guy with the sunglasses smiles at Jack and says, "*Loved* your movie, man. When can I expect the sequel?"

As Jack watches the others, they seem to be waiting, curious to know the answer. Not wanting to disappoint them, Jack finally says, "Comes out next year. It's called *Shake It Up.*"

The guy with the Kangol nods. He smiles wide and makes a clicking noise with his tongue against his teeth. "That's the shit, my man. Like I said, I *loved* that picture." He holds out a fist towards Jack, and Jack touches the front of it with his own.

The women start to exit the room, followed by the guy in the blue suit. Turner and Junius pause to look at Jack one last time. Jack takes a shot in the dark, guessing at what might get Junius to talk. "I wanted to talk about the Russians," he says.

Junius stops. He looks at Turner and motions for him to keep walking. "Meet you outside," he says. Then, when the other man is gone, he looks at Jack. "What you say?"

Jack looks up at him, wants to ask if he can get up off the floor yet, but, remembering Freeman, he doesn't. "I said, 'Let's talk about the Russians you know.' That's my interest."

Junius nods at this, looks like he's thinking it over. "You wait here," he says, and goes out of the room.

Jack looks up at Freeman, says, "What am I going to do?" For a moment, the big Samoan appears as if he might laugh, but then doesn't. Alone with the giant, Jack would love to lighten the mood, but Freeman stands cold, arms folded.

Jack waits a few breaths. Then he asks, "Mind if I just get up now?"

Freeman unfolds his arms and stares at Jack. "Mr. Ponds will be back soon." He shrugs just slightly. "He won't mind if you're standing."

Jack puts one foot in front of himself and braces his hands on his knee. He pushes himself up to standing slowly—it isn't that he's getting old, but he's getting tired of being knocked down and having to pick himself up. Looking at the Samoan, he figures he's shorter by at least four or five inches, a state of affairs he's not used to. "You played for the Jets."

Freeman nods. "Four years. All-Pro twice. But when I blew out my knee, that was that."

"But still."

"Right man. Still. Those were some good fucking years."

Jack wants to shake his hand, pat him on the arm—something—but doesn't. "You know," Freeman says. "That picture you did. All Hollywood, but it wasn't that bad." Jack nods. "You must've had some good times there, on the L.A. scene and shit."

"Yeah," Jack says. "It wasn't bad by any means. But All-Pro is something to be proud of. Playing in Hawaii."

Junius comes back into the room carrying two chairs and sets one down next to Jack. The other he puts back a few feet and sits down on himself, crossing one leg over the other. "Sit," he says motioning at the chair with an open hand. Jack does. "So what about the Russians?"

"Who sent them?"

"Right. That'd be what you'd want to know." He shakes his head and checks his watch. "Listen, man. I got my people outside in the car waiting. You have about five minutes, *tops*. Make the most, as they say."

Jack takes a stab at putting the pieces together. "How'd you know about The Mirage?"

"Mirage," he says. "That don't have nothing to do with this."

"But you told the Russians to go there."

"What the fuck with you and the Russians? Stop. I did not send any Russians to The Mirage. What you're trying to find out involves someone else."

"Who?"

Junius looks at Freeman with pronounced disdain. "What'd I just say to this motherfucker?"

"You said enough about the Russians."

"Right."

Jack shakes his head. "Did I miss something?" When neither man answers, he starts at the beginning. "What was your relationship with Ralph?"

"Easy, man. He rolled a bit at the clubs for me, moved some product. Mostly small time."

"I was a friend of his. That's why I want to know. I'm trying to find out why he got rubbed."

Junius nods. "That's real cute, you saying 'rubbed' like that. You learn that from TV?"

"So who popped him?"

"Yo, popping Ralphie was almost a community service out here, man. I mean I did business with the fat fuck, but he was not what you'd call the most above-deck motherfucker, if you get me."

"Then just tell me why he stopped doing business with you?"

Junius looks upset at this, as if Jack's brought up a bad memory, or made him think of something he didn't know. He shakes his head. "That motherfucker stop? Shit. He couldn't stop buying if he had to."

"OK," Jack says. "So you don't know anything about the deal he was working with a Colombian named Castroneves?"

Junius shakes his head. "I fucking hate Colombians, man."

Behind him, Jack hears Freeman say, "*Scarface*."

Junius points at the big Samoan. He laughs. "No," he says to Jack. "In seriousness. I don't know anything about that."

"Or who hired the guys to drop by his house and leave a hole in his head?"

"Here's what I can tell you, Jack Palms. And I tell you this out of a friendly gesture, not anything more." He holds up his hand with his pointer finger extended. "The Russians you talk about? I know them, and have worked with them. But if they're the ones who put a hole in Ralph's head, *and I'm not saying they are*, it was not me who sent them. I just did some business, made a few trades to see what their supply line was worth and then I backed off it. Truth is, they're more headache than they worth."

Then, from inside his jacket, Junius's cell phone starts ringing. He takes it out and looks at it, and then holds up one finger to Jack. He pushes a button, holds it up to his ear. "Yeah." Junius nods, listening to the other end. "Really," he says, nodding again. "No shit?" Then he looks at Jack. "I've got Jack Palms right here in front of me now." He listens. "No, for real." More listening. "No, just big Free and myself. Sure. Sure." Then he listens and looks at Jack, laughs, and hangs up the phone.

"That's the man Vitelli," Junius says. "He say he got Alex Castroneves with him right now. That Colombian motherfucker you just spoke of? Tony tells me that you two just did size business for Ralphie-boy's visiting friends. Is that true?"

Jack holds up his hands, palms up, beside his knees. "This is why I'm trying to talk with you, Junius. I just want you to know what's going on, so I can find out what's what in this town. I want to know how I'm involved."

"Oh, you involved now, Jack," Junius says, nodding. "You involved here in this motherfucker." He stands up and goes over to the table, turns and kicks the chair across the room. "Ralph got you doing business with the Colombian?" He has his hands in fists, his forehead furrowed. "What the fuck that fat fucker thinking?"

Jack gets up and prepares himself for anything. Caught between a giant and an angry man is not where he wants to be. "So I take it that you didn't know that was coming?"

"Motherfucker." Junius takes a deep breath, trying to settle himself. He holds up one finger and starts breathing like he's in a Lamaze class. "The thing you don't understand," he says. "Is that I made that little bitch."

"But then you knocked him down, too."

"Right. That'd be how you want to see this, wouldn't it." He shakes his head.

Jack looks at Freeman to see what to expect: the Samoan has his arms folded, a serious look on his face, from what you can tell from his non-tattooed side. The side with the tattoo looks serious or angry all the time. Suddenly Jack wants to ask him if he had the tattoo when he was in the NFL.

"What you looking at?" Freeman says to Jack.

Jack turns and sees Junius pick up the chair he kicked over and set it back upright. It made a mark on the wall that he smoothes his hand over, then knocks just above it. "This place ain't all that sturdy, Free. Just a bullshit partition here, really." He stands up straight and looks at his friend. "We ought to check out for ourselves whether we want to keep coming here. Bullshit like this can walk right in." He tilts his head toward Jack. "And who knows who's listening on the other side of this wall?" He knocks on it again.

Freeman nods, his arms still folded. "I'll look into that, J."

"Thank you." Junius slides the chair in front of Jack's, but doesn't sit down. He brushes off his hands. "Now, Mr. Palms, my friend. We got the car outside, and my people are waiting. So this conversation is over." He takes a card out of the inside of his jacket and drops it on the floor. "You call me when you're ready to start rolling," he says. Then he nods at Freeman and leaves the room.

Freeman bumps Jack from behind as he heads toward the door, knocking over Jack's chair. "Later, bro."

Alone in the small room, Jack bends to pick up the card as one of the waitresses comes in to start clearing the table. The card is Junius', with just his name and a cell phone number, nothing else except one word: product.

33

After a fast exit from the restaurant, just a wave to the maitre d' and his two friends in suits, Jack stands outside in the cold air, breathing hard, trying to calm his nerves. He walks around the corner, paces back and forth, then crosses the street to the park to sit on one of the concrete benches. He looks up at the Peace Tower, its concrete platforms looming above him, and at the night, gray and full of light reflecting back down onto the city. There's enough fog in this town to keep any night stars away for most of the year; the city lights shine up against the clouds and make a bubble of reflected fluorescence.

He gets up and decides it's time he saw Maxine. The last thing he needs is another encounter with people who have bad tempers or want to do him harm, especially if those people have extra-large body guards. Though he'll have to talk with Junius again and probably Tony before the night is through, it's been a long, crazy day, and he wants to relax, at least for a little while.

About a half-hour later, Jack shows up at Maxine's with Japanese take-out—noodles and sushi—as a peace offering. He didn't call ahead, but he can see she's home because her lights are on, so he knows she can't ignore him when he rings the bell. "Delivery," he says into the speaker box when she comes on. The door buzzes—was she expecting food?—and Jack goes inside, walks up the stairs and to her door.

When he knocks, she calls out, "It's open."

Jack opens the door, and she's standing in front of him, hands on hips, wearing jeans and a gray hooded sweatshirt cut open partway down the front to show her chest and a little cleavage. "Jack Palms," she says.

Jack smiles. "That's me."

He goes over to the table to set the food down and then wraps Maxine up in his arms. "You were expecting a pizza?"

She laughs, puts her hand on his chin and turns his face to the side. "You know you got new cuts today?" she says. "I might not be able to let you leave here again, if this keeps up."

"Baby," Jack says. "Don't make the offer if you won't keep it."

"What's wrong?" she says.

"Someone shot the Mustang."

She pulls back to see Jack's face and as soon as she does her face gets doubly serious. For all Jack knows, there might be tears in his eyes. "Oh, Jack," she says. "The Mustang?"

He nods and she comes closer, holds him tight.

"I'd be glad to stay here and stop getting bruised," Jack says. "I'll stay inside with you forever once this thing is done."

She pulls back. "But?" she says.

"But tonight I've got to go out, fix a few things, collect some money from the Czechs, and point a cop in the right direction. Then everything will be OK."

She leans forward and stands on her toes, kisses Jack on the lips. "That's not so bad," she says.

"Good. Keep reminding me of that."

"I will." She takes him by the hand and brings him back through the living room to her bedroom. She dims the lights, but Jack can see she has more bookshelves in here, some lamps with scarves draped over them, a tapestry on the wall, a couple of pictures on the shelves. She takes off his jacket and starts unbuttoning his shirt. "So how was your day, darling? Tell me what happened."

"Not bad. Just a few meetings, a conference call, some Russian fucks shot at us and then I chased them down, crashed their car, and made sure they were dead."

"That was you?" Maxine says. "I saw that on the news tonight. It looked *awful*."

"Then I drove a few friends to the wharf, got the Czechs the coke they wanted. The Colombian came through. You know: just your average day in the city."

"Standard," she says.

"Tell me about it."

"Now will your friends take off?"

"Monday, I think." He kisses the top of her head, runs his fingers along her bare shoulders.

She pushes him backward and down onto the bed, and then climbs on top of him, straddling his chest, and finishes unbuttoning his shirt, peeling it open like a present. She slides her fingers across his pecs and then down along his sides toward his back. He winces a little as she goes near his ribs, and she moves closer to take a look. "You have a *nasty* bruise here," she says. She gives it a light kiss. Then she leans back to take her top off, and Jack starts touching around her navel, below it and around the rim of her jeans. When she comes back down to him, he kisses her neck, then her lips, and then raises her up and kisses her chest. He takes one of her nipples in his mouth and teases at it with his tongue.

It hurts when she touches his face, kisses his ears, but he can hear the music come on soft and gentle when she reaches to the dresser and puts on a CD. He's glad for the sound, glad to know his ears and some other parts of his body are still working, that he can still feel pleasure after the considerable pains of the day. She takes his pants off slowly, kissing along his legs as she does, finding a few more bruises, and for a few minutes Jack lets himself lie back and enjoy it. Then he takes her in his arms and pulls her up onto the bed and moves over her. He touches her skin with his fingers, opens her pants, and eventually takes them off. Seeing her firm body in the dim light, he feels better than he has in a long while.

When they've finished, they lie still for a time, hearing the soft music and feeling the slow, small movements of one another's breathing. Finally, she gets up and disappears, comes back with the food, brings it to the bed, and they eat with chopsticks out of the white Styrofoam containers, taking turns feeding one another.

"So you know about how my marriage broke up?" Jack says.

Maxine shakes her head. "No. And don't tell me."

Jack takes another maki. "OK by me."

"I've got some cigarettes in the night table next to you," she says. "You ever eat sushi while smoking?"

Jack laughs. "I'll wait for later."

She stops with her chopsticks near her face, a clump of noodles hanging from them. "Do you really have to go back out tonight? Why not just call the Czechs tomorrow and go get your money."

He shakes his head. "Can't. They made that mess downtown today, and now I've got to give the police something by tomorrow or else they come after me looking to clean it up. That and I still have to find out who killed Ralph."

Jack remembers Junius getting the call from Tony at the restaurant earlier. He wonders why Tony would call Junius, especially if he was with Castroneves. What was happening there?

"Remember when you first called me?" he asks. "And you said you wanted me to come down to The Coast so you could tell me something about Ralph."

She nods, taking a piece of salmon nigiri and putting the whole thing in her mouth.

"So what'd you want to tell me? I never got the full story because Tony showed up."

"Yeah," she says. "That bastard made me go turn up the music, only you can't turn it up from behind the bar. You have to go upstairs to the office. And the office was locked. So I had to get one of Tony's boys to let me in. Then the thing's already programmed to go up at eight o'clock, and it was like five minutes to eight."

"So Tony wanted to get rid of you."

She shrugs. "Who knows what that bastard ever wants. He wanted to get rid of you in a minute. Maybe he was trying to get rid of you then."

"So what'd you want to say?"

Jack can feel Maxine's body next to his under the blankets: their sides pressed together and her smooth skin against his leg. She nods, puts her hand under the blanket and runs her fingers along Jack's thigh. "You're all right, you know that Palms?" She kisses him on the cheek. "The thing is," she says, "Tony wouldn't let

Ralph come around The Coast anymore because he found out Ralphie was dealing to a couple of the girls."

"And Tony didn't want Ralph around the girls."

"No," Maxine says. "That wasn't it. Ralph dealt to his girls for a long time and Tony was OK with it. He said he liked how it made them dance, that it made the new ones dance better and not worry. When my friend Michelle started dancing there, he even *gave* her coke to get over her nerves the first few times."

"So what happened?"

"Tony told Ralph to stop. Then he started dealing to the girls himself."

"Tony?"

"Yeah. He got himself a new supply line and then he started dealing to the girls. He cut Ralph out. Then he found out Ralph still sold to a few of them and he wouldn't let Ralph around the club anymore. After that he started dealing to the customers too."

"And that stuff about Ralph touching the girls?"

She shakes her head, hair falling onto her face that she brushes away with the back of her hand. "Not really."

"Fuck," Jack says. "So Tony Vitelli wanted to set up a new business for himself and he had his own supply? Someone must have been getting him the coke to sell at The Coast. Junius?"

Maxine shakes her head. "That I don't know."

"OK though." Jack starts getting out of bed and putting his pants on. "OK."

Maxine puts down a maki with her chopsticks. "Where are you going?"

"I think it's time I go talk to the man: Tony Vitelli."

34

Jack calls Niki to come pick him up: he's ready to leave the Mustang behind for a while, let it rest out of harm's way. Niki agrees, but says he'll have to bring the others too: coked up in the hotel room, they're all too ready to go out, which they figure may as well be finding Tony Vitelli, regardless of where he is or how he'll receive them, as long as it gets them out into the night. Jack tries to convince him to leave Al and David behind; he doesn't want any more of Al's recklessness and gun-toting bravado, but Niki says that won't happen. He puts Vlade on the phone, and Vlade says they'll be there in fifteen minutes.

Maxine calls The Coast, asking if Tony's there, and the manager won't tell her anything. But when she calls the dancers' changing room, one of them tells her that Tony's at The Mirage tonight, taking care of some business, she says.

Jack's not sure if this is supposed to mean dealing, fucking someone up, or just watching the club. He wonders where the club kids get their ecstasy, whether Tony's got his hand in that as well. And why wouldn't he? It's as good a business as any other, probably better than coke even, a definite line to some hard cash. He wonders how many people Tony has dealing under him.

While he's waiting for Niki to show, Jack and Maxine share a cigarette in her living room. "I don't want to come," she says. "But I will if you want me to."

"No." Jack touches her leg through her robe. "You just stay here and get some rest. With any luck, I'll come pick you up in the morning and we'll head up to my place to get some breakfast."

She puts her arms around Jack. "Or we'll just stay here and you can get into the bed with me."

Jack has to admit it: "That sounds pretty nice. When this shit is over, I'll be ready for a few *days* in that bed." He starts thinking about the scene ahead of him at The Mirage, what that'll be like, and it's stuck in his head about Junius: whether he was Tony's supply or if Tony went outside of him too.

In the car, after Niki's buzzed up and Jack has kissed Maxine goodbye, he's still thinking about whether Junius would turn over Ralph and start supplying to Tony. But he doesn't see why Junius would turn over his own man, even if he and Ralph weren't that close.

"Hey Jack," Vlade shouts from the back seat. "We can fuck up these guys tonight!"

"It's OK, man. I can hear now."

Then Vlade leans forward. Without shouting, he says, "Yes. I know. We can do this."

Jack looks at Niki, who shrugs and smiles. "He talks like this way when he is high." Vlade says something in Czech, and Niki laughs. "He says to don't fuck with him or he'll kill us all."

"Right," Jack says. "I believe it."

The Czechs have insisted on playing loud techno music in the Escalade—so they'll be ready for the club when they get there, or because they're in that kind of mindset, Jack doesn't know. It's loud and he wants to be back with Maxine, in bed, but after a little while the music starts to pick him up and help him feel ready for the task at hand.

"Pull over up here," he tells Niki. "I need a coffee."

Outside the SUV, Jack gets his phone and tries Junius at the number on the card. He stands under the bright fluorescents of a gas station, heading inside to buy coffee. The Man picks up on the seventh ring. Jack can hear loud pumping music in the background, barely understands Junius when he says, "Who this?"

"Junius. This is Jack Palms. I got to talk with you."

"Where you at?" he shouts.

"I'm on my way to The Mirage."

Junius laughs. "That's good. Because I'm already here."

"You dealing through Tony?"

"What you say?" On the other end of the phone, it sounds like the music just got louder.

"I asked if you're his supply?"

"You better come here, brother."

Jack says he will, but Junius has already hung up. He makes his coffee strong and black, no milk or sugar. As he's paying for it, Jack thinks over Junius' call from Tony, and the fact that he's already at the club. He hopes he isn't walking into a mess. Maybe it'll turn out better to have Al and Vlade around, he considers, though he hopes he won't need their guns. Whatever the situation may look like, getting caught in the middle of a gun fight is not something Jack wants to go through again.

35

When they show up at The Mirage, Jack's already finished his large coffee and he's still miles behind the Czechs. They're talking and gesturing wildly with their hands; Vlade and David seeming to be concerned with calming Al down. Jack figures Vlade and Niki are packing guns, but he doesn't push to ask them, just hopes they'll get into the club. For that matter, he's hoping *he'll* get into the club without having to walk over Tony's bouncers. Not that that wouldn't be a pleasure.

But at the front entrance, the security seems happy to see him; it's the same guy he's seen there before, the one who likes his movie. He says, "Jack Palms, man. You're starting to be a regular around here," and opens the ropes for Jack and the Czechs right away. "Where's that girl you were with last night? She was smoking."

Jack shrugs. "At home."

"All right, player," the bouncer says, hitting Jack on the arm. "Ready for somebody new?"

Jack looks at the guy and at the line to get in through the regular, non-V.I.P. entrance: it's twice as long as it had been last night, at least. "What's going on here tonight?" he asks the doorman.

The guy smiles wide. "People like the action, my man. Heard we might stay closed tonight after that shit getting out on the news, but turns out people wanted to come out *more* because of what went down last night." He shrugs. "I guess they read it in the papers and wanted to say they been here. You're back. What's your excuse?"

"Go figure," Jack says. "And I thought the place had just gotten shot up."

"Yeah," the guy says. "That's the whole thing of it, man. That shit be cool now!"

Jack sees Vlade look funny at one of the bouncers on the side, a white guy who's wearing a thick gray sweater, not the cool-looking black stretch shirts or leather jackets the others have on. He's bald, his head fresh-bic'ed, like the shooter from last night, but he has a thick brown beard, overgrown, as if he's been living in some place cold and trying to cover his skin. He seems disinterested, but looks in their direction, clearly noticing Vlade and his friends.

As he and the Czechs make their way through the velvet ropes, Jack turns to one of the other bouncers, a short guy with an ear-piece attached to his head. "How'd you guys get this place ready to open again after last night?" Jack asks him.

He looks at Jack like Jack's just done something wrong, points inside with his finger like he's showing him the way to go, as if it wasn't abundantly clear already. He shakes his head.

Inside, Jack asks the girl at the register the same question. She lifts her shoulders. "I been wondering that myself. Somebody must have some good connections and pull with the boys downtown."

"That and some fast contractors," Jack says.

She shakes her head. "Most of it's not even fixed yet. They just put up plastic over the broken glass. People love that shit!"

"Right," Jack says, and he thinks about his own connections on the force, wonders whether Sgt. Hopkins would want to know where he is. "There's no way they'd come bust this place two nights in a row, right?"

The girl laughs. She smiles while she takes a handful of twenties from the Czechs, and then points them through a set of velvet curtains.

"That better not be coming out of my cut," Jack jokes.

"Oh, no," David says. "We have for you at the hotel."

Jack nods. "Good." He wants to call Hopkins, find out for sure that there's not going to be any bust here tonight, but he can't try making a call now that they're inside. It's just too loud.

They're coming out into the big dance room. It looks a lot like it did last night—kids and glow sticks, a very similar brand of deafening music, a few people dancing above the crowd on high platforms, the area above them on the balcony level—but now it seems twice as crowded and the people look like knock-off copies of the previous clubbers: as if this set wants to be the ones who were here last night, the people they've just read about in the newspaper, and they're trying their hardest to fit what they imagine those people to be. But with only a day to get their shit together, they look just slightly out of touch, a little behind the others. Jack can see it in their pants fitting a little tighter, their sneakers somehow not looking as fresh; fewer people are dancing. Jack's not much of a connoisseur of these things, but the extra effort shows around the edges, even to the eyes of someone as out of touch as he's become.

Another difference is that now the music has to compete with Jack's other deafness and it seems less loud. There's definitely something less infecting about tonight's beats.

Vlade comes up close to Jack and pulls his shoulder down to speak into his ear, "That man outside. The one who looks different is K.G.B."

"You sure?"

"I am sure. He is K.G.B."

"What's that mean?"

Vlade shakes his head. "I don't know. But I guess it is bad."

"Nice." Jack walks back out through the entrance and to the girl who took their money. Here the music is less encompassing, quiet enough that he can ask her, "Where can I find Tony Vitelli?"

She shakes her head. "Tony's around. I seen him tonight. But I can't say where he'll be."

"He's here though?"

She nods.

"Then I'll find him."

Back inside, moving through the tight press of bodies to catch up with the Czechs, Jack looks around: up above them, Junius will probably be on the balcony, and Jack wants to talk with him first to see where he stands in it all.

He looks around for Tony: it's hard to see the walls of the place because they're painted black, so with the flashing lights, kids, and the various bars spread around the dance areas, Jack has a hard time seeing the perimeter of the room. But looking for a while, he makes out the few guys stationed here and there with wires in their ears— these are the security. They look far more serious than the bouncers outside, other than the asshole who would only point Jack in one direction. These guys aren't dressed for the chill air or for clubbing. They wear black, which makes them even harder to see, but they're there when you look hard enough. Jack counts five.

He starts to make his way toward the balcony with the Czechs. Up above he can already see how some of the walls are covered with plastic sheets where the mirrors used to be. "You don't think they'd bust this place two nights in a row, do you?" Jack asks Niki. "That'd *have* to be bad for business."

Niki doesn't respond, but Jack is starting to believe in people thinking it's cool to be at a club that just got busted. For them it's a major change from the ordinary, the standard weekend and then going back to work on Monday. But for him it's not cool, more of last night's mess, and to be on the safe side, Jack takes his cell phone out of his pocket and tries to work the text message feature. It's not something he's familiar with—why he would use it other than when he's in a loud club, he's not sure—but with a few attempts he manages to find Mills' message from last night and then the option to reply. He writes in just one word, *Mirage*, and hits send.

They make their way around the outside of the room and to the ramp up to the second level, Vlade and Niki just behind Jack, David and Al hanging back, scoping out the scene, David even dancing a little. Al talks to himself, gesturing in several directions at once, looking like he's trying to decide who he should start a fight with. At the bottom of the ramp, the security's tightened up: they have more guys now and a list of names for who can go upstairs. But Vlade steps up and gives the man with the list the twenty-dollar handshake when he tells him their names. The guy actually does a passable job of acting like he scans the list, going onto the second sheet before pretending as if he's found the name of their party and then waving them through. Jack gives the kid credit for that, figures he's probably an aspiring actor, maybe someone with a little actual talent.

As they start up the ramp, Jack catches a glimpse of Tony: he's in back of one of the bars on the main floor, listening in on a head-set, hard to notice at first because he's wearing a black suit over a black shirt: the Johnny Cash look. He has a walkie-talkie that he says something into. Then, from across the room, Jack sees him look their way. Tony sees Jack see him, and the two make eye con-tact, Tony taking his time to look Jack over, then shaking his head slowly. Jack doesn't change his expression, just stares at Tony like he knows why he's here, what they're both doing. Tony winks.

"Motherfucker," Jack says, hoping that Tony can read his lips. But Tony's no longer looking; he says something else into the walkie-talkie and goes through a door behind the bar.

At the top of the ramp, Jack sees Freeman ahead of them, stand-ing close to another bar, the one that got shot to pieces last night. Now, where there were glass shelves along the wall last night there are just clear plastic sheets tacked up and dim light glowing through them. It gives the place a very industrial, not-yet-open-for-business kind of aura, that Jack can guess is very *in* these days.

The big Samoan would never be hard to spot, regardless of the lighting and his surroundings: he's almost a foot taller than most of the people around him. Thinking that wherever Freeman is, Junius must be close, Jack heads over. When he gets to the bar, he sees the fancy bottles of liquor stacked in boxes on the floor below the sheets; what used to be top-level is now like somebody selling drinks at a yard sale. But Freeman's paying big money for a martini and a beer regardless. He points toward the rail and Jack can see where Junius and his friends have a couch and a table not far away, overlooking the dance floor. Jack nods at the couch and asks, "No waitresses over there?"

"No," Freeman says, taking a long pull off the beer that drains half of the bottle. "We have them. They're just slow tonight, and I don't like to wait." He raises the martini. "Neither does J."

Jack can see that even up here, the crowd is different from last night: more trend-followers and real money than the people who were just here to get fucked up as a precursor to sex. The suits are nicer, the groups larger, and the conversations more involved, like these people are actually talking instead of just feeling the drugs buzz around in their heads.

Freeman takes Jack over to where Junius and the same people from the restaurant are seated, the same two women still close to Junius, and the two men sitting in chairs at either end of the couch. The guy with the black Kangol gives Jack a wave. Vlade keeps the Czechs up at the bar, telling Al and David that he's buying them a round of drinks, and Niki comes along with Jack.

Junius stands when he sees them, takes the martini from Freeman, and waves for Jack and Niki to follow him as he walks away from his friends towards the wall beside the bar. He opens a door that Jack hadn't noticed, it looks like just a part of the wall, and invites Jack and Niki to enter. They go through into another room, a quiet one with gray walls and a leather couch on one side, a large leather chair on the other, and a low, black table separating the two. Junius and Freeman follow them in and, as soon as the door closes, the music level drops off; they're cut off from the pounding beats by a few inches of heavy soundproofing along the walls. Junius sits down on the chair and motions for Jack and Niki to take the couch. The chair isn't the type you sink into; it has a straight back and Junius looks tall in it, not swallowed up. Jack sits down and Niki stands. So does Freeman.

"So, Jack Palms," Junius starts. "What brings you down here? You really after a discussion tonight."

Jack starts to respond, but Junius cuts him off. "You know," he says. "This meeting is a *little* better than the last one because you called, but it's still not what I'm looking for here. I'll indulge you, but we don't normally do this." He points to Freeman and himself. Freeman finishes his beer and tosses the bottle into an industrial-sized garbage can against the wall. Then he crosses his arms.

"Spare me," Jack says. "I'm here to help your ass and talk about what's been going down with your boy Tony, the one who sold you out."

Junius laughs. "You think Tony sold me out?"

Jack looks to see that Freeman is still reserved, standing in the same place. He's not sure what to say next, but having started into his bluff—trying to scare some form of truth out of them—he may as well keep going. "Tony wants to supply this town, his clubs, with *his* blow. And his X. You probably know this, but you're not admitting it to yourself yet."

Niki looks concerned. He has his hand near the lapel of his coat, but Jack knows he doesn't have a gun because nothing went off when they came through the metal detectors. Maybe he knows some martial arts from his time in the K.G.B., but if he's thinking about whether he can take Freeman, he can't like his chances against the big Samoan.

Junius shakes his head. "Jack, you have to be grasping at shit here, my man. How do you know I'm not supplying Tony myself?"

"Are you?"

Junius shakes his head. "Motherfucker. Now you want to know *my* business? What you think this is?" He looks at Freeman like he can't believe what's going on, then looks hard at Jack, his eyes narrowed. "You know what you're talking about here, or not?"

"You didn't hire the Russians, right? But you've worked with them in the past."

Junius nods. "I known a few Russians."

"But you didn't have them kill Ralph."

"What? No." He waves his hand in front of him. "I don't care enough about Ralph to have him dropped."

Jack's cell phone starts buzzing inside his jacket, vibrating against his chest. He jumps at the unexpected feeling.

"What's wrong man, you got the shakes?" Junius and Freeman both smile. "Don't tell me you still stuck on that H kick." They laugh at this, and in their moment of distraction, Jack takes out the phone and sees that he's received one message. "Sorry," he says. He pushes the "view" button and sees a message from Sgt. Hopkins: *Just heard: Mirage going down. Don't be there.*

"Shit," Jack says.

"What's up?" Junius asks.

Niki looked expectant, Junius and Freeman still relaxed, enjoying the comment about Jack having withdrawal symptoms from his old drug addiction.

"The fucking cops are coming down on this place again."

"Impossible. I'm here to do business with Tony V. himself. You think he let the pork in here when he's making a move?"

Jack stands up. "I think he will if he wants to get you locked up."

Niki says, "Last night we barely got out."

"Ho!" Junius does a double-take looking at Niki. "Quasimodo speaks. I didn't even know you had a tongue, my man. What you say?"

"Who you supposed to meet with tonight? Alex Castroneves? Tony?" Still trying to get Junius to tell him something to make things clear, Jack says, "I have a cop friend who just told me they're busting this place tonight. My guess is Tony called it in to get your ass pinched, just like he tried to get us and Alex pinched last night. I'm saying he's trying to take you down."

Junius stands up, drains off what's left of his martini in one long swallow, and fishes out the olive with his fingers. He shakes his head clear and looks at Jack. "This is what you really think?"

"Shit." Jack's feeling it now, and he lets it go. "I think Tony popped Ralph and used the Russians to make it look like it was you, tried to have Alex and maybe me killed in here *and* busted by the cops last night, and now he's trying to do the same to you, or at least get you arrested. *That's* what I think."

Junius looks at Freeman and then back at Jack. Jack has the sudden feeling that he's said more than a mouthful. But now that he has it all out in the air, it actually sounds more than half believable.

Junius stares. "You *know* this?"

Jack figures it's time to come clean. There has to be some honesty in things for people to believe you. "Part of it is I know this," he says. "Part is me trying to put things together the only way they can go."

"No, no, no, man," Junius says. "Sit down. Let's talk this back through again." He sits down on his chair. "First of all, fuck the police, like N.W.A. say. They come in, they won't even know there's a room here. We got time. Talk to me about Ralph." He points at Jack and then brings his finger down, presses it against the table. "The first thing I want to know, is why he's cutting around me and going to Castroneves."

"That's a good question," Freeman says, stepping closer to the others.

"Because that's enough to get popped right there." Junius points at Jack *and* Niki now. "And then trading with that fucker after, that's another thing that might get someone fucked up." He raises his eyebrows, moves closer.

"Hey," Niki says. "Ralph connected us to him. You want to sell us more?" He holds his hands at his sides, his thumbs pointed out, and curls his fingers towards him, waving for Junius to bring it on. "We will buy."

"Ho!" Junius and Freeman exchange glances. "OK, my man. We can talk business." Junius laughs. He points to Niki and says to Jack, "Your boy talks big. Is that safe?"

Jack looks away. He wishes he had a drink or something he could throw against the wall, a bad reaction he probably learned from Victoria. "You don't get it. All this means is we have to get out of here."

"Because there's a problem."

"Tony's the problem."

"Oh he is? Let's call him in here." Junius brings his phone out of an inside pocket in his jacket and flips it open. It makes a beep sound, like the walkie-talkie phones do. Into it he says, "Vitelli!"

"Yo!" Tony says back. "Jack Palms is here."

"Jack's up here. Says we got a problem."

"On my way."

Junius closes the phone and looks at Jack. "See that? Not so hard. We can resolve this all right now."

Jack leans back on the couch, pats himself down for his cigarettes but doesn't find them. He nods at Junius. "Got a smoke?" Junius takes a pack out of a jacket pocket and flips it onto the table. They're not Jack's brand, but they're not menthols, so they'll do. Niki steps forward to give him a light. Jack takes a puff and leans back on the couch. He's not sure if Tony's going to come with the police, his bouncers, a Russian army, or *what's* going to happen.

Junius says, "So tell me why would Tony pop Ralph?"

"One," Jack says. "He wanted to deal to his girls and these guys." He nods at Niki. "Two, he figures if he can make it look like you're the guy who did it, he can get you off the streets, get your spot and deal your share too. I'm betting on this guy as a ladder-climber, trying to make it to the top. He got a new supply line and wants to make good."

Sitting down next to Jack, Niki takes out a cigarette and lights it.

Junius shakes his head. "Shit," he says. "Dog eat dog is the only world I know. We all trying to eat each other out here." He takes a cigarette out of the pack and lights it himself. "But Tony buys from me. He's strictly middle."

Jack takes a shot: "You supply him with the X he sells to those kids out there?" He looks around for an ashtray, but the table's empty and there isn't one around. He ashes on the floor.

"No man." Junius frowns. "I don't do that techno shit. Shit be all *technologized*."

"Then who is?" Jack looks at Junius and knows he has him. Someone's selling the ecstasy in this place, Junius has to realize, and if it's not Tony through him, then Tony must have found a different supply.

Junius's brow furrows. He leans back in the chair, takes a long drag off his cigarette, and exhales smoke straight up into the air.

36

Tony comes in with two bouncers holding Alex Castroneves up by the arms and a third in tow. Castroneves looks like they've been using his head for a soccer ball. They drop him on the ground in front of Jack and Junius.

"Here's your friend," Tony says to Jack and Niki. "Make a trade with him now."

Jack snuffs his cigarette out on the tabletop. "This how you treat all your guests?"

Tony laughs. "No. You didn't get the full hospitality because you had your mommy there to beg for us to let you go." He looks around. "But I don't see her now, so maybe we can accommodate you."

"That's OK." Jack stands up next to Niki and takes a step toward Tony. Niki drops his cigarette, grinds it out against the floor. "Where your guys? The ones that whacked Ralph?"

"Fuck!" Tony says. "What the fuck is it with you and that dirt bag?" He takes one step closer to Jack and then lunges, punches Niki in the stomach. Niki groans and doubles over, looks up at Tony like he's ready to rip his muscles from his bones, but Jack holds his hand out to restrain him, watching the three bouncers move closer. These are some of the guys from the inside, the perimeter players, not the muscle guys from outside. Now that Jack sees them from close up, he can tell these aren't the normal goons you'd find on the streets of San Francisco. These are pros: they've each got on a tight black long-sleeve shirt, and a wired mic on their head. They have black pants on and tight belts with what looks like mace and a taser gun mounted within reach. They're white, but don't look like California boys: they're too clean cut. Jack hopes they're not more ex-KGB. He looks to see that Freeman is still standing in the same position.

Junius gets up slowly, adjusting his suit. "Jack here has been telling me about how you wanted to cut me out of the city, trade up my ground, and get me in the clink for popping Ralph."

Tony shakes his head. "How about we beat the fuck out of both these bastards, all them for going around us to this piece of shit." He points at Castroneves. "I could right now—" Then he goes to kick him and stops, pulls back at the last second.

Jack helps Castroneves stand up. He's wearing just a shirt and pants now, no tie or jacket, and through these clothes Jack can see that he's in bad shape: his shirt torn, he has cuts across his back and blood on the side of his mouth; his nose looks broken. Jack helps him to stand, but Castroneves can't stay up on his own. He slumps against Jack's shoulder.

Jack looks at the big Samoan. "Freeman, you want to help me with this guy?"

Freeman shakes his head, his arms still folded in front of him.

Castroneves falls to the couch. "You are cocksuckers who will pay," he says, glaring at Tony.

"Oh?" Tony says, "We'll pay? And you bring that fucking Colombian army in here to make it happen, OK?" He waves at one of his guys, who moves over to Castroneves and points for him to get up. When he puts his hand on the taser, Castroneves stands.

Junius shakes his head and clicks his tongue against the roof of his mouth. "I mean I know this guy's competition, but you treating him *hard*."

"Fuck," Tony yells. "Somebody get rid of the fucking conscience on this guy."

Junius points to Jack and says, "This guy's saying you wanted to cut Ralph out and deal at the clubs yourself, T. What's up with that?"

Tony shrugs. "So? You give a fuck about that bastard? What if I do want to deal this whole city? What then?" He looks hard at Junius, maybe more brash then he wants to come off, but with his guys to back him up, he's feeling strong.

Jack wonders what's happening with the other Czechs, wishes they were in the room, but they probably can't even find the door. "When are the police showing up *tonight*?" he asks.

Both Tony and Junius stop and look at him. "Police?" Tony says. "There's no police coming *here* tonight. Why would you think that?" He steps away from Junius, closer to Jack. Both of his bouncers have their arms folded, but they can get at their belts. They're not big like Freeman, but they're ready.

"This motherfucker's undercover," Tony says, pointing at Jack.

Jack holds up both hands. "Now let's just wait a second. If anyone's working for the cops, it's the one who called in our meet here last night, the one who brought the cops down on this place."

Tony laughs. "I called the cops on my own club? Why'd I do that?" But then he looks serious. "Matter of fact, who told you I did that?"

Jack says, "The only cop I know is the one who busted my house and made sure my picture got all over the tabloids, the asshole who helped destroy my career."

Tony shakes his head. "Junius, you going to believe what this nut job tells you?" He waves his hand at Jack. "If you do, you're as fucked as he is. Get rid of this guy."

Junius looks at Freeman and tilts his head in Jack's direction. Freeman starts toward Jack and Niki, his arms unfolded. "Let me show you boys the door," he says.

"You take me out of this, he'll cut you out next, Junius," Jack says. "Listen to me. You know what I'm saying is right."

Freeman gets close enough to Niki that he could hit him if he wanted, but he brushes past to the door. He opens it and the sound of the club comes in strong. Niki starts in that direction.

"Junius," Jack says.

"This fucking guy is not leaving this club in one piece tonight," Tony says, turning to his guys.

Jack holds up his hands. "OK." He starts heading toward the door. With his hand on his head, Junius looks like he's thinking; his brow wrinkled, he paces away from Tony and then back toward him. "You know I'm right," Jack says, backing toward the door. "Ask yourself what happened to Ralph."

"That's it," Tony says, waving at his guys to move. "No more mentions of Anderino. Kick his ass."

One of the guys says something to another in a language that's not English and sounds different from the Czech Jack's been hearing. Niki gives Jack a quick look, then the three bouncers start forward, but Freeman puts his arm out to stop them, holds them back. "No," Freeman says. "Give him one for his movie. That shit was decent."

Jack heads toward the open door, following Niki. Outside, the music in full blast, he turns back and sees Tony say something to Junius, something he can't hear. Then Tony takes his walkie-talkie off his belt and speaks into it. The door closes in Jack's face and he's cut out, he and Niki in the club with the other Czechs already coming over, asking Niki where they were. Jack goes to the rail and looks down at the guys around the perimeter: they're listening in on their headsets and then they look up, almost in unison, to the balcony.

They start to move.

"Shit," Jack says. He starts toward the Czechs, standing in a group holding drinks and talking to Niki. Here we go again, he's thinking, but this situation's worse than last night, with more of these bouncers coming after them, not to take anything away from the hit men with guns and what a joy that was to deal with. "Come on," Jack yells, breaking into a run. The only advantage this time is that now he knows the way out.

The Czechs take their time to pause and find out what's happening, so Jack pushes Vlade toward the exit behind the men's room. "We have to get out of here before every bouncer in this place comes down on us."

Al stands firm. "We don't run."

Jack stops pushing Vlade and stands next to him, looking at Al, yells in his face, "You want to end up tasered and maced, then found by the cops when they get here in five minutes?"

Al starts to move, following Vlade and the others. Despite their suits and the fact they've been taking blow for a few hours—maybe *because* they've been taking the blow—they actually move pretty well, heading not in the direction Jack had expected, but to a new exit that he just now notices, probably the one Maxine used to take them out last night. Niki hits the door first, and Jack looks back to see three of the bouncers at the top of the ramp, one of them waving the others back down and talking into his headpiece. "Fuck," Jack says, hitting the door and entering the dark stairwell. Small lights are set in a string along the base of the stairs on the outside wall, and in this light Jack can just make out the handrail and the flight of stairs, see the Czechs start down. He looks for a way to block the door and doesn't see one, but then he makes out a fire extinguisher on the wall and grabs it, bangs at the door's handle a few times and finally knocks it off. Then he pushes the rest of it back in through the hole, hoping this will slow the black shirts down.

Now, with his eyes starting to adjust, Jack can see the stairs and starts down them, jumping over the first half-flight and making the turn around the rail. On the second flight, he hears Tony's guys hit the door above and for a second it holds. He keeps running, one flight up from the Czechs, who are already going out into the alley behind the club. Jack hears Niki say something loud, but it's not until he comes into the alley himself that he sees why: a few of the guys, four of them, are waiting with their tasers out.

"Hold it," one says, and lunges at Niki, who grabs his arms and runs the taser into the wall. He starts kneeing the guy in his midsection. Al gives a howl and rushes at another of the bouncers, followed by David. This leaves Jack and Vlade with two of the guys to themselves.

Jack shrugs as one guy comes at him with his taser, waits until he's close enough, and dives at the guy's legs, basically tackles him full out onto the asphalt of the alley. It feels good to move again, to have a moment of action without being outnumbered or sore, and

Jack takes the guy down fast, turns him onto his chest, and takes the taser out of his hand. The guy's struggling underneath him, but with one of his arms locked behind his back, there's not too much he can do. With his taser in one hand, it's too much for Jack to resist. He hits him with the full stun of the voltage. The guy goes limp.

Jack looks for a way to restrain him and sees a set of flex-tie plastic handcuffs conveniently strapped to the back of the guy's belt. He puts them on the black shirt's wrists and gets up just as Al and David lift their guy up to chest level and deposit him into a nearby dumpster. Vlade's got his guy pushed up against a wall, his face against the bricks and his arm pinned behind his back.

That's when Jack first hears the sirens. At the end of the alley, toward the front of the club, he sees the flashing lights of the police. Niki stands over his guy and kicks him once in the side.

"Let's go," Jack yells, waving and then moving the other way down the alley, away from the lights. The Czechs start after him, moving slowly, as the stairway door opens right behind them and three more of the bouncers come out. Standing with them is the odd Russian Jack noticed when they first came in, the bald guy with the beard and the sweater. The one whom Vlade recognized. The Czechs start to move faster, breaking into a run behind Jack.

At the top of the alley, on a broad, brightly lit, downtown street, Jack turns and sees the bouncers by the exit, helping up their boys and taking off the handcuffs.

37

"Well, we fucked that up," Vlade says, back in the SUV. Niki's got them headed toward the hotel, Jack in the back with David and Al. Al's hand is bleeding, mostly around his knuckles, where he missed hitting the bouncer and punched the side of the dumpster instead. He's got a thin handkerchief wrapped around it, but the blood's already starting to come through.

"No," Niki says in the front. "Nothing we could do."

"I think Junius was cracking," Jack says. "I was guessing about most of what I told him, but I think he was starting to believe me."

"You think Junius Ponds is responsible for killing Ralph?" Vlade asks.

"No, it was Tony, I believe," Niki offers.

Vlade turns around in his seat to face Jack. "You think Tony Vitelli killed Ralph?"

"The guy's fucked," Jack says. "I'd say it's more than a theory."

Vlade nods, turns back toward the front of the car. Ahead of them, downtown glows in the late-night action, the bars crowded full and people walking the streets.

"Time to leave town," Vlade says. "It is too bad here. Messy. We have to go."

Al says something in Czech, and David rips off part of his shirt and wraps it around Al's hand. "Did you see the cops coming again back there?" David says. "They are everywhere we go. Vlade is right."

"Too many police," Vlade says.

David nods. "We must leave."

"Fuck this you are saying," Al tells them. "Let us go back to there and kill them now."

"Shhh," Vlade says to Al, holding one finger over his lips.

Jack just pats Al's knee. "It's all right, big guy," he says.

They come out onto Market and everything turns brighter, the shops glowing now inside and out. Soon they'll turn onto Stockton and head toward the hotel. Jack resigns himself to looking out the window, wondering what he'll do about Sgt. Hopkins now that he's got nothing real on Tony or Junius Ponds. Anything he'd say about Tony would slide off, leaving him mad enough to send the bald Russian, or a couple of the other guys after him, and Hopkins probably has more on Junius than Jack can offer. Not wanting to piss off Freeman, either, doesn't leave him many options. On a whim, he takes the cell phone out of his inside pocket and checks to see if he's gotten any calls or messages. It merely states the time: 1:45AM, meaning no one has called, and it's too damn early in the morning.

At the hotel, Jack goes up to the suite with the Czechs. Al's yelling about the police, and that he wants more blow, but David leads him to one of the bathrooms to soak his hand in a sink. The others start packing. Jack drops himself into one of the couches, feeling like he's really ready for a drink. If he's going to be on the inside for a while, he won't get drugs or alcohol there, and he can go into a whole new detox.

Niki walks out of the room with a heavy leather bag and brings it over to Jack. He offers his hand; Jack gets up, shakes it. "We want to thank you for being our guide in this city," Niki says. "We are very sorry about Ralph."

"I'm sorry about Michal," Jack says.

Niki bows his head.

"Yo!" Vlade comes out of the bathroom, drying his hands on a towel. He comes over to Jack and hugs him. "You have helped us here very much," he says. "Thank you for showing us your hospitality and to your friend with the blow."

Niki says something to Vlade in Czech. Vlade clicks his tongue, shakes his head. "I am sorry to hear that the Colombian is not doing well. Perhaps he tried to settle a score he could not pay?"

"I don't know," Jack says. "As far as I'm concerned now, those three, all of them—Tony, Junius *and* Castroneves—they can all go to hell." He reaches out for the bag, tired and ready to go home.

But Vlade takes it from Niki first, looks inside and nods approvingly. He closes the bag and hands it to Jack. "This is the fifteen that we negotiate. There is more here also, to cover the damage to your car." He nods, hugs Jack again, and starts into one of the rooms to pack his things. Jack shakes Niki's hand again and calls out to the others to have fun across the states. Niki walks with him to the elevator and pushes the button.

Jack judges the weight of the bag: it seems pretty good, heavy enough, he hopes, to pay off all the bills and keep him relaxed in Sausalito for a while, or on the road if he needs to be on the move to get away from whoever Tony V. will send, or to skip town on Sgt. Hopkins. By Monday morning he could be in Brazil, he realizes, choosing a country at random.

"You have done well for us here, Jack," Niki says. "What you will do with the police?"

Jack shakes his head. "That's one thing I don't have figured."

The elevator door opens and Niki pats Jack on the back. "It will go. Those people in downtown will go away when the police look up their records. You do not need to worry. Go home. Get some sleep."

Jack steps into the elevator. David comes out of the bathroom, stands at the couches with Vlade, watching Jack go. He holds up his hand. Jack watches them standing quiet, seeing him off, as the shiny metal doors close and his own reflection replaces the view of their suite.

As the elevator starts to descend, Jack begins to assess the damage, the lines around his eyes and the creases in his forehead. His hair's dirty and he has a fresh cut on the other side of his face to match the one under the bandage. He runs his fingers over his head telling himself it's been a long day. Though he looks more tired and beat up than he's known, worse than he has in as long as he can remember, tonight's exhaustion feels better than any he's had from working out. Something inside him feels good, alive. He steps closer to look at the side of his face, realizes the cut under the gauze will probably need stitches when he can get to a doctor. He closes his eyes; he's seen enough.

38

Outside, on the cold streets, Jack remembers that the Mustang is parked at Maxine's, so he lets the bellman hail him a cab. In the warm backseat, he opens the bag and looks inside, sees the clean stacks of twenties and fifties and runs his finger along the edge of one, feeling the soft tickle of the individual bills brushing his thumb. When he brings his face down to the opening, the small bag smells like new leather and fresh money: a musty smell, pungent and maybe just a little bit wet. It's not a smell he's especially used to, but it's one he'll remember, one he'll want to smell again.

As the taxi makes its way west toward the Sunset, getting onto Fell, one of the fast four-lane roadways that pass through the city like highways, Jack sits back and closes his eyes. He knows there's no smoking in the taxi but soon he'll have a cigarette, maybe even get some sleep and wake up with Maxine next to him sometime tomorrow afternoon. Then he'll start to put some of the pieces back together.

Jack leans forward toward the driver and asks, "Excuse me. Do you mind if I smoke?"

The driver shakes his head and says he doesn't mind. The window next to Jack is already starting to lower as he feels around for his pack. He's at the end of his options, he's afraid, and has pissed off too many people. The thought of Freeman showing up at his house, tattoo and all, or a couple of Tony's guys from the clubs, even the bald Russian, all of these fears come to Jack, and he worries his life will never be the same, that he'll never be able to relax. Then there's Sgt. Hopkins too, his concern about the shootout downtown and what he's already said about getting Jack into a small cell. Even if he hides out at Maxine's, that can only last him a little while. Maybe Brazil's not such a bad option after all. He's definitely got the money to hop Sunday morning's first plane to South America.

But then he feels a buzz, his cell phone vibrating against his chest from his inside jacket pocket. Here we go again, he thinks, taking it out and seeing Junius Ponds' number. "Oh yeah, baby," he says out loud, and then, flipping open the phone, "Hello?"

"Jack Palms. You were right, man. That bastard had the police drop in not five minutes after you left. And guess who skated out before anyone could find him?"

"Tony V."

"That's right."

"What happened to Castroneves?"

"That motherfucker? Shit. Tony probably had his boys take him out the back way, take him *out*, or gave his ass to the cops. But I don't see him down here."

"How'd you get out?"

"I didn't, bitch. This is my one call, and I'm calling you because if you know the cops are coming before they get there, then maybe you can get my ass out of here. I'm in the clink, motherfucker."

Jack exhales at that concept: he's supposed to be giving Sgt. Hopkins the big dealers in the city and now they've got one, if not two of them, behind bars, and Jack's supposed to help him get out?

"Who's your lawyer?"

"Man, this is inside shit, strictly. You know someone on the force, right? If not, you'd be in here now. And I need out. What we both need is to take Tony V. down. We work together, we make that happen and *then* we turn him over. We make that happen and *everyone* is happy."

"Everyone but the guy I have to call at two in the morning to get you out."

"Now you talking, Jack Palms. That's the form of discussion I like to hear."

Jack shakes his head. Outside his windows, he can see the first parts of Golden Gate Park as they make the turn onto Stanyan. The fog is heavy across the trees and over the green lawns of the park. It'll be cold outside, colder than downtown. He rolls up his window.

"OK," Jack says. "Let me see what I can do."

"That's good, Jack. You all right, man. And don't worry. If it don't work out, Freeman knows to call my lawyer in the morning. Not that that's good."

"I hear you," Jack says, and hangs up.

"Shit," he says in the silence of the car, dreading the call to Sgt. Hopkins to wake him in the middle of the night. But then again, Jack figures, why not? *Fuck* him.

The driver asks Jack again for directions, thinking he's made a wrong turn. "We are there almost?" he asks.

Jack tells him what he needs, directing him the rest of the way to Maxine's.

Across the street from Maxine's apartment, Jack stands with the bag by his hip looking up at her windows, trying to decide if she might be awake. He paid the cab driver with a fresh fifty from one of the stacks, enjoying the crisp feel of it and the ease of paying with cash in one lump sum. It's been a while since he's had this kind of liquidity.

There's one light on in Maxine's, but it's dim, maybe a reading light or maybe just a light to leave on so she can find the bathroom. Jack's not sure. But he's here, so he might as well drop in, he figures. At least to leave off the money. He takes out his cell and tries calling her, thinking it'll be easier to answer the phone that's close to her bed than to get up and answer the door. But Maxine doesn't answer, and after a few rings the answering machine comes on. "Maxine, I know it's late," Jack says onto the message. "But I'm outside. I came back for the car and I thought I'd come up for a minute if you're awake."

He waits a little while for her to pick up, and then ends the call. "Too many cell phones," he says, walking up the street to his car. He tries her on hers to see if that's any better, and it goes straight to voicemail. At the Mustang, he opens the trunk and puts the bag down into the bottom of the well. He opens it, takes out a fifty and two twenties in case he'll need them later. Then he closes the trunk and locks it. The old American car has a firm lock, no push-button release switch, all hard metal surrounding his luggage. Jack knocks once on top of the trunk and feels good about the deep, resonant sound.

He takes a long look at the new tire, the spare, and kicks it to make sure it'll be fine. If anything else happens to one of his tires, he'll be screwed with a flat in the trunk, but he's not going to find a new tire at 2AM on a Saturday night anywhere. He opens the car door and, once inside, takes the cigarettes out of his jacket pocket and mouths one out.

Jack lights up and takes out his cell phone, dreading the call to Sgt. Hopkins that'll wake him up, but also ready to rattle the old bastard's cage a little more for all the trouble he's brought. But first Jack smokes for a minute looking up at Maxine's apartment. He wonders if she's sound asleep or if she went out somewhere, doesn't think either one seems probable. He tries to shake it off, stop thinking about it; he knows the trust road isn't one he wants to start down again after the trouble its already gotten him into with her, that he's better off not worrying. He thinks about calling again and instead dials the sergeant's cell.

After three rings, Jack hears the phone pick up but no speaking. "Mills!" he says. Then he hears the sergeant breathe, mumble something and swear. "Mills."

"Fuck is this?"

"Jack Palms, Mills. Hate to wake you, but at least I don't have the papers there with a camera in your face, right?"

"Fuck you Palms."

"Now you're starting to talk to me." Jack takes a pull off the cigarette, flicks the rest onto the asphalt. He waits a second, exhales, and then says, "I'm sorry, man. But I need you right now."

"I hear you."

"That favor you owe me. I need it now."

Hopkins makes a coughing sound on the other end. "Favor? We finished that."

"Did we?"

"Oh yeah. When I didn't pick you up after that shit downtown." He breathes into the phone. "That was all your favors right there. You know, that shit that involved two people who don't exist. What the fuck is that?" Hopkins says, waking up.

"That is you finding your terrorist warlord boys already, like I told you."

"What happened at The Mirage?" Jack drums the steering wheel with his fingers, turns on the engine so he can start the heat.

"What's that?"

"I'm in the car. Here's what I need." Jack waits to hear the sergeant's answer.

He hears breathing, then, finally, "Go ahead, Jack."

"The guy you need is still on the streets. Your boys missed him tonight, but they got the guy I need to bring him in."

"Who's that?"

"Junius Ponds."

"Fuck, Jack. You want me to release Junius *Ponds*? That fucking guy has a sheet as long as my—" Jack waits, hoping the sergeant will come up with something good.

"Your what?"

"Fuck, I don't know. I'm too tired. He's bad."

"Right. But I can give you worse. I'm talking ecstasy, coke, murder and a guy who's connected to the Eastern Europeans you've been looking for, probably using them to hit Ralph and come after us. This is more than just the shit that Junius runs. This is the new supply."

"Keep talking."

"Tony Vitelli is trying to take over Junius's operation and bump everyone else out of town. I think he's also trying to set up his clubs so he can distribute ecstasy. I don't know his supplier, but Tony V. is ready for a fall."

Sgt. Hopkins yawns into the phone. "Right," he says. "You want me to give you Junius and then you give me Tony Vitelli and we're even?"

"Murder, Mills."

"Right."

"Plus I give you his new supplier, someone bigger than Ponds. *And* the Europeans you're looking for. I'm this close. Everything you want I can get you. I just need Ponds to show me how."

The sergeant doesn't respond. Jack waits him out.

"I'm listening."

"That's it, Mills. I give you Tony Vitelli and your friends there, the ones who caused the mess downtown today. I can lead you to more of them and give you Tony's supply line above and beyond Junius Ponds."

"What makes you so sure there is someone bigger than Ponds?"

"Tony V.'s bringing ecstasy into his game. He has to be getting it from someone who's not Junius. He's also going somewhere else for his blow all of a sudden. I put those together, I get a new supply line in town, a bigger one. Plus, with Tony looking to squeeze out Junius and Castroneves, he must have something big. You spring Junius for me, he'll think I can walk on water. Then there's no telling what he'll lead us to."

"OK." Jack hears the sound of shuffling at the other end of the line—probably Hopkins getting out of bed. "I'll make the call. But you got until noon tomorrow and then, if I don't have Vitelli and your buddies, you're going to be inside instead of Ponds."

"OK, Mills. But that's where I was anyway. This works out, you get the mob leader you want *and* the supply."

"That's good, Palms. I fucking better."

39

Figuring he'll have a while until he hears from Junius again, Jack
looks up at Maxine's windows: sees the same dim light. "Shit," he
says, cutting the engine and opening the car door, getting out into
the cold. He stands and walks up the block to Maxine's doorway,
flips open his phone and calls her house line again.

This time she answers, groggy, after four or five rings. "Max,"
Jack says. "I'm downstairs."

"You OK?"

"I'm OK, but I can only stay for a minute." He leans his head
against the glass of her front door. The buzzer goes off, and he
pushes the door open, almost falls into her front hall. He looks at
his phone and sees she's already hung up. As he feels the sudden
warmth of her building, Jack knows how tired he actually is, but he
fights it off: he stumbles to the stairs and starts up them, sees her
there at the door. At the top of the stairs, he takes her in his arms.

"I'm glad you're here," she says.

"I know the feeling."

"Can't you stay?"

Jack pulls back so they can see each other. "I think Tony had
Ralph killed. My guess is he wanted a piece of the Czechs' action
and Ralph wouldn't give it to him. Now he's pushing Junius out of
the game and trying to take over. That's the theory I'm working off
of."

Maxine's eyebrows go up. "You sure you're not just trying to fit the story to get the guy who beat you up?"

"No," Jack says. "I'm not sure. But I'm making the story the only way I can see it." He shrugs. "If things change, they change. I could be wrong."

She waits, then says, "But what?"

"But this feels like it's right. That's all."

"Come inside." She takes him into the kitchen. He sits down at the table, and she turns on the fire under her kettle. "You want some coffee?"

Jack shakes his head. "Tea."

She smiles, gets a box of tea bags down from the long shelf above the stove.

"How long did you work at The Coast?"

She shrugs. "A couple weeks. Why?" With her back to him, Jack looks Maxine over, sees her nice legs and her long, plaid, flannel nightshirt just covering to the back of her thighs. He gets up and runs his hands up her side, kisses the back of her neck. "Oh," she says. "Oh, Jack."

"This should all be over soon."

"Did you get the money?"

Jack steps back. When Maxine turns around, she has a small revolver in her hand, a snub-nosed .38 that she's pointing at him. Jack sits down hard on the kitchen chair, shakes his head in disbelief. He feels like he's just been punched in the gut. "Damn, Max," he says. "Damn."

Her face is cold, hard when she says, "Did the Czechs give you the money?"

"What money? Did Tony put you up to this?"

"Shit, Jack. Don't play fucking dumb. Did they give you the cut they've been talking about?"

"No. I told them to keep it. To use it for Michal's funeral."

Moving fast, Maxine kicks Jack once across the face with her bare foot in a wide-arcing roundhouse. He sees her panties when she's doing it, sees she's just got on a thin lace thong under her shirt, and part of him is more turned on than hurt. Then he's sur-

prised that it didn't knock him down or out of his chair and he
touches his face.

"That was your warning, Jack," she says. "The next one is real."
He realizes she only meant to touch his face with her foot, that she
could've done worse. She still has the gun aimed at him and now
Jack's in the uncomfortable position of being turned on, pinned
down, and not sure what will happen next.

He holds up his hands, a motion that's starting to feel too familiar. "You really going to shoot me, Max?"

She blows a few hairs out of her face, holds the gun steady with
both hands. "I haven't decided yet. You going to tell me the truth
about the money?"

"So you've been with Tony the whole time?"

"Shut up," she says. Behind her the kettle starts to whistle, and
she half-turns to shut off the flame, keeping the gun trained on
Jack. She takes a step back from him to stand beside the stove.

"The money's in the trunk of my car. You want it?" Jack goes to
take the keys out of his pocket, and she shakes the gun, juts it out at
him. "Relax. I'm just going for my keys." He sits back and takes the
keys out of his jacket pocket, holds them in front of him. "Is this
because I wasn't a good enough lover?" he asks.

She shakes her head. Her eyes look big in her face.

"Because I've been getting these emails that tell me how I can
get better—"

"Shut up!" she yells, and takes a step toward Jack. He throws his
keys at her face and she turns, shying away from the flying object as
he'd hoped, and he throws himself onto the floor at her feet, his
legs on either side of hers; he scissors her calves between his legs
and rolls over, taking her down onto the floor of the kitchen. Her
gun goes off as she's falling—it's loud but not as bad as the guns
going off in the car—and Jack grabs her hands, wrestles the gun up
over her head and then knocks her arms against the floor until she
drops it. She's trying to knee him in the stomach or the groin, but
he's got his legs still tight around hers and she can't accomplish
more than a pronounced squirm against him.

"Fuck, Jack. Fuck. You. Jack," she's saying.

"Maxine," he says. Their faces are close but there's no intimacy now that she's trying to break away from him and has just held him at gunpoint. "Did you just want the money?"

She doesn't say anything; her lips are pale with how tight she's holding them closed; her face is furious.

"Max," he says. "Why couldn't we just relax together when this was over?"

"Because fuck you, Jack. You think I just like dragging guys I don't know home and taking care of them? You think that's my idea of fun?"

Jack wants to let her go, but she's still fighting. It seems so crazy that they're on the floor of her kitchen, their bodies pressed against one another, his legs around hers and both of their arms over their heads, and yet she's trying to kill him. "I actually liked you," he says, feeling like an idiot.

"Yeah, well that was dumb, wasn't it, Jack?"

He kisses her on the cheek. "You're the one who was dumb, Max. What's Tony giving you?"

"Fuck! Why don't you just let me go and leave?"

"OK," Jack says. He holds her arms with one hand so that he can take the gun off the floor, and then he pushes her back and sits up, pointing the gun at her. "Don't get up just yet," he says. "Let's us talk for a minute."

She pulls her shirt down around her thighs and sits up, legs crossed, with her hands in her lap. Jack moves back slowly, reaching behind him. He finds the chair and sets it right, sits down. "Now," he says.

"What do you want Jack?" Her eyes are cool, without any of the emotion he thought he'd seen in them in the past few days.

"I guess I just want to know why."

"You really going to shoot me?"

Jack looks at the gun. She's been staring at it, and now he has a look at it himself. "I don't know," he says. "Would you have shot me?"

She turns her head to look away, then down at her hands. She shakes her head. "Tony wanted me to follow you and see what went down."

"But that doesn't make sense. He found out about The Mirage from Castroneves. So why'd he need you too?"

She looks up, and Jack can see tears in her eyes. "He just wanted me to stay with you in case anything happened. He didn't know that you guys'd be dumb enough to meet *in his club*." She laughs, looks down at her hands, plays with the silver ring on one of her fingers. "I told him no for as long as I could. I swear it, Jack."

He puts the gun down on the table. "Didn't you feel anything this whole time?"

"I don't know." She nods. "Yes." She stands up and looks at the gun, but Jack's got his hand over it. There's a moment where he can see her considering another run at him, but then it passes.

"Good decision," he says.

She moves back to the stove. "You want some tea?"

"Why don't you just sit down with me at the table." He points to the chair across from him: a good distance from the kettle, any knives, any heavy objects. She moves across the kitchen and sits down.

"So," he says. "What was in that for you?"

She sits down, fixes her shirt around her shoulders and tightens it to her body. She shrugs. "I did this for Tony," she says. "He asked me to and so I did it."

Jack feels like he just realized half-way through his marriage that he's been spending his time with someone he doesn't really know. It's not unlike what happened with Victoria. It took him a lot longer to see what was really happening there, but this isn't so different. It really all just comes back to trust: Jack trusting the wrong person— the wrong woman—yet again. He tries not to wince.

Maxine laughs once, covers her face. "Oh, Jack," she says.

"Tony Vitelli. You did all this for him?"

She nods. "He's the boss."

"What's he giving you?"

"Money, dumbass. Bartending I'm making like a hundred a night, if I hustle; then you walk in, Tony offers me five grand to watch you and keep him up to date on the Czechs. That seem like a hard decision?"

Jack looks down at the gun on the table, frowns. "It's a hard decision if you don't consider yourself a prostitute."

She hits the table hard, with both hands. "You motherfucker!" Maxine starts to stand, but Jack takes the handle of the gun, grips it properly again. He holds it on her until she sits back down.

"Get the fuck out of my house."

"I'll leave." Jack stays where he's sitting, looks around the small kitchen. He's not sure of what to say next yet, can't believe that she's actually rolled him over. "For fucking Tony?" he says. "That sleaze ball?"

She shakes her head. "Green money, Jack."

"You fucking him, too?"

Then, before he can lift the gun, she's standing; she swings and connects with his face as he lifts the gun. He takes the hard slap and nods. "OK," he says, though it hurts. "I guess I deserved that." He touches his cheek. "If you are I don't want to know, I guess. Matter of fact, I don't care."

"Think whatever you want, Jack. You're an asshole." She sits back down.

"Tell me why Tony's so hot after the Czechs."

She shrugs. "He's got something going with a guy who knows them. That's what I *think*. Some guy from over there." She waves her hand toward the living room, beyond. "This guy is a whole new line for white products: pills and powder. He's Tony's new guy. Now he has a problem with your friends. Turns out he wants to know where they are, what they do, what they're involved with. It becomes Tony's concern."

"What's he look like?"

"He's bald. Ugly bald. Bad beard. That's all I know."

Jack shakes his head, still unable to believe that she's been working for Tony the whole time. "Didn't you know I'd get the money, that it'd be worth more to you to be with me?"

She laughs. "Yeah. I see all that money rolling in from the DVD sales of 'Shake Me Down' just falling off of you. No offense, Jack. Your house is nice, but if you plan on entertaining, you should lose some of the 'third notice—unpaid' envelopes off your dining room table."

Jack nods, stands up from the table. "That's cool, Max. I see how it is. You couldn't wait. I have the bag of money outside, actually, and all you want is to relieve me of the whole amount. Right? Take it at gunpoint?" He walks close to her, holding the gun down by his side. "That's good, Maxine. Nice way to be." He reaches to touch her face and she slaps his hand away.

"OK," he says, walking out of the kitchen. "Then thanks for the bandage job. You did a good job of patching me up."

He lets the door close softly behind him, doesn't give her the pleasure of hearing it slam.

40

In the car he goes straight for his pack, doesn't even bother to try and hold back from smoking. He's got about ten cigarettes left, half the pack, and if he goes through that tonight, it's fine with him.

Then he's driving and for a while he's not even sure where he's headed. It occurs to him that he's got to go to The Coast, but he needs Niki with him, at least, so he heads for the hotel.

Jack can't quite wrap his mind around what happened with Maxine: that she was playing him the whole time. There was that part of him that never trusted her, and then she made that part seem so wrong. So much for the idea that he has to trust somebody, or maybe he just has to be more careful about who that person is. Jack knows he's done it wrong now twice at least with women, fucked up and let them take him down, mess him up. He can only be glad this didn't cost him as much as his time with Victoria. Maybe he should just give up on trust for a while. Maxine did him successfully, made him play her game, but he still doesn't understand why. It's just another question for Tony Vitelli.

He just wants a drink more than anything else now, thinks of himself at a bar with the smokes and a scotch in his hand. Then he lets himself think about going up to the Czechs and joining them in the powder, and it's the first time that he's thought like that in a long while. He shakes his head and puts out his cigarette, curses into the empty car. He knows she hurt him bad if his mind goes that far, if he's that far out of where he'd worked himself back to being. But the temptation's been there for the past few days, the whole time this thing's been going on. What he needs now is to just finish it up, go back to Sausalito, get back into his routine, or maybe even leave town for a while, head up to Seattle or the San Juan Islands, even Vancouver. He can get away and let it all blow over, which it hopefully will, and then worry about getting healthy again.

But what he needs now is to get through this; he takes a new cigarette out of the pack and lights it up.

At the Regis, he leaves the car outside and goes right to the bank of elevators for the penthouse. When the operator sees Jack, he recognizes him and takes him right up. In the car he looks himself over again, checks his reflection in the doors and actually decides that he looks better now that he's had it out with Maxine and he's determined to get this thing over with. There's a new look of determination on his face that's stronger than coffee, overcomes even the exhaustion he'd seen before.

"You guys are having some night, it looks like," the operator says to Jack.

Jack looks at him, a kid not more than twenty, working his way through the night at a fancy hotel. He nods. "It's all good times with us."

"You were in a movie, right?"

Jack shakes his head. "You must be thinking of somebody else."

The doors open, and Jack sees David and Al sitting on the couches, watching TV. Al's got his hand in a bucket of ice. "You're back," David says. He doesn't get up, just raises his glass: another scotch.

"Boys," Jack says. "I need a drink." They point him to the bar, and Jack walks over. Al gets up off the couch and comes with him carrying the bucket of ice. He starts to question Jack about what's happening next. Jack has his hand on the decanter of scotch, whatever they're drinking, and he's going to tell Al to sit back down when he hears Vlade.

"Jack's back!" Vlade comes out of one of the rooms, holding a small travel bag. "What is up, Jack?"

Jack laughs. "You want the good news, or the bad?"

"Good news, of course." Vlade comes around the outside of the room and over to the bar. He claps Al on the back and takes a low-ball glass off the shelf, pours it half-full from the decanter that's still in Jack's hand.

"Where's Niki?"

"Niki is sleeping. But we will get him up."

"You call my name?" Niki stands on the far side of the room in a pair of pajama bottoms. His chest bare, Jack can see he's wider in the shoulders than he expected, and big through the chest.

Vlade takes the bottle out of Jack's hand, pours another lowball and adds a few chunks of ice from the refrigerator. He puts the glass into Jack's hand, where the bottle had been. "The good news, Jack."

"Shit," Jack says. Even now, this close, he thinks of what he's seen drinking do to Victoria, what he remembers it did to his father, and he puts down the scotch. "I need a coffee."

Vlade laughs and claps Jack on the shoulder. He gives him a light slap on the face, just enough to touch and not hurt—it gets the point across.

"OK. The good news is that Junius is getting sprung from prison as we speak. How's that for good?"

Vlade raises his lower lip and tilts his head at the same time, as if he's considering this and isn't entirely sold on its merit. He takes a drink, shakes his head. "And the bad news?" he says.

"Maxine sold me out. She was working for Tony this whole time."

"Oh!" they all make the sound at once, a communal groan.

"Ouch," Vlade says. "Shit, Jack."

This even gets David to turn around on the couch and look at Jack with a long face. Al just shakes his head. He puts down the bucket of ice and pours himself another scotch.

Niki comes into the room. "What is next?" he asks.

"The Coast, baby. It's definitely time to take Tony Vitelli *down*."

"Shake him down!" Al says.

Vlade puts his hand on Jack's shoulder. "You sure you are up to that tonight?"

Jack shakes his head. "Fuck. This is the time and I see plenty of reasons. I came to recruit guns and drink scotch. And I'm not drinking scotch, so who's coming?"

Niki raises his hand, disappears back into his room to get changed. Vlade says, "Your friend on the police. Why can't you just tell him to arrest Tony? Why do you have to go there?"

"I don't know," Jack says. "He wants names and faces, who's doing what in this town. It's not just about Tony, it's about finding his supply, finding out what he has going with Maxine. It might be about finding his connection to the K.G.B. I want to find out for myself what happened to Ralph, who sent the guys that shot up my car, who killed Ralph's dog. I want no guesses, so I can rest when this is all over. I'm not going home until I find out for sure."

"What guesses?"

Jack takes a step back and counts them out on his fingers. "Maxine working for Tony? That's not a guess. She told me she was. Junius getting put in the lock-up as part of Tony's design to help get him off the streets, I still don't know for sure, but Tony didn't go in. That's one. Tony killing Ralph and sending the Russians who shot Michal, that I still don't know. That's two big ones. Why would someone kill Ralph?" He looks at his hand, and then puts it on Vlade's shoulder. "This guy with the beard being Tony's new supply? I'm getting close on that one but I want to know it for sure. I still don't know what're my guesses and what I've actually figured out. That's what's killing me."

"Why not go home, Jack? Wait it out and let the police sort through this?" Vlade puts his opposite arm on Jack's shoulder so now they're in a kind of odd yin-yang embrace. "Take the money and relax, as they say."

Now Jack gives Vlade a light slap on the face and he takes his hand off Vlade's shoulder. He steps away. "I can't do that, V. The money will be there. I can go home to rest tomorrow." Part of Jack wonders if maybe Vlade's right, but the greater part of him knows he won't sleep for weeks thinking of the Russians or Freeman knocking at his windows, wants to ride this thing out so he can personally put all the pieces in place. "Tonight I got to get to the bottom of this. Tomorrow I go home and know that the people who killed Ralph and put Maxine up to this are taken care of, that they're not going to come looking to find me. That," he says. "That, Vlade, is for *me*."

41

Jack calls and leaves a message on Junius's cell phone for him to call back when he gets out of the clink, and then not five minutes later, he calls back: "Yo, Jack! It's J."

"That was fast, man." Jack's still in the Czechs' penthouse, drinking room service coffee now and standing close to the windows, looking out at the night skyline. "Nice work."

"Shit, man. You're the one did the work. Now tell me what's next."

Jack takes a sip of the hot coffee, liking the way it burns going down. It's not scotch, but it'll leave him one-hell-of-a-lot better off for what he's getting into tonight, and keeps his two-year wagon intact. He rests his forehead against the glass. "We take The Coast," Jack says.

"That's what I wanted to hear."

"We go into The Coast and say hello to Tony. My sergeant on the force needs a bust out of this shit bad, and I need to give him one: the new supplier. Bad as I want Tony, I'm going down there to piece this shit together for myself, and then we send in the cops."

"I like the sound of that as long as I get to say what's up to the man Tony, myself."

"Freeman with you?"

"Yeah. He here. Where you want us to meet you at?"

Twenty minutes later, Jack pulls up next to Junius's Mercedes on Minna, a small street parallel to Market, just one block south and not yet into SOMA. In the Fastback, Jack's got Vlade next to him up front, and Niki in the back.

Junius rolls down his window. "Ow! Jack Palms. That's one *damn* nice ride! '67?"

"'66," Jack tells him. "K-code."

"Fuck! Hi-po! Those things are rare as shit. You just rose up about ten pegs in my book, son."

"Thanks. This afternoon some of these fucks shot up my driver's side. That's another reason I'm here." Jack tells Junius who Vlade is and they lean forward to see Freeman wedged into the front passenger seat of the Mercedes like a bull in a chute. He just nods at the two of them, holds up two fingers.

Jack guns the engine of the Mustang, and Junius howls. Then he holds up his hand. "One word, Jack?" he says, opening his door.

Jack looks back over at the Mercedes. "What?"

Junius stands up out of his car, motions to its rear end with his hand. "Let me just talk to you for a second."

Vlade gives Jack a look like he should be careful, that maybe they'd be better off just driving away now, but Jack shakes him off. Vlade takes a gun out from below his seat and presses it against the door, pointing at Junius. Jack looks in back at Niki: he's got his knees pressed up into the air in front of him and he's sunk way back down in the seat. He nods once, pats the side of his jacket.

Jack looks back up the street in his rear-view, making sure no one's coming down behind him, and sees it's empty. At this hour of night, Market may be busy with cabs, but no one's coming down the one-way side-streets; most of them don't even run for more than a few blocks. He gets out of the car and walks around the back to meet Junius at his Mercedes.

Junius waves him closer and walks around to his trunk. "What you need, man?" he says, opening the trunk. Jack sees an array of weapons—guns mostly, but some brass knuckles and knives—that would make most any urban warlord giggle. There, in front of him, the weapons are all neatly laid out inside a foam-covered trunk-liner. He sees a few small automatics, a couple of assault rifles, an assortment of handguns, including a shiny silver Magnum with a barrel long enough to poke your victims' eyes out.

"I'm all right, man," Jack says, holding up his hands. He takes an inadvertent step back away from the trunk.

"No, man. Listen." Junius says, "You might need some of this shit if things get tight in there." Jack looks back at the Mustang: Vlade and Niki watch with their full attention.

"I'm OK." Jack produces Maxine's revolver from his pocket, drops it into the trunk.

"You sure?" Junius asks. "You heard what happened to the Colombian?"

"No."

"Police found his ass in back of The Mirage, stuffed in one of the dumpsters. Motherfucker had *holes* in him, Jack. I mean plural."

"Shit." Jack spits onto the asphalt, rubs it out with the toe of his sneaker. A car starts down the street behind them, its light bright in Jack's eyes. He holds up his arm to shield them from the light. "I'm all right, J.," he says.

Junius grabs his arm. He regards Jack with complete seriousness as he presses the side of a gun against his chest and tells Jack to take it. Jack can feel the gun in his hand: it's warm, like molded black metal made to fit your palm.

"This is the Glock, Jack." As the oncoming car gets closer to where they are, it honks once. Junius pats Jack across his collar. "You'll be glad when you need that."

The car honks again and Junius rushes at it, his hands raised, yelling at the driver to get out and fight or shut the fuck up.

Jack walks back around to his side of the Mustang and gets in. He hands the Glock off to Vlade and guns the engine. Vlade nods at the weapon. "This is good, Jack. A nice gun."

With the driver of the third car sufficiently scared and quieted, Junius goes back to his Mercedes, closes the trunk, and slowly gets in.

"He gave you this?" Vlade says. "Does he think we do not have weapons?"

"I don't know," Jack says. "And I don't care."

42

As they drive to The Coast, Junius follows the Mustang lazily, as if he knows their path even better than Jack, dropping back and then coming up close to them at turns, fading off and drifting behind them for blocks on end. Jack smokes a single cigarette, taking his time to enjoy it. Vlade and Niki smoke too, hurrying through their cigarettes like normal smokers, and Jack watches them, monitoring his own inhales and exhales, watching the road, putting in a tape of some slow bass-heavy jazz to calm his nerves.

For all he knows, he's the only one sober at this point in the night, the only one who's not on coke or something else. Junius was drinking at The Mirage and probably with dinner, and it's Jack's guess from the smell around their car and coming out of the trunk, that he and Freeman smoked something potent after he got out of jail. With a gun he should feel safe, in Junius's view, but Jack actually feels less safe with a loaded weapon. Long term, it just doesn't make sense if he's going to get out of this and go back to his life. He thinks of the bag in the trunk, the bills he's had on his kitchen table for the past few months and how he'll be able to pay them off now, get the bank and the mortgage straightened out, push the credit card bills off his back. Then he'll get back into his routine of healthy living: running, weights, cereal for breakfast. At least that's something to hope for.

But now that all seems dull, boring. Something far away.

They pull up outside The Coast and Jack sees Maxine's VW Bug among the few in the lot. He's seen it a few times in front of her house, and she mentioned it when he dropped her off at home this morning—how that's still part of the same day is more than he can imagine at this point. Thinking back to last night at The Mirage, the shooting feels like last night, but waking up in Sausalito with Maxine this morning feels like months ago. Somehow it seems like the whole arc of their relationship has happened since then.

Now he's sure he'll be awake to see it when the sun comes up in a few hours, and there'll be something good to that. He says to Niki and Vlade, "Breakfast when this is over?"

"Yes," Vlade says. "Fucking steak and eggs, mother-fucker."

Jack laughs at Vlade's accent around the familiar word that he must've picked up from Junius or someone along the way. "That's right," he says.

Jack pulls the Mustang around the corner to park on the side of the club, where the front doormen won't see them coming. Judging by the number of cars, The Coast is close to empty at this hour, not long before closing. There are just two guys at the front door, and they didn't look familiar to Jack as he checked them out driving by.

"You boys ready for this?" Jack asks. He gets out of the car and waits while Niki and Vlade get out on the other side.

"I am ready," Niki says.

Vlade puts his chin to his chest, looks down at his body, his stomach mainly—a small-to-medium-sized protrusion around his middle—and then agrees.

Junius is slow to park his car, getting it into the spot just right, and then gets out, stands wearing a black fleece over his shirt. "Yo!" he says. "Let's do this." He goes around back to his trunk and takes out a black, stocky submachine gun with a big sight on top and something thick below the front barrel. He bounces it a few times in his hands, feeling the weight, and then slams the trunk closed. He looks at Jack. "H and K MP7, motherfucker. Let's roll."

Freeman steps out of the car stretching his arms and cracking his knuckles. He stretches one arm across his chest, then does the same on the other side. Then he hits his chest with his forearms. When he makes fists, his knuckles crack, and Jack can imagine him doing something awful to somebody's head. He's got on big, black warm-up pants and a top that goes with them, and Jack wishes he were wearing the same thing, something more comfortable than the jeans and button-up he's had on all day.

Niki and Vlade have their guns out, look as if they need to be doing something. So Vlade drops the clip out of his weapon and checks to make sure it's full. When he nods, Jack can see that he already knew this would be the case.

"Long night?"

Vlade and Niki agree quickly, Vlade putting one finger over his nostril and inhaling deeply, then putting both hands together on the side of his face, as if they were a pillow, and resting his cheek against them.

He laughs, pushes both eyes open with the first finger and thumb of each hand. "Let's go."

"Plan of attack?"

Junius and Freeman walk over to join Jack and the Czechs. "This place has a front and a back," Junius says. "That's all. Tony's office in the back. That's where he'll be with his boys. Whatever's going on, they be doing it there." He points around the opposite side of the club. "Front is the part you already saw: the tables and stages, the bars. They got some private rooms in there, but those mostly just for hand jobs and shit."

Vlade laughs, tilts his head two inches to the side to grudgingly admit that he knows what Junius means.

"So we will go in the front, you three go in the back?" Niki says, pointing to Jack, Junius, and Freeman.

"I'm not going in shooting, just so you all know," Jack says. "I want to talk with this guy. We find any hard evidence of him killing Ralph or Castroneves, something that can lead us to his supply, I call the cops, we bring the heat down on this place. That's all they want."

"Shit," Junius says. "We can all say boo right now." He looks around at the others. "I'm not saying I'd testify, but we know enough between us to say he killed both Ralph *and* Castroneves."

"And had Michal killed," Niki says.

"No," Vlade says. "That was K.G.B."

"I don't know." Jack kicks the ground. "Why's that Russian with the sweater still hanging around? If he's not hooked to those guys, what were they doing at The Mirage?"

Vlade shakes his head. He looks at his gun and then at Jack. "That is what we need to know."

"Right." Niki looks firm in his readiness to go in and get something done. "What about Maxine?"

Vlade puffs out his lower lip, shakes his head at Niki.

"No," Jack says. "That's all right." He points at the club. "I think she'll be inside. She said something about that guy being Tony's new supplier. We'll just have to find out."

"Oh," Niki says. "I am sorry."

Junius cocks his gun and the parts engage, make a locking sound. "This your girl, Jack?"

"Was. Maybe."

Junius squints, grimaces. He looks like he's imagining one of his women ending up with Tony Vitelli. "Shit," he says. "Come on, then. Let's do this."

Jack starts to walk around the back of the club with Junius and Freeman. Niki and Vlade say something in Czech and then start for the front door. As they go around the other side, Jack loses sight of them. The outside walls of The Coast are all black, tall—about two stories, though it's all one high-ceilinged level inside—with a small parking lot stretched around the perimeter in the area the real estate allows. Where they are in SOMA, there are a couple of streetlights on the street and not much else: cars and taxis going past to get to or from the Bay Bridge, and just a few people walking from the clubs to their cars. After the regular bars close, places like this stay open for "After Hours," but it's officially late, part of the night where you can already start to feel some of the pain you're going to be feeling the next day.

Freeman looks like he's had some sleep, though reading him is like reading a vending machine; he's moving all right, fluid and without any hitches, but Jack can't guess what the big man's thinking. He'd guess Freeman caught a few hours of sleep somewhere in the night before Junius started calling to pick him up, but he can't tell for sure.

Junius still wears his suit pants, but the tie is long gone. Jack still wishes he had on something more like the warm-up suit he wore back when he went to Ralph's.

In his mind, he's not all there; the day and the lack of sleep in the past few days is getting to him. But he tells himself that it'll all be over soon, that if he takes care of this he'll be able to sleep in his own bed instead of a small cell with bars for walls for the next few years. And that's compelling. That and the thought of the bills piled up in the leather bag in his trunk. Jack leans his neck toward his shoulders and cracks it, pulls his arms back toward each other behind him, and feels a good crack in his back. There's a release that comes from this, and if there was time, he'd spend a few minutes stretching out and trying to loosen up, get his blood flowing again. But Junius gets to the back door of The Coast and starts banging on it with the back of his fist.

"Stay in the moment," Jack says, just to feel his lips moving over the words.

"Open the fuck up," Junius says, and when one of Tony's boys opens the door just slightly, Junius slams it against him with all his weight, pushing the guy back to the floor. Jack and Freeman follow into a dark corridor with a concrete floor and gray walls. Junius moves to the guy he just knocked down and holds his gun against the guy's temple. He puts his finger over his lips. "Shhh," he says.

Freeman produces a roll of duct tape from somewhere in his pants and rips off a strip that he puts over the guy's mouth. Then he flips him over and runs the duct tape quickly around his hands and feet. Jack's having a hard time hiding how impressed he is with all this precision, actually says, "Wow."

Junius just winks at Jack, once, and points down the hall toward a door not twenty feet away. From farther inside the club, Jack hears the music, Sir Mix-A-Lot doing "Baby's Got Back"—a song that's sure to accompany a special performance on stage. Freeman closes the door behind them and makes sure it locks.

Wondering where the Czechs are, Jack stops for a moment, thinking, but Junius is already headed down the hall.

43

They come to a door and Junius puts his head against it. After listening for a few seconds, he points at it and whispers, "They in there."

"OK." Jack nods. "Do this."

Junius and Freeman exchange a glance, and that's when Freeman kicks the door open, loud and hard. Junius jumps into the opening, yelling, "Boo!" After a quick look to see the scene inside, Jack follows Freeman into the room.

What they come into is a big play den for Tony and some of his boys. It's something of an extension to the club: there's a big glass window on the back wall that you can see the girls on stage through, the other side of a two-way mirror—Jack realizes—the lights dim enough inside the room to keep it reflective on the other side. Tony sits behind a big desk off on the right-hand side with a significant pile of blow, about the size of a softball, and a small mountain of white pills that must be ecstasy piled up in front of him. He starts nodding when Junius walks in and then laughs when he sees Jack. He reaches up to the back of his head and straightens his pony tail, pulling it tight. "Jack Palms," he says. "This is fucking hilarious. Call this your next movie, right?"

"I'll get you as the big star," Jack says.

Tony laughs. "But this ain't no play acting here." He looks around the room. "And I don't see any stunt doubles to protect you, you fuck."

In the middle of the room, two of Tony's bouncers in black shirts have been playing pool with one of the clean-cut, slick bouncers from The Mirage. Now they stop and stand, holding their pool cues and looking at Jack and the other visitors. Two of them are the ones who beat Jack up when he got under Tony's skin a few nights ago, The Surfer and a black guy with a shaved head that reflects the ceiling lights. These two smile especially wide smiles at him. The other one is the asshole from outside The Mirage, the one who wouldn't answer Jack's question, one of the clean-cut professionals.

The shiny Bald Head says, "We're glad to see you back here, Jackie."

Another guy leans against the pool table, smoking. He's got on khaki pants and a light blue polo shirt. He looks at Jack with pure contempt. He's hard to place without the uniform, but Jack remembers his face from somewhere he's been with Hopkins, maybe from the Hall of Justice.

Beyond the pool table, on the left, is a sectional leather couch with Maxine stretched across one part, lying back with her wrist on her forehead. She sees them come in, doesn't make a move to sit up or change position. "Jack," she says, smiling. "What a dumbass."

The bald Russian with the beard sits bolt upright on another section of the couch, smoking a long cigarette out of a plastic holder. He's got his other arm draped over the back of the couch, an automatic resting on one of his thighs. The way he looks, the gun seems like the furthest thing from his mind. He touches his moustache with the first fingers of his cigarette hand as if he's considering the situation.

"No, movie man," Tony says, "No stunt doubles here."

Jack says, "Right. Just you, your stooges, a cop, and a Russian mobster."

Junius steps farther into the room, waving the gun around to make sure everyone sees it.

Tony stands up, clapping his hands. "That is very good, Junior. Nice work with the flashing of your thing there. How are you with the business end?"

Junius points his gun straight ahead, between two of Tony's guys, The Surfer and the Bald Head, and lets off a few shots into the wood side of the pool table. They both jump back, but the cop stays put. The Professional throws his cue down on the floor. On stage, the stripper keeps dancing, kicking her legs high, the music bumping through the wall.

"Fuck!" Tony says. "That's a three thousand dollar table, you fuck! What are you thinking?"

Junius holds the gun up, makes a show of blowing off the barrel. "I was just checking to see I could shoot this thing." He holds the gun out away from his body as if he's looking it over, and then levels its barrel at Tony. "I'd say I can."

Tony raises his hands lackadaisically, as if he's just playing along with a game. "So what is it you boys want? Would you like a share of my coke? Do you want to buy some X? Or," he looks at Junius, "Do you want to know where I get it now? Because I think *that* you must already know."

Jack nods at the guy in khakis and the polo shirt. "Maybe we want to know how you got to be so comfortable with the force here."

Tony laughs. "That's right. You haven't officially met our friend, Officer O'Malley. Sorry I didn't do the introduce."

"Man, fuck." Still aiming the gun at Tony, Junius turns to Freeman. "What is the deal with this guy?"

Freeman cracks his knuckles, starts toward the little man.

"Ah ah hah." Tony waves his finger at Freeman, turns his chin an inch toward the Russian, who now has his gun in his hand, the barrel leveled at Freeman's head. The guy's twenty feet from Freeman and the desk, but his gun has a laser sight on it that shows where he's pointing, even from this far away. Whether Freeman knows it or not, he now has a single bright red dot in the middle of his forehead.

"Man, fuck," Junius says. He turns his gun toward the Russian. "You better put that down."

"Really," the Russian says, still pointing at Freeman. "Had I better?" He raises his eyebrows.

Jack feels the tension in the room rise a few levels. There's a moment when he thinks Junius considers blasting the Russian, blowing him away, wondering whether Freeman would live through it. But it seems there'd be a chain reaction, that somehow the Russian would pull the trigger—at least that's the decision Junius makes; he doesn't do anything.

"Oh, carnage in here," Tony says, stepping around the desk. "Wouldn't that be awful?"

"Shut the fuck up!" Junius turns to hold his gun on Tony and as he does, in the moment of that move, the Russian turns his gun onto him, shines the light across his eyes and then trains it on his chest, over his heart. Junius looks down and sees the bright dot. "Shit," he says, still holding his gun on Tony.

Jack steps forward toward the Russian. "I just want to talk for a minute here. Let's all keep calm."

Now Maxine sits up. "*You're* doing the talking? Why don't you just shut up, Jack?" She's slurring a little, must have been drinking since she arrived. Jack sees an empty glass in front of her on the coffee table.

Tony clicks his tongue against his teeth. "Oh," he says, nodding toward one shoulder. "A lover's quarrel?"

The cop, O'Malley, drops his cigarette on the floor and grinds it out. "This is a nice party you got here, Tony, but I think I should be going. Don't want to interrupt any family business." He steps forward as if to start walking out.

Tony shakes his head. "Why would you leave now, Joe? This is the perfect place for you to be. You just witnessed a breaking and entering. Maybe you'll even get to make some arrests. Hmm?"

The Surfer taps the cop on the shoulder with the thin end of his pool cue, making sure he realizes that Tony's demanding, not offering.

"This shit's getting ugly," Freeman says. He takes a quick step to his side, moving surprisingly fast for a man his size—showing he still has some NFL speed—and reaches out to backhand Tony across the face, knocking him into a cabinet behind his desk. Tony's fall breaks the glass front of the piece, and he drops to the floor. He scrambles up fast and then looks at his hand, holds it up with blood running down the side of his wrist.

"Ahh," Tony says. "Will you look at that?"

Jack realizes he's probably fully coked out of his mind.

Freeman raises his hands, but the Russian says, "Don't!" loud enough to stop him before he can move on Tony again.

"Can you please waste these fucks right now?" Tony asks the Russian.

The Russian tilts his head, as if considering this possibility. Then he shakes just the middle of his face—just his mouth and nose—holding his head still. "No. Not *quite* yet." He looks at Freeman. "Though one of those is certainly enough. OK, friend?"

Freeman backs a step away from Tony.

"Very well," the Russian says. "Now here's what *I'd* like to know." He takes a long time making a very pronounced move to fix his gaze on Jack. Then he raises his eyebrows. "Where are your Eastern-European friends? I believe I have some business with them."

Jack looks away from the Russian; something about the way his eyebrows rise up on his bald head—it almost looks like they've become his hairline, gone beyond his forehead—creeps Jack out. He looks out of the two-way mirror and sees a big-busted stripper wrap her arms around her back and undo the tie of her top. She's bringing the ends around, when suddenly she stops, screams and drops out of sight below the bottom edge of the mirror.

Jack hears a gunshot, and a second outside in the main room: shots from handguns.

He turns back to the Russian, who's got his gun still on Junius but his attention in the direction of the mirror. Jack says, "I'd say that's them outside now."

44

From outside in the club, Jack hears the spray of an automatic weapon followed by a scream. The Russian looks at Jack, expectant. Jack shakes his head. "*That* is not them."

The spray of the automatic comes again, and Jack hears glass breaking, shouting, a chandelier falling and crashing to the floor. Women are screaming in the larger part of the club. Tony looks like an animal that's just gone on full alert: his eyes opened wide and his back straight to raise his ears higher. He points at his bouncers, and they start for a separate door out the back of the room, behind the pool table, just to the right side of the two-way mirror. As they start to move, the shots come again, and the mirror shatters. Shards of glass burst into the room and onto the pool table. The three of them hit the deck as glass showers them in crystals. Then big pieces of the glass fall from the top and bottom of the frame, some breaking on the way down, some smashing against the floor. The cop is crouched low, almost under the table.

From a crouch—Jack ducked at the sound of the automatic tearing through the mirror—he notices that the others are down as well, but that the Russian still sits with his gun trained on Junius. The music in the exterior of the club blasts into the room for a few beats of something and then stops altogether. For a moment, they're surrounded by silence.

"Motherfuckers!" Tony says. "What the fuck is happening out there?"

Then, from the other side of the wall, Jack hears, "Puta madre! Maricon! Come out here Vitelli!"

Tony waves at his boys to go see what's happening on the other side of the wall. They get up slowly, brushing the glass off their clothes, looking at him like he's the insane bastard he is. But then slowly they start toward the door. Just then the little annoying guy, The Talker, comes in through the back door, the one Jack and Junius came in. He trips and falls on the floor as he comes into the room, and then pulls himself up to a sitting position. There's blood covering his leg and half of his body.

"Who's out there?" Tony demands. He's crawled behind the desk for protection, but stands up to see his little manager, hear his report.

"Mexicans, Mr. Vitelli. There are Mexicans with fucking Uzis out there!"

Jack looks at Junius, who's looking back at him. They both nod in agreement, and then they both say it at the same time, not loud, but they know the word when they see it mouthed: "Colombians!"

Again, Tony waves at his boys. "Get out there!" He throws a set of keys across the room and points at a large gun cabinet next to the door. "Get yourselves some fucking artillery!" The Surfer picks the keys up off the floor and starts to open the cabinet.

Jack looks at Junius to see his lead, but Junius is watching this all happen, just like Jack is. He's pointing the gun around the room at Tony's guys and at Tony, but never staying on one target for long. He slowly backs toward the wall.

Then Jack feels a punch in the back of his neck, and he turns to see Maxine falling onto him, swinging wildly. Before he can move, she's on top of him, her weight taking them both to the floor. Once they're down, Jack's able to roll her off of him. He pushes her away and slides back from her kicks. She's got her hands and feet flying; where she was a tough woman before, now she's just a drunk trying to kick and punch blindly. Jack grabs her wrists and wards off her feet with the other hand, pushing her away. Then he stands and keeps backing up.

"Fuck you, Jack Palms," she screams, sitting up.

"What did you guys do to her?" Jack looks at Tony, but he's watching his men head back towards the far door. Now holding shotguns, they move toward the door slowly, and then The Professional breaks through it, fires off two shots and falls back in. Jack's watching The Surfer, hoping he'll go through the door next and catch a few shots in the chest. Then The Surfer and The Pro push their way out, followed by more shooting, and the spray of the machine gun comes again. Jack's hoping it finds them both between the eyes.

Jack takes another step back and walks into the Russian, still watching Maxine to make sure she doesn't make any more crazy moves. "Excuse me," the Russian says, pushing Jack to the side. He has his gun trained on the door behind the pool table, following the bouncers' movements out into the club. Junius is doing the same, watching with his gun ready.

Maxine starts to get up, and Jack holds out his hands in front of him, his arms straight. He yells, "Stay down!" and thankfully she does, whether from his suggestion or fear of more shooting, he's not sure.

The door that Jack came in opens again, this time hitting The Talker in his back. He winces and drags himself toward Tony's desk, holding his leg. "What the fuck is wrong with you?" Tony says, handing him a gun from his desk. "Get your little ass up and get out there."

Vlade and Niki come into the room through the open door now, their guns raised. When Vlade sees the Russian, he trains his gun on him immediately, but the Russian already has his laser dot over Vlade's heart. They each say something in another language.

Beyond them, The Talker shows Tony where he's been shot, and asks him to call an ambulance. Tony tells him to fuck off, grab a gun and get back out there. At this the little guy pulls in his breath and collects himself. Then he tells Tony to fuck off. He raises himself up to standing by using the desk. "Fuck this whole place," he says, and starts to make his way toward the door, attempting to push Niki out of the way. But before he can get five steps, Tony raises the handgun he'd offered, says, "This fucking place is home to you, you ungrateful motherfuck," and shoots him in the back.

This breaks the standoff between Vlade and the Russian for a moment, as they all turn toward Tony.

"What the fuck are you doing?" Junius says.

Then Freeman moves on Tony again, grabs his hand and takes the gun away. He knocks Tony back down onto the chair behind his desk. "Stay there, little white man," Freeman orders.

Jack wants to cross the room to get to Tony, find out what's been going on, the truth about what he's guessed at and pieced together, whether he's the one who had Ralph killed, but the Russian and Vlade are in his way. Junius starts toward the far door where Shiny Bald Head is trying to find something to shoot at with the shotgun. He does, shoots, and falls back into the room. Then he reloads and looks up at the others. "What the fuck are you all waiting for? Stop looking at me and shoot these motherfuckers!" He turns out into the club again, fires off a shot.

Junius starts toward the door.

"What the fuck is going on out there?" Jack says to Vlade and Niki.

Niki's got his gun trained on Tony. "Did this motherfucker kill Ralph?"

"You're God-damned right I killed that pig. That fat fuck was taking good business out of my hands. He can't come in here and do business right under my nose and not expect me to get in on it! He can't hold me out of my business here in my own club. That fuck shouldn't even have tried. And I used your fucking thugs, Junius."

Junius looks at Jack and nods.

"Hell yes!" Tony yells. "But that didn't get you locked up because the police are too fucking stupid to put two and two together."

Junius says, "You a real dumb bastard, you know that. I don't have no connection to these crazy-ass Russians." He looks at the bald Russian, sizes him up from his feet up to his head. Then he says, "No offense," tilting his head at the Russian's feet. "When you came in with product, our business ended." He looks back at Tony, trains his gun on him.

Maxine, having lost her floor space to Vlade and Niki, has now crawled away from the standoff between the Czechs and the Russian, and reached the couch. She crawls up onto it and then goes over the back like any smart person would when surrounded by this many guns. Jack sees the last of her tight jeans going over the back.

"No," the Russian says. "You are nothing." He waves his hand at Junius. "Small business. *Now*," he looks at Tony, the two piles on his desk. "Now we sell directly to his clubs. Make real money here."

"So who killed Ralphie's dog?" Jack asks, looking at the Russian. "Was it your boys?"

The Russian makes a face with his lower lip pushed up, tilts his head to the side. "It had to be done," he says. "But you have killed those who did it now."

"The K.G.B. fucks," Vlade says.

"So you're the fuck who sent them to shoot up my car?" Jack moves toward the Russian.

The Russian says something to Vlade in another language and fires a shot into Vlade's shoulder. From this short a distance, Vlade's shoulder looks like it explodes with the impact of the shot; he doesn't just fall back, blood shoots up out of his shoulder onto his face and into the air. Vlade stumbles back a few steps, swearing in Czech.

Jack is on the Russian before even thinking about it, before anything else can happen; he's flying at his upper half, taking him down from the top, his arms around the Russian's shoulders and neck as they fall to the floor of the room. The Russian lands hard under him—Jack's done this enough times in football to know how to make the impact of the fall go fully into the other guy—and his head hits the floor. In the moment he's stunned, Jack pushes the gun out of his hand and slides it toward Niki. But now the Russian starts punching, hitting Jack in the side of the head from underneath him. Jack tries to pin the Russian's arm, but he knees Jack in the side, and suddenly Jack's off him, on his hands and knees. From a crouch, the Russian punches him in the ribs, hard enough that his world goes black for a second with the pain. Jack falls against the couch, holding his side—he'd almost forgotten about his ribs, but now they're his whole world again, a world of red. Jack rolls onto his back, eyes closed. He hears Niki yell something and, thankfully, the Russian doesn't hit him any more.

For a few seconds, Jack only knows internal space: the loud sounds of his own breath struggling to get in and out of his body, his heart beating. Then a full breath comes, its sound resonant, and finally another brings light back to the room.

And sound: the blasting spray of the machine gun comes again from out in the club.

When Jack opens his eyes, he sees Niki over the Russian, one hand holding the Russian's neck and the other pressing the muzzle of his gun to the Russian's temple. Niki says something Jack can't understand.

Holding his side, Jack rolls on the floor and against the couch. He opens and closes his eyes for a few breaths and gradually the pain ebbs back to the point where he sees the world without a circle of small dots of light around the edge of his vision. He sees Vlade standing against the wall, holding his shoulder. Vlade has his gun pointed at the Russian, but he's clearly in a great deal of pain. He says to Niki, "Just kill him."

Tony yells to the room, "Will someone tell me what's going on out there?"

"It is the Colombians," Vlade says, through clenched teeth. Then he makes himself inhale a deep breath and he raises his chest from the sternum; he gets up off the wall and opens his eyes completely. "There are guys out there with automatic weapons, as you know. They are shooting."

Junius turns to Tony. "They want your ass, you fuck. Come over here." He waves his gun at Tony to come around the desk. As soon as Tony stands up, Freeman grabs him and throws him across the desk, onto the floor in front of it. Tony's foot goes through the stash of blow and knocks a good-sized portion of it into the air. Tony knows this even before he hits the ground, starts screaming about *his blow*.

Jack pushes himself up to sit against the couch. The pain in his ribs has gone from an inferno to a three-alarm-fire. He concentrates on his breathing.

"Fuck your blow," Junius says, shooting into the pile of white. This sends more of the coke into the air and breaks through the leather back of Tony's chair, shatters glass in the cabinet behind his desk. Junius starts laughing in a way Jack doesn't feel comfortable about.

"Ahh, guys?" The cop starts to get up from underneath the pool table, his hands raised above his shoulders. "I'm just going to leave now, OK?"

Junius, Freeman, Tony and Niki all look at him and yell, "No!"

Outside the room, the volleys of automatic fire have ceased. Jack can see Shiny Bald Head standing at the door with a shotgun, but The Surfer and The Pro are still out in the club. Jack hears a shotgun blast, then another. The automatic follows it with another volley.

"The fuck is going on out there?" Jack says, not loud enough for anyone to hear.

Niki looks at Jack, still holding the Russian down. "Are you OK?"

"Give me a few minutes." Jack touches his lips and checks his fingers for blood.

Then Jack hears a scream and more yelling in Spanish. To the side of Vlade, the door Jack came in bursts open, and a small man wearing mirrored sunglasses and a loud shirt bursts in holding an Uzi. He sprays in the direction of the pool table, and Vlade simply raises his arm from pointing down at the Russian to point at the guy's head, and fires from about three feet away. The guy drops to the floor without the top of his head, blood draping the back of the door. Jack hears more shooting from automatics that sound like they're getting closer, and he ducks for cover beside the couch. It sounds like one or two people come over the stage and through the mirrored window. When Jack looks up, he sees two Colombians on top of the pool table spraying Tony's desk, sending more blow up into the air, and shooting Tony to pieces: he's crouched on the floor and stands up as the bullets start tearing through him. He takes one, one-and-a-half steps toward the pool table and the Colombians, raises his arms and yells at them to fuck themselves. All the time they're still shooting him, and bullet holes are riddling his body. Finally, his face and chest torn apart from the shots, his knees collapse and he falls to the floor in a pool of his own blood.

Jack can't see the far door where the bouncers are, but he sees one of the guys on the pool table shoot in that direction and then leap up into the air, his arms limp and his middle pushed back as if he's just been shot at close range with a shotgun. Maxine's screaming from the other side of the couch, and the Russian knocks Niki to the floor with his legs. Niki aims at the Russian, but now he's got his hands on the gun too, over Niki's, and it goes off. "Stop," Vlade says, but now he's crouched against the wall; he holds the gun at the guy on the pool table. Niki and the Russian wrestle.

Jack can't see where Junius is, but soon he hears the isolated and regular shots from Junius's gun coming from the far side of the room. He scrambles around to the far end of the couch, where he finds Maxine curled up in a ball with her hands over her ears. She shakes her head when she sees Jack. "I don't like this," she says.

He touches the top of her head, smoothes her hair. "I'm sorry, Max."

But the Russian seems to be gaining an advantage over Niki, so Jack scrambles forward as best he can, and grabs the Russian's arms, pushes them back enough that Niki can pin them over his head. Niki says something that Jack can't make out. Now the automatic fire is coming rapidly all around them, tearing up the couch. Jack gets down flat on his stomach. The Russian and Niki are already flat down. Vlade starts firing in the direction of the pool table, Jack can't see at what, but assumes it's at a Colombian who's going crazy with his Uzi.

Niki starts punching the Russian in the face with his non-shooting hand and knocking his head against the floor. Blood's coming out of the Russian's nose and soon the pressure of him pushing his arms against Jack's hands subsides.

"Shit. Fuck!" Jack hears Junius's voice on the other side of the room come in a scream. He sees Freeman move in a crouch across the wall from the desk to the door that they came in through, and slip out. An abrupt burst of automatic weapons fire comes from the hall, and then it ends just as suddenly as it started.

Jack and Niki exchange a look that Jack wants to mean, *this place has turned into a hell storm*, but Niki has a wild look on his face that contains something different entirely. He sits up and shoots over the back of the couch, at what Jack can't even see. Then there's quiet in the room, a lack of shooting in the club. In the silence, Jack hears Maxine crying at the end of the couch, her sobs consistent and her struggle to breathe in between them, and the other people breathing around him. The Russian's is labored, coming in fits and starts. Vlade's chest is heaving.

"Junius?" Jack calls.

He hears coughing, then, "I'm here," from the far corner of the room.

"You OK?"

More coughing. "I don't know."

Jack starts to sit up, looks around the room: he sees glass and plaster, a thin film of white in the air that might be coke, or plaster dust from the walls, or smoke from gunfire. Lines of bullet holes criss-cross the wall from the desk to beyond the door and over Vlade's head, to the wide screen TV in the corner. This has bullets holes through it too, the screen smashed and destroyed. Vlade's on the floor against the wall, his gun beside him and his hands covering his shoulder. Jack throws him a pillow from the couch, and he presses it to his wound. "Thanks," Vlade says.

"Anybody there?" Jack recognizes the voice of the cop coming from the other side of the room, probably still under the pool table. "I'm coming out now. I'm done here."

"Fuck you!" It's Maxine's voice, coming from the other end of the couch.

The cop comes into the center of the room and turns toward Jack and Niki for a moment. Then he continues in the same direction, heads out the doorway to the hall, and is gone.

Vlade looks at Jack. "Who was that?"

"Crooked cop," Jack says. "That's all I know. But it's OK. I know someone who will know him."

From what Jack can see, the area behind the desk is a mess of destruction: the cabinet where Tony held some trophies—they look like baseball and Little-League—and a few china plates, crap really, is all shot up and broken far beyond what happened when Freeman knocked him into it. Now the shelves themselves hang at odd angles, their items in pieces. The chair-back is broken, cut off with bullets and hanging backward, holding on by a piece of leather at one side. Slowly rising to a crouch and higher, Jack sees a couple of Colombians, Alex Castroneves' guys for sure, splayed out on the pool table, the two-way mirror completely broken out, glass all around them.

As Jack stands, he sees Tony lying on the floor in front of his desk. He thinks it's Tony, what's left of him: in a great deal of blood, Jack can make out Tony's ponytail, his black clothes. He sees one of his hands and can recognize the rings. He's been more than significantly sprayed by fire from the automatics.

Through the space where the mirror used to be, Jack sees the wreckage of the club: tables turned over and most of the bottles and glass shattered with automatic weapons fire. On the far side of the room, a woman holding a dressing gown to her chest walks across the floor. When she sees Jack, she screams and raises her hands beside her shoulders, still holding the gown to her body with her arms. When Jack shows her his own hands are empty, she smiles, crying steadily, her makeup running down her face in streaks. She keeps walking toward the front exit of the club. No one else moves outside. One of the front door bouncers lies draped across a table, and on the floor a couple of Colombians lie cut up with bullets, losing what's left of their blood.

Niki stands too now, still holding his gun on the Russian. "Shit," he says. "This did not go well."

"Yeah," Jack says. "That's the truth. Other than the fact that we're alive."

He carefully makes his way around the couch to make sure there's no life on the pool table: just two dead Colombians. Beyond them, by the door to the club, Shiny Bald Head is crumpled against the wall, still holding the shotgun in his arms, but with a line of black across his chest and red underneath it, where one of the Uzis cut across him at close range.

Just to be secure about the Colombians, Jack takes the automatics—both Uzis, hot to the touch—and slides them on the floor into the corner, away from anyone else. He hears Junius cough from behind the desk. "Jack?"

Jack turns toward the desk and as he does, through the far door, he gets a look at The Surfer and The Pro, both still holding shotguns, laid out on the floor in a great deal of blood. They look as if they set up behind a table turned on its side, but somehow lost this cover or got shot up—what's left of them does anyway.

Jack walks over to the desk as Niki takes out a set of flex-tie handcuffs and puts them around the Russian's wrists, attaching him to one of the legs of the couch.

"Junius?" Jack says.

"Yeah, man."

Coming around the end of the desk, Jack finds Junius pressed up against the wall in an awkward pose, his shoulders hunched against his chest, as if he's fallen into this position and it's not one he would choose. His gun rests next to him on the floor.

Junius shakes his head. "I'm fucked up, man," he says. He coughs, and a bubble of blood forms over his mouth, then pops. He looks down at his body. Jack can see that he's been shot in the stomach a few times, maybe also in the chest, in his leg. It's hard to tell where the bullets went in and where he's just bleeding. He spits a gob of red onto the floor. "What the fuck can I do, man?" He looks up, his eyes glassy, but not without some hope.

Jack bends down, crouches beside him, and takes his arm. "This isn't the scene where the drug dealer dies at the end, OK?"

Junius laughs. "This ain't your fucking movie, man. This shit be real out here." He coughs. Jack hears Vlade yell and, turning around, he sees Niki helping him up to his feet. Niki raises his chin at Jack and points toward the door.

Jack pats Junius on the arm. "Where's Free, baby? We'll carry you out of here."

Junius shakes his head. "Find that motherfucker man, but I ain't going make it. I'm fucked." He spits. "Is Tony dead?"

Jack nods. "He's shot to pieces."

"That motherfucker *did* have this whole shit planned. I used the Russians once. Now he's their boy." He takes a few breaths to collect himself before going on. "You heard him say that bald mother-fucker was his new connection?"

Jack shakes his head. "I heard that part."

"Yeah. The dude. He said that." Junius nods, then he shakes his head, coughs. "Maybe he didn't say it; I don't know. I bought from him before. He's size."

Jack pats Junius' shoulder. "Relax, man. It's OK now."

"Just the fact that that bald fucker's here means he was selling to Tony. Man, he *only* does size. Probably set to have Tony run this whole city."

"OK, J. OK."

Junius spits. He looks at the desk. "There still blow up there?"

Jack looks, sees there's enough left for them all to do a few lines tonight, and cups some of it in his hand. "Will this help?"

Junius looks at the blow and his eyes widen. "Is a pig's pussy pork?"

Jack holds the blow under Junius's nose, and Junius does his best to inhale, but when he tries, he coughs and blood runs out of one nostril. He laughs, shakes his head. "I'm so fucked, man." Jack holds up his hand again, but Junius says, "It's OK, Jack, man. Be good. You did OK." He looks at the desk, the gun cabinet. He nods, and then he's quiet.

Jack drops the blow onto the floor, claps his hands clean. He waits to see if Junius will breathe again, and then closes the dead man's eyes.

Niki's hand falls onto Jack's shoulder. "We need to go."

"OK," Jack says, standing. He starts to back away from the desk and then hears the spray from an automatic firing and ducks back down again. The bullets cut across the wall to the side of the desk, over the gun case. "The fuck?" He turns and, peering around the desk, sees Maxine holding the Colombians' Uzis, one in each hand. Niki rolls against the wall and comes up with his gun trained on Maxine's chest. He yells for her to put the weapon down.

"No," Maxine says. She's standing at the end of the couch, where she's been the whole time, where Jack stupidly threw the Uzis.

"Maxine," Jack says. He starts to stand up slowly, shaking his head. "This is over. Just put them down, and we all leave, never think about this place again."

"You don't," she says. "I worked for this motherfucker." She's crying even harder now, her hair covering her face and mascara running down her cheeks. "I *worked* here."

"That's OK," Jack says. "Just calm down." He reaches for Niki's arm and lowers the gun. "Just put the guns down, and we leave. OK, Max?" He starts across the room toward her, and she points the guns at his chest.

"Don't make me use these, Jack."

"Hey," he says, raising his hands. "You don't have to do anything here. It's all real easy."

"No," she says. "Everything is fucked now, Jack."

Jack opens his arms. "You're a beautiful girl, Maxine. You'll be OK." With his right hand, he gestures toward what's left of Tony. "You really think you needed this little fucker?"

"I needed his money."

"You want money?" he says. "Go sell these guns, sell some of the coke lying around here, some of the X. Come out to the car and let me give you a few grand for your troubles."

"Like fuck," she says, shaking her head.

"Look around you, Maxine. You see what this kind of shit brings down?"

She lowers the guns, still holding them ready as Jack moves closer, but no longer aiming at him. "Give me the guns," he says.

She drops them onto the couch, leans forward, rests both her hands on its back. She takes one deep breath and then screams, lets out everything inside her in one huge, penetrating cry that sends Jack and Niki both a few steps backward. Then she stands up straight, looks at Jack. She waves her hands. "I'm OK," she says. "And I'm done here."

She walks out from behind the couch, and Jack goes to her, his arms open, ready to give her some comfort, but she holds up a hand, keeps walking. "No thanks," she says. "I'm better off."

She walks to the door, nodding at Vlade and Niki. As she passes them, she says, "Boys." Then she walks out.

"Shit," Jack says, taking the clips out of the Uzis and throwing them aside.

Niki's eyebrows are half-way up his forehead. "Chick is fucked," he says.

Jack laughs. "Tell me about it. But she can get it together when she needs to." He starts toward the door, looking around him to see if there's anything he should take. The place is pretty much destroyed; the only piece of furniture that hasn't been completely taken apart is the couch, and even that has a line of gunshots across its top, the fabric torn and stuffing sticking out of it. Jack looks at the coke, decides it's not in his best interest to try to do anything with it. The same goes for the guns. He claps his hands off, looks down at them, and sees the blood on his pants, probably Junius's, and the coke on the front of his shirt. He tries to clean himself off, but knows this'll take a long, hot shower—maybe more than one.

Jack looks at the Russian, lying on the floor with his hands cuffed to the couch. "Can he move that?" he asks Niki. Jack tries lifting the couch, and moves it a little, enough to worry about the Russian leaving when he comes to.

Niki's already started to cut off the plastic cuffs, and Jack helps him drag the Russian across the room to the pool table. He starts to wake slightly as they move him, his eyes opening slowly, and Niki punches him in the face again. Jack can see he's still breathing when he looks at his chest, but he's out again, his eyes closed, blood around his nose and mouth.

"Nice work," Jack tells Niki. "Very thorough."

With another pair of plastic cuffs, Niki attaches him to the pool table, an object that's so heavy he definitely won't be able to move.

"The cops will want this guy," Jack says. "He's been dealing blow and X, his set up's big enough to give Tony V. delusions of grandeur, and they've been hearing about him through the wires. Shit, they even think he's an international terrorist. War on Terror and some shit. They get a case against him, make it stick, and maybe all our troubles go away."

"Troubles?"

Jack shakes his head. "That thing downtown today? The cars?"

Vlade raises his gun. "No. He is K.G.B. coming after us. We should kill him."

Jack looks up, surprised to hear Vlade getting involved. "The police come across this shitstorm, they're going to need someone they can bust. You want that to be us or you want it to be him?"

"But we haven't killed anyone here," Niki says.

"Exactly." Jack fixes Vlade with a hard stare. "Well most of us haven't. Let's keep it that way."

Vlade still holds the gun aimed at the Russian. "He sent his men after us and now he will want to kill us." He looks down at the blood coming out of his shoulder. "And," Vlade yells, "He just fucking *shot* me!"

"Calm down, big fella." Jack stands and goes over to Vlade, pats him on the good shoulder. "Seriously. We need the police to find this guy alive. They'll take care of him." Jack looks at Niki and then back to Vlade.

Vlade bites his lower lip. "He sent his men to shoot at us. They shot your car."

"That's right," Jack says, turning back to kick the Russian in his legs. "He's a fuck, but we leave him."

"We got to go." Niki straightens up to his full height.

"He's right," Jack says.

Vlade puts up the hand on his good side to show that he won't argue anymore.

"Plus," Jack says. "We have to get you fixed up."

Niki comes over to Jack and Vlade, claps his wounded friend on the good shoulder. "I will fix you," he says.

"Then let's go."

"One second," Niki says. He goes over to the desk, where he puts a small pile of coke onto a credit card. After cutting it into two lines with his finger, he brings it over to Vlade. "This will help with the bullet."

"OK," Vlade says, and then, after snorting the lines, "Yes!" Now wide awake, glowing, he shouts it. "Yes! Take this fucking metal out of my shoulder!"

Niki looks at Jack guiltily, shrugs. "It will help with pain."

Jack laughs. He has to: Now he's got a shot-up, coked-up Czech-Russian, ex-K.G.B. man to deal with. He just points to the door. "Let's go."

45

They find Freeman in the hall outside the office, partly awake. He's been shot, but he knocked the hell out of the Colombian who shot him, beat the man with his own gun, using it as a club. They help him up; it takes Jack *and* Niki to lift him, but soon he's supporting most of his weight on his own, starting to walk. Jack asks him if he'll be OK, and Freeman laughs. "This's just a few shots, is all."

Jack and Niki exchange a look behind Freeman's wide back, Jack wondering how much coke the big guy's done, and Niki raising his eyebrows, probably thinking they should give him more.

They walk outside into the pre-dawn glow of the city, the lights above the parking lot still on, and the dark night sky beginning to lighten. But it's not daylight yet; the dim glow of the city is still the only light. The cold, wet air surrounds them, the moisture of the fog starting to seep into their clothes and their bones. This is where the city finds its life.

They walk in silence around the corner, Freeman dragging his bad left leg, and Jack and Niki still supporting part of his weight. Vlade comes up behind, breathing with some effort.

"I'm driving my ass to the hospital," Freeman says as they come around the corner to where they can see the cars. "NFL Players' Union insurance for life, bro." He claps Jack and Niki on their backs, moves away from them to limp toward Junius's car on his own.

"You have the keys to that thing?" Jack asks.

Freeman laughs. "In the car." He turns to regard Jack and the Czechs. "Rule number one," he says. "You ever go into some shit like this, you leave the keys in the motherfucking ignition."

Jack nods. "That's sage advice, big guy. What about Junius?"

Freeman just looks at them. Even with the tattoo covering half of his face, blocking his expression, Jack can tell he doesn't like the question. "He's dead, right?" None of the others says anything, but Freeman reads the answer from their expressions. "He's dead. If he wasn't he'd be here now. What else can I do?"

He shakes his head. Then he limps around the car to the driver's side, opens the door, and waves without looking back as he gets in. "I'll see you all when I see you," he says.

When he's in, the car dips down noticeably on his side. The engine starts and the rear lights come on. All the windows in the car are tinted black, so Jack can't see him, but he imagines Freeman giving them a last wave before he backs out and pulls off.

Mouthing a cigarette out of the pack, Jack looks at Niki and Vlade: Niki looks serious, taking out a knife and wiping it against his pants. After Jack lights his cigarette, he hands him his lighter, and Niki nods, runs the flame underneath the blade.

Vlade says, "Now we eat!"

Jack laughs, watching Niki sterilize the knife that he'll use to dig the bullet from Vlade's shoulder. Vlade glows, triumphant in the morning buzz of the two big lines of coke, luminescent in the fog and the blur of the streetlights above them. Niki was right, Jack realizes; Vlade's not about to feel any pain.

They talk Jack into letting them take the bullet out in the back seat of the Mustang as he drives them to breakfast. He's not a fan of the idea, but when he hears the sirens in the distance as they stand in the parking lot, he goes along, moves to get by. Even if the cops aren't headed for The Coast, it's time to get the hell out of this part of the city, as far away as they can manage, and operating on someone's bullet wound isn't the kind of thing you want to be doing out in public, even in this section of town.

Jack gives Niki a towel out of the trunk, an old one, to catch any blood that Vlade might lose, and Niki tells him not to worry. "OK,"

Jack says, taking a look at the leather bag full of money. He touches its side, feeling the heavy leather. "It'll be OK," he says.

Vlade barely screams as Niki goes to work in the back seat. He's cut off a part of the towel for Vlade to bite down on, and he's biting so hard that Jack can see lines sticking out on the sides of his neck in his rear-view. There's sweat on Vlade's brow, but he still doesn't make a sound.

"No bumps, Jack," Niki reminds. "Or you tell me first."

"Either of you see any bullet holes in the leather back there?" Jack asks. "You see where any shots went in?"

"I am looking at where the bullet went into Vlade, actually."

Jack sees the Market Street trolley tracks coming up and slows the car. "We're going to bump."

In the rear-view, Jack sees Niki stop what he's doing with the knife and blot Vlade's shoulder. He says something in Czech and Vlade nods.

Niki points up ahead on the road. "Will you pull over ahead?"

Jack turns to really see them for a moment: Niki's holding the towel hard against Vlade's shoulder, and Vlade's really starting to sweat. He turns off Market and slows as they head onto Van Ness, going toward the Tenderloin and the Cable Car diner. When Jack stops the car, he watches Niki insert the tip of his knife into Vlade's shoulder at least three inches. Vlade screams into the towel in his mouth, and it comes out muffled but loud enough for people outside the car to hear, if there were any. Luckily, there's no one on the streets here at this hour. Even the homeless have gone to sleep in their makeshift beds; the shoppers have all long gone home. Niki works the blade for a second, takes something in his hand, and presses the towel against Vlade's skin.

Niki holds up a small, round, bloody piece of metal. "He's OK," he says. "Let's go get some food."

46

At the Cable Car—the only other diner Jack knows in the city is the Blue Diner, the one across from The Hall of Justice, and he's not about to go there with a bloody, coked up Czech, blood on his pants, and whatever other remnants of what's just happened clinging to the three of them—Jack just eats, drinks enough coffee for the ride home, thinks about the shower he'll take and how well he'll sleep for the next three or four days. They sit at the opposite end of the dining room from where he sat with Ralph before this all started, but Jack looks at the booth, knocks wood three times as he thinks of Ralph.

After he's eaten most of his steak and eggs—the eggs sunny side on top of the steak so he can let the yolk run over it—and had a full cup of coffee, Jack excuses himself to go outside. He's reached the point in the meal where he'd rather have a cigarette than more food. Out in the parking lot, he leans against the hood of the Mustang as the sun comes up around him. The light of day began when they were eating, and now Jack stands in the twilight of the morning, finally done, finally clear into Sunday, and smoking, finally almost ready to go home.

He takes a long drag of his cigarette, enjoying it as much as anything he can imagine. If he has to chain smoke for the next two weeks, months even, he's going to smoke now and for the rest of the next few days, as much as he wants.

He watches the cars cruise past him, still in a trickle of early Sunday morning inactivity, feeling the cold chill in the air. He'll go back up to Sausalito this morning to relax for a few days, eventually go to a doctor to have his ribs and face checked out, then get back into the gym and start up his morning running, but not right away—not anything right away. Jack nods at the thought, exhaling smoke through his nose, enjoying that feeling and the cold, icy buzzing around his bones that comes from the exhaustion mixed with coffee and ignited by the nicotine. There's something about the feeling that's so wrong it's good. A shiver runs through him.

In the diner, he can see Vlade and Niki talking fast. Now that the bullet's out and Vlade's through some of his pain, he's flying on the coke, drinking coffee; he only wants to talk about their road trip and the places they'll go. Jack has just heard his plans about Yosemite, Yellowstone, Montana, and then driving down across the plains into Las Vegas, clear through to L.A. from there.

Jack looks up at the sky, takes his cell phone out of his jacket to call Sgt. Hopkins. It's not something he's eager to do, but it's a part of the job he has to finish.

The cop answers on the fourth ring, groggy when he says hello, clearly still sleeping at this hour on a Sunday. It's not even six-thirty.

"Sergeant, this is your friend Jack Palms, calling you in less than twenty-four hours from the last time we spoke, the time when we decided on our deal."

"Uhngh. What is it Jack? This better be good, you ungrateful, sleep-depriving fuck."

Jack can't help himself from enjoying the moment, waking Hopkins, hearing him struggle to deal with the phone for the second time of the night. "Not such a good night for you sleep-wise, was it Mills?"

Hopkins grunts.

"Me, I haven't slept yet, so I feel OK. But I expect I'll be crashing soon."

"Yeah. Good. What is it?"

"I wanted to call and let you know that some of the city's big drug traffic can be found down at The Coast in SOMA, that their supply line is currently handcuffed to a pool table in a back office of the club, very much alive. You'll find him to be a bald Russian guy with a beard, not very agreeable, but I have it on good terms from Junius Ponds, now deceased, and Tony Vitelli, also now deceased, that this was The Man. Plus, I think he's your Eastern European problem. Your terrorist."

"Really?" Now Jack can hear the sergeant coming to his senses, waking up as his police mind thinks through the implications of what Jack is saying: the busts, the investigations, the trials, thinking about the possibility of a promotion.

"I'm serious. Tony V. offed the wrong Colombian, and his army tore up The Coast this morning. You'll find a bunch of them sleeping the big sleep, along with Tony, Junius, and a bunch of Tony's thugs. Any other Colombians that were there will be long gone by now." Jack's even a little surprised by the upbeat sound of his own voice, but he has to allow it: right now, he feels good to have this all done.

"Wait a minute, Jack," Hopkins says. "I'm sitting up now. Tell me all this again."

"The Russian was Tony V.'s new supply line. He's sold here to Junius and Tony before, and now Tony was trying to cut out Junius and Ralph, also the Colombian, Castroneves. I think that's what pissed Tony off."

"Pissed him off enough to kill Anderino?"

Jack takes another drag, lets some of the smoke out through clenched teeth. "Enough to have a couple of Russians take him out. Those would be the John Does you found downtown today."

"I know," Hopkins says. "I could still recognize the one we had in custody last night."

"So there you go. Tony V. was behind it, but the guy you'll find at The Coast was his outside help, his new connection. For all I know, he was the Eastern European you've been looking for. He's definitely a well-connected guy. Ex-K.G.B., from what I understand."

"I'm on it." Now Hopkins sounds very much awake. "You have a good morning, Jack."

"Thanks. And one other thing. You have a leak on your force. I'm assuming you know that."

"Right." Hopkins grunts. "I'm getting dressed. Tell me something I don't know."

"It's O'Malley. He was there."

Hopkins whistles. "Shit. He was *there?*"

"He was. Now he isn't, but you know your man. Seems he was pretty tight with Tony."

"OK," Hopkins says. "Thanks. I guess I won't have to meet at the diner anymore."

"No," Jack says. "I guess not." He looks at his sneakers: scuffed and discolored from the blood, what were recently some new-looking Nikes are now not a pretty sight.

"Go home, Jack."

"Hopkins," Jack says, standing up to head back inside. "Don't let's talk for a long time, OK?"

47

After finishing his breakfast, Jack takes the Czechs back to their hotel, Vlade still talking road trip, planning the Miami-Atlanta-Charlotte leg of their ride. Jack's already told them the police will be very serious about picking up the Russian, taking him in and making sure something sticks. All along, it's the supply line and the mob guys that Sgt. Hopkins had wanted; now that he has both in one man, he'll do what he needs to make some convictions stick.

"You don't want to see Orlando?" Jack asks, joking. "Disney World? Epcot? You know they have a whole display of the world in there, even your country, probably."

Vlade shakes his head, very serious. "No Disney."

In front of the hotel, they pull up to the lone bellhop working this early on a Sunday morning. The Czechs get out of the car and Jack gets out with them, receives big hugs from both: a one-armed from Vlade and a long, two-arm squeeze from Niki.

"I want to thank you guys for coming with me."

"No," Niki says. "We started you in this. We help you to finish."

Vlade nods. "We needed to see our friend again." He claps Jack on the shoulder, squeezes his bicep. "And you too," he says, his face breaking into a smile. He laughs.

Jack fakes a punch at Vlade's stomach but Vlade doesn't flinch. He pats his chest. "You hit me. Anytime you like." He laughs again. With the big coat on, it's hard to make out the lump of the towel over his shoulder if you don't know what to look for. In the diner, the waitress didn't even flinch. Now the bellhop hardly notices them; he's clearly more interested in Jack's car.

"Is that a 68?" the kid asks.

"66," Jack says. "K-code."

"Yeah," the kid says, but then he sees Jack, really sees him, and he stops. "Fuck! You're Jack Palms?"

Jack nods. He points at the kid. "Shake 'em down!" he says.

"Too awesome!" the kid grabs for his cell phone behind his stand and starts taking pictures as Jack and the Czechs walk away.

"Tell Al he missed some good violence," Jack says.

"Don't worry." Vlade nods. "He will be asking us about it all day."

Jack yawns, realizes he can hardly keep his eyes open. He tells the others he has to go, that they should look him up if they're ever back in town. "We'll go out, have some fun." Jack winks. "But less next time."

They laugh, are already heading into the building as Jack starts back to his car. He gives the kid a wave as he revs the engine, pulls out of the drive.

Going home through the City, Jack sees the tall green trees, a few of them redwoods, and the grass of Golden Gate Park shrouded in fog. The streets are quiet until he gets to Highway 101, where he meets more cars, still not that many, but a few. The sun is brilliant on the Golden Gate Bridge, and Jack can see that the day is going to be one of those especially beautiful ones that make living in northern California all that much more worthwhile.

In front of him, the tan hills climb up into Sausalito and his days of peace and quiet. He yawns, crossing the bridge, knowing he'll be in a shower, then in his bed soon. It'd have been nice to end up there with Maxine, finish this whole ordeal by going home with her, having someone to share his bed with. Given the way that worked out though, it's hard to be too upset with her loss. Jack realizes he's more sad at the loss of *someone* than with the fact that *she's* not around; and still he knows there are other women out there. He'll get out; he'll meet them. There's plenty of nightlife left in the city, now that he knows he's ready to find it.

But for now, he needs to sleep. Home inside of a half-hour, his whole body hurting now that the caffeine has lost a fight with his exhaustion, he drops his jacket on the floor in the hallway and his shirt outside the bathroom. He starts the water in the shower, strips off the rest of his clothes, and climbs in under the hot spray. In steam and with heat running all over his body, he watches some of his dried blood run down the drain, stands and lets the stream work out some of the muscles in his back, his neck.

From the shower, he's in bed and under the sheets as soon as he's dry, before he's even looked around the house yet. The only thing he sees is his alarm clock on the dresser, the time just coming up on eight o'clock.

He sleeps through most of Sunday, gets up in the late afternoon and orders Chinese food for dinner, eats it in a daze, watching TV, and then goes back to bed again.

The clock is the next thing he sees when he wakes up the following morning, Monday, the time 9:07, and his front doorbell going off. He realizes that it's been ringing for a long while, that he's brought the sounds into his dreams, incorporated them, and now, finally, he realizes it's a reality that he needs to get up and deal with. He shakes his head, not happy with this situation.

Jack rolls onto his back and looks up at the ceiling, feeling his ribs with his hands as he takes a deep breath: nothing seems to be loose there. Just bruises, he hopes, no broken bones. Taking a few more deep breaths, he feels the sleep slowly fall away from him as the doorbell rings again. He still has an ache in his bones and a tiredness that's not going to leave for some time, but he manages to sit up, and then stumbles to the closet, takes out a robe. In what works of his mind at this point, he imagines Mills Hopkins at the door, a bright, Monday morning crew of cops in blue uniforms and photographers behind them snapping shots of Jack going off to jail again, this time in his robe, going away for accessory to murder or organized crime. The thought of this scene jolts him further awake, enough to be mad as he walks out into the hall, tying the robe closed around him.

In the living room, he can hear pounding on the door, a harder knock than knocking, and someone calling his name. "Fuck!" he yells, getting close to the door.

The noises stop.

Jack looks through the peephole and doesn't see anyone. He's expecting the police, rows of cameras, newspaper reporters, and, at this point, he's capable of imagining them hiding on either side of the door, in the bushes. "Who is it?"

"It is us," Niki says, the voice unmistakable.

"Shit." Jack opens the door and sees three motorcycles parked in his driveway, one with a big red sidecar, and the four Czechs standing along the sides of his front stairs. They're all smiling, wearing leather pants and tight leather jackets. They look like something out of the future, versions of bikers descended from outer space or Eastern Europe, helmets on the back of their bikes and wide smiles on their faces. If they're not coked out now, they will be, and that's all part of the futurism of it, Jack guesses.

"Jack," Vlade says, grabbing him into a tight one-armed hug. He's got his other arm in a sling close to his body and it gets in the way when they hug, makes Vlade call out in pain but he pulls Jack closer, laughing and saying his name.

Al laughs. "Nice robe."

Jack looks down and sees that he's got the robe open in the front. He's tied one of the ends of the belt into a knot without having done anything to join it with the other. He's wearing just boxers and nothing else, greeting the neighborhood in his stripes and paisleys. He laughs, pulls the sides of the robe closed and properly ties the belt.

"Guys. What's up?" Jack rubs the sleep out of his eyes, trying to get his body and mind both to start.

"Look at these bikes!" Vlade says. "Look at these!"

Jack looks. At the end of his driveway are two Ducati and a Harley Davidson with a sidecar—some nice-looking machinery.

"Damn," he says, starting out onto the steps before realizing he's not wearing shoes. "Those are fine."

"Yes they are, Jack Palms," David says. "Yes they are."

"Nice," Jack says.

Niki claps a hand onto his shoulder. "We just came to say good-bye," he says. "And see if you want to come."

"Come?" Jack says.

"Come along for the ride," Vlade says. "The open road."

"We will take you to where we got our bikes," Al says. "You can pick. This fucking trip is going to be *awesome*, my man."

Jack laughs. He comes farther outside the house, sees the morning sun glorious on the streets, the bikes shimmering in their newness. The leather seats look big and comfortable, the Ducati sleek and fast. Each of the bikes has compartments along its sides, hard ones on the Ducati and saddle bags on the Harley, more than enough room to put your essentials: a few clothes and who knows what else. A toothbrush?

"The Ducati for you?" Vlade says, practically singing. "We will buy…"

Jack thinks of the money in the leather bag on his couch, enough to make a trip across the country, pay off the bills on his kitchen table, and *then* some. He thinks about the big house behind him, its empty rooms, his morning runs and the taste of the cereal and the milk, the fact that it's not as good as the cigarettes. He thinks of his solitary afternoons in the gym listening to the music he doesn't like, and the nights with no one else in his bed. He thinks about the San Francisco tabloids and the people who still recognize him when he goes out, admittedly not as bad an experience over the past few days as he'd have thought, but still. That and the fact that one of these days, not today and maybe not the next, but one day soon, Mills Hopkins will call and Jack will have to go downtown to talk about something, testify, sit in a small room and discuss all that's happened, that he'll be lucky if he gets out when it's over.

And he looks at the bikes in the sun, new and gleaming and fast-looking, *very* fast looking, and the Czechs in their futuristic riding outfits, all four of them smiling.

Then Jack feels himself start to smile too.

"Well…" he says. And his thoughts run to what he should start packing first.

ABOUT THE AUTHOR

Photo by Jarda Brych

SETH HARWOOD grew up in the Boston area, graduated from the Iowa Writers' Workshop in 2002 and currently lives in Berkeley, CA with his wife Joelle and their dog. He teaches writing and literature at City College of San Francisco and Chabot College.

In July 2006, Seth started podcasting *Jack Wakes Up*, the internet's first podcast-only crime novel. It didn't take long for the novel to catch on and become a web sensation. Nineteen episodes and almost five months later, *Jack Wakes Up* was complete; the Jack Palms Crime Series was born.

Seth's other jobs have included commodities floor trading clerk, bartender, copy-editor for Avon Products, rare book cataloguer, librarian, high school English teacher, and freelance journalist.

His stories have been published in over a dozen literary journals including Post Road, Ecotone, Inkwell, and Sojourn, as well as online at Storyglossia, Thrilling Detective and zeek.net. Portions of this book appeared in Storyglossia and Spinetingler Magazine.

For more information, visit sethharwood.com

ALSO AVAILABLE FROM BREAKNECK BOOKS

By Jeremy Robinson
"...a rollicking Arctic adventure that explores the origins of the human species." -- James Rollins, bestselling author of Black Order and The Judas Strain

www.breakneckbooks.com/rtp.html

By James Somers
"...a nice read of battle, honor, and spirituality... that left me wanting more." -- Fantasybook spot.com

www.breakneckbooks.com/soone.html

By Sean Young
"...captures the imagination and transports you to another time, another way of life and makes it real." -- Jeremy Robinson, author of Raising the Past and The Didymus Contingency

www.breakneckbooks.com/sands.html

BREAKNECK BOOKS
PUBLISHING COMPANY

ALSO AVAILABLE FROM BREAKNECK BOOKS

By Eric Fogle
"This will definitely be one of my top ten reads of the year and I would recommend that this book makes everyone's 'To Read' list..." – Fantasybookspot.com.

www.breakneckbooks.com/fog.html

THE LAST KNIGHT

By Craig Alexander
"*...an action packed race against time and terrorists. Absolutely riveting.*" – Jeremy Robinson, bestselling author of Raising the Past. And Antarktos Rising

www.breakneckbooks.com/nineveh.html

By Michael G. Cornelius
"*A dark and dangerous book with suspense and surprises aplenty...a remarkable novel.*"--A.J. Mattews, author of Follow and Unbroken

www.breakneckbooks.com/ascension.html

BREAKNECK BOOKS
PUBLISHING COMPANY

ALSO AVAILABLE FROM
BREAKNECK BOOKS

By Jeremy Robinson
"[A] unique and bold thriller. It is a fast-paced page-turner like no other. Not to be missed!" – James Rollins, bestselling author of Black Order and The Judas Strain

THE DIDYMUS CONTINGENCY

http://www.breakneckbooks.com/didymus.html

MASTER OF THE WORLD

By Jules Verne
This Special Edition of the original high speed thriller features discussion questions, a design challenge and the complete and unabrideged text.

www.breakneckbooks.com/mow.html

By Edgar Rice Burroughs
This Special Edition features all three Caspak novels (*The People that Time Forgot* and *Out of Time's Abyss*) in one book, the way it was originally intended to be read.

www.breakneckbooks.com/land.html

THE LAND THAT TIME FORGOT

BREAKNECK BOOKS
PUBLISHING COMPANY

ALSO AVAILABLE FROM BREAKNECK BOOKS

By Kristina Schram
"An amazing adventure to a unique and mysterious subterrainean world." – Jeremy Robinson, bestselling author of Raising the Past and Antarktos Rising

www.breakneckbooks.com/anaedor.html

By David S. Michaels with Daniel Brenton
"This is not just among the best first novels I've read in years, it's among the best novels, period. Red Moon is a masterpiece." -- Paul Levinson, President Science Fiction Writers of America and author of The Silk

www.breakneckbooks.com/redmoon.html

By Paul Byers
"A high flying thrill ride exploring the Nazi's last ditch effort." -- Jeremy Robinson, bestselling author of Raising the Past and Antarktos Rising

www.breakneckbooks.com/catalyst.html

BREAKNECK BOOKS
PUBLISHING COMPANY

Printed in the United States
105685LV00004BA/7-9/A